Bride and Groom

The Dogfather

The Wicked Flea

continued . . .

Stud Rites

A DOG LOVER'S MYSTERY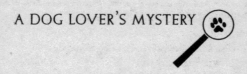

Susan Conant

BERKLEY PRIME CRIME, NEW YORK

THE BERKLEY PUBLISHING GROUP
Published by the Penguin Group
Penguin Group (USA) Inc.
375 Hudson Street, New York, New York 10014, USA
Penguin Group (Canada), 10 Alcorn Avenue, Toronto, Ontario M4V 3B2, Canada
(a division of Pearson Penguin Canada Inc.)
Penguin Books Ltd., 80 Strand, London WC2R 0RL, England
Penguin Group Ireland, 25 St. Stephen's Green, Dublin 2, Ireland (a division of Penguin Books Ltd.)
Penguin Group (Australia), 250 Camberwell Road, Camberwell, Victoria 3124, Australia
(a division of Pearson Australia Group Pty. Ltd.)
Penguin Books India Pvt. Ltd., 11 Community Centre, Panchsheel Park, New Delhi—110 017, India
Penguin Group (NZ), Cnr. Airborne and Rosedale Roads, Albany, Auckland 1310, New Zealand
(a division of Pearson New Zealand Ltd.)
Penguin Books (South Africa) (Pty.) Ltd., 24 Sturdee Avenue, Rosebank, Johannesburg 2196,
South Africa

Penguin Books Ltd., Registered Offices: 80 Strand, London WC2R 0RL, England

This is a work of fiction. Names, characters, places, and incidents either are the product of the author's imagination or are used fictitiously, and any resemblance to actual persons, living or dead, business establishments, events, or locales is entirely coincidental.

STUD RITES

A Berkley Prime Crime Book / published by arrangement with the author

PRINTING HISTORY
Berkley Prime Crime mass-market edition / March 2005
Bantam paperback edition / March 1997
Doubleday hardcover edition / June 1996

ISBN: 0-425-20159-7

BERKLEY PRIME CRIME®
Berkley Prime Crime Books are published by The Berkley Publishing Group,
a division of Penguin Group (USA) Inc.,
375 Hudson Street, New York, New York 10014.
BERKLEY PRIME CRIME is a registered trademark of Penguin Group (USA) Inc.
The Berkley Prime Crime design is a trademark belonging to Penguin Group (USA) Inc.

PRINTED IN THE UNITED STATES OF AMERICA

10 9 8 7 6 5 4 3 2 1

To Virginia,
in memory of her beloved husband, Howard Devaney,
whose caring and generosity
were the foundation of the
Alaskan Malamute Protection League

ACKNOWLEDGMENTS

Many thanks to Jean Berman, Judy Bocock, Fran Boyle, Gail Castonguay, Virginia Devaney, Dorothy Donohue, Grace Franklin, Judy Kern, Roseann Mandell, Amanda Metzger, Devin Scruton, D.V.M., Jan and Rocky Smith, Geoff Stern, Margherita Walker, and Wendy Willhauck. I am also grateful to my husband, Carter Umbarger; to my muses incarnate, Frostfield Firestar's Kobuk, C.G.C.; and Frostfield Perfect Crime, C.G.C.; and to an editor to kill for, my beloved Kate Miciak.

For the appearance of American and Canadian Champion Williwaw's Kodiak Cub, R.O.M., the inimitable Casey, I want to thank his breeders and owners, Al and Mary Jane Holabach, and his co-owners, Frank and Lynda Sattler. Special thanks to Al Holabach for handling Casey in my fictional ring. I also want to thank Robin Haggard, Jim Kuehl, and Cathy Greenfield, D.V.M., for the appearance herein of Champion Poker Flat's Rainman, C.D.X., T.D., W.W.P.D., W.T.D., C.G.C., known as Joe; and Robin and Jim for joining Joe in my book and for letting me borrow Champion Poker Flat's Paper Chase, C.D., W.T.D., W.L.D., W.W.P.D., W.P.D., C.G.C., Champion Poker Flat's Snow Flurrie, C.D., W.T.D., C.G.C., Poker Flat's Risky Business, W.T.D., W.W.P.D., and Poker Flat's Hell's Belle. Jim has given me permission to mention the underground video classic known as "Poker Flat Presents: Malamute Obedience Bloopers." Vanderval's Tundra Eagle, C.D.X., W.P.D.X.,

W.L.D., in whose eyes I see the brilliance of my beloved first malamute, Tasha, reappears in this series with the permission of her breeder, owner, and handler, Anna Morelli. In real life, as in this book, rescue malamute Czar is owned and handled by Lorraine Rabon.

PREMIUM LIST
SPECIALTY CLUB DOG SHOW & OBEDIENCE TRIAL,
NATIONAL SPECIALTY SHOW
(UNBENCHED)

ALASKAN MALAMUTE CLUB OF NORTH AMERICA

DANVILLE MILESTONE HOTEL
AND CONFERENCE FACILITY
DANVILLE, MASSACHUSETTS

THURSDAY, OCTOBER 31: OBEDIENCE TRIAL & FUTURITY CLASSES

FRIDAY, NOVEMBER 1: SWEEPSTAKES, REGULAR CONFORMATION CLASSES, NON-REGULAR CLASSES

SATURDAY, NOVEMBER 2: REGULAR CONFORMATION CLASSES & NON-REGULAR CLASSES

JR. SHOWMANSHIP COMPETITION

SHOW HOURS—6:00 A.M. TO 8:00 P.M. DAILY
ALL JUDGING WILL BE INDOORS

Entries Close at Show Secretary's Office at 12:00 Noon, Wednesday, October 16, after which time entries cannot be accepted, cancelled or substituted, except for in Chapter 14, Section 6 of the Dog Show Rules.

Mail All Entries with Fees to:
Lisa Tainter, Show Secretary
P.O. Box 2161
Georgetown, MA 01833

Mr. and Mrs. Harold Jenkinson request the honour
of your presence at the marriage of their daughter

Crystal Marie
to
Mr. Gregory Philip Lofgren

on Saturday, the second of November
at three o'clock
Okalani Banquet Hall
Danville Milestone Hotel and Conference Facility
Danville, Massachusetts
and afterwards at the reception

R.S.V.P.

PROLOGUE

Late in the evening on a narrow street in Providence, Rhode Island, the handsome woman catches a stiletto heel in the antique-brick sidewalk. As she regains her balance, the diamond on the third finger of her left hand refracts the inadequate light of a pseudo-gas lamppost. She curses aloud. A phrase comes to her: *one little candle.* Better to light one than to curse the quaintness. She smiles. She has gained in wit far more than she has lost in looks. Besides, in preparation, she has shed forty pounds. Her rings are loose on her finger: the diamond and its friend, the platinum band. Her legs are as good as ever, and the tweed suits packed in her leather suitcase will serve their intended dual function of proclaiming her essential, if adopted, Englishness while disguising the dog hairs she is bound to pick up. Blocks ahead of her, a dog walker pauses to let a little terrier mix lift a leg on a tree. Owner and dog move on, turn a corner, vanish. The woman's eyes search for what she has been told are the interior lights of her hired Porsche, her rental car, as it is called on this side of the Atlantic. An American car, she reflects, would have come equipped with some sort of automatic device, bells or whistles to warn her that she had flipped the wrong switch or failed to close the door all the way. The Porsche itself, an intelligent and subtle machine, may have issued an elusive caution that, if heeded, would have spared her this late-evening nuisance of running out to make sure that the battery did not drain. As it was, an anonymous neighbor had rung up her cousin, who could hospitably have volunteered to dash out instead of sending a long-lost relative on this bothersome errand.

This dark street, however, threatens none of the famous *violence in America* so beloved by the British press. This is a safe street in a charming neighborhood. Except for the click of her heels on brick, the swoosh of autumn leaves, and the distant hum of traffic on some unseen thoroughfare, the handsome woman hears nothing. Reaching the Porsche, she is more irked than alarmed. Fumbling with the key, she peers through a window in the hope of spotting a low glow of light, a sign that she will not, after all, need to delay her morning's departure to have the wretched battery recharged. She is eager to arrive at the final destination of her journey. She looks forward to hearing that she is as beautiful as ever, that she hasn't changed at all. Her last feeling is one of mild irritation. Her last thought is that the miserable battery has, after all, gone dead. The blow is swift, powerful, and fatal. As her body falls, the dim light again catches her diamond. Hurried hands slip the rings from her finger. Frightened eyes do not see the woman as handsome. In the murderer's view, she has not aged well.

More than twenty-four hours later, in a poorly lighted parking lot on a second dark night, the old man impatiently awaits his companion. What can be taking so damned long? The pollen count must be high. The air is damp and thick. Breathing is difficult. The old man is in a foul mood. His position entitles him to respect. His gnarled hands pat his pockets in search of cigarettes. He never coughs. Rather, he admits to a frequent need to clear his chest. The sound could be mistaken for the low rumble of a big dog. Hearing it now, the murderer is not deceived. This blow, too, is swift and powerful. This blow, too, is deadly.

CHAPTER 1

Relics: venerated remains.

Buddha's tooth, snatched from his funeral pyre.

The shroud of Turin. If not Christ's image, whose?

The stole of Saint Hubert. Presented on the occasion of his consecration by an angel of the Virgin Herself, it was a narrow, yard-long band of silk interwoven with gold, but of incomparably greater spiritual than commercial value. Sacred coin, it was bound to appreciate. And so it did! When Saint Hubert died in A.D. 727, he bequeathed the stole to his budding cult; and for a thousand years, from all over France, vast hordes of pilgrims trudged in haste to a small abbey deep in the Ardennes in search of the miraculous healing that flowed from the Donor through the saint to the sacred relic. The need of the pilgrims was great. In the stole lay their only salvation. All, you see, had been bitten by dogs.

As had we—Heaven preserve us!—the hundreds of souls who'd made the pilgrimage across the globe, from Great Britain, from Holland, from Japan, from Canada, and from all over the United States, to the site of our annual gathering of the cult, which, like the cult of Saint Hubert, was the cult of the dog, although in our case, not just any dog of any breed or none discernible, but the cult of the living relic of the ancient peoples of the Kotzebue Sound, dog of dogs, breed of breeds, the highest link in the Great Chain of Being Canine, the noble and glorious Alaskan malamute.

But I exaggerate. Only a few people had come from overseas. Many proud breeders, their vans and RVs packed with dogs, had come from Washington, Oregon, California, Colorado, Wisconsin, Texas. With or without dogs, some had flown. Scores had driven for hours or even days to this little town in Massachusetts. I'd lucked out. I was a fifty-minute ride from home and could have driven from Cambridge to Danville and back each day. Instead, I'd been saving up for a year to splurge on a room at the show site itself, the Danville Milestone Hotel and Conference Facility. There wouldn't be another Alaskan Malamute National Specialty in New England for ten more years. Damned if I was going to miss a second of the five days, the first of which, Wednesday, October 30, had already elapsed when my story begins, and the last of which would fall, as celestial design would have it, on Sunday, November 3, the Feast of Saint Hubert, the French patron saint of dogs, whose principal relic, as I've explained, was a miraculous garment.

Now, at eleven o'clock on the morning of Thursday, October 31, twenty-four hours after my arrival, I stood behind the Alaskan Malamute Rescue Booth in the exhibition area, the heart of the show, as Sherri Ann Printz presented me not with Saint Hubert's stole, of course, but with a relic of equally legendary association.

The Presentation of the Lamp was not, I might mention, any kind of re-creation or reenactment of Saint Hubert's consecration. I, the recipient, was merely a follower of the cult, no founder, no leader. Besides, I'm a woman. And I'm no saint. The donor, Sherri Ann Printz, didn't fit my image of the Virgin, either, whom I imagine as having a clear, radiant complexion, whereas Sherri Ann's was pale, lumpy, and doughy, like a yeast batter in need of punching down. Indeed, I found it impossible to envision Sherri Ann as even the lowliest and most improbable of angels, whom I see as akin to the Alaskan malamute in the sense that both breeds exhibit considerable natural variation in size, shape, and coloration, but are never marred by coarseness or, in Sherri Ann's case, outright dowdiness. A national specialty is an Occasion, with a capital *O*. Consequently, most of us had made an Effort, with a capital *E*, in the manner of appearance. Sherri Ann's capital *E* Effort had, alas, produced a lowercase effect. Her gray hair was cut painfully short, and a heavy perm had given it so dense and wiry a texture that her coiffure resembled a small terrier victimized by overenthusiastic plucking and stripping. Sherri Ann wore what I think is called a duster, the sort of loose, knee-length blouse with buttons down the front in which persons quaintly known as "housewives" were once apparently encouraged to drape themselves so that they wouldn't need to wear bras and thus wouldn't have any to burn. But, as I've said, Sherri Ann had made an obvious, if lowercase, effort: The robe was of a heavy pseudo-satin in the particular shade of pale rose-red that does a splendid job of camouflaging malamute undercoat.

So I was no saint, and Sherri Ann was neither the Virgin nor one of Her messengers. As a stand-in for the sanctuary in which Saint Hubert was consecrated, the exhibition hall was, however, approximately the right size: larger than a chapel, if smaller than the interior of a cathedral. Exposed steel beams elevated the ceiling toward the heavens, and the industrial carpeting was a deep stone gray. I seem to recall that early medieval churches didn't necessarily have pews. I'm positive, however, that even Saint Hubert's didn't devote most of the empty floor space to baby-gated show rings.

The event taking place here, however, the competition

known as the Futurity Sweepstakes, did suggest a satisfying timelessness in spiritual theme: the Hereafter, the world to come. The Futurity actually was a bet on the future, an innocent flirtation with organized gambling. The long, complex process of nominating the teenage pups now in the ring had begun before or soon after they were born. Now that the future had arrived, the payoff would be in cash.

In place of shrines and confessionals, booths lined the four walls. A few concessionaires offered all-breed, any-breed goods or services, but two or three vendors whose wares I'd only glanced at sold dog sleds, harnesses, dog packs, snow hooks, gang lines, and expensive three-wheeled rigs that looked like giant tricycles. Artisans stood behind tables piled with hand-knit sweaters, hats, mittens, wooden carvings, weather vanes, mailboxes, silver earrings, pewter pendants, and a bewildering number of other items that paid tribute to the object of our annual rites and, with few exceptions, did so with unusual accuracy. The depictions, for once, showed Alaskan malamutes that looked neither like Siberian huskies nor like mixed-breed sled dogs, but could only have been our Arctic bulldozers: big, heavy-boned sledge dogs with blocky muzzles, smallish ears set on the sides of the head, and plumy tails sailing over the back.

On display at our national breed club's booth lay dozens of items that would be auctioned on Saturday night after the banquet that would follow the Best of Breed judging: Copenhagen collector's plates, oil paintings of malamutes, books autographed by authors' dogs, framed photographs of puppies, drawings in charcoal and pastels, decorative little wooden dog sleds, and a battered old board with faded paint and the words "Cleo, BAE I," a relic of the Chinook Kennels, the lower forty-eight home of the Alaskan malamute, the very sign that had proclaimed the name of a veteran of Byrd's first expedition to Antarctica. It was a treasure I couldn't begin to afford. But someone could! The high bidder would pay dearly. And rightly so! Ceremonies don't come cheap! Ever paid for a wedding, a bar mitzvah, a lavish wake, or even a modest funeral?

Ever paid vet bills? Behind the Alaskan Malamute Rescue booth, I was filling in for Betty Burley, who was the national vice president of the organization, which has nothing to do with the search-and-rescue dogs that sniff out earthquake victims, but is a combination dog-rehabilitation-and-adoption agency and cult-within-a-cult that devotes itself to the malamutes that no one else wants. More often neglected than actively abused, some rescue dogs are given to us by their owners. Others have been abandoned at shelters or just found wandering. Before placing the rescue dogs with adopters, we check out their health and update their shots, and to avoid creating additional business for ourselves, we have them spayed or neutered. In rescuing dogs, that's what costs: the rehab. Our booth consisted of two long tables laden with issues of our newsletter, an album bulging with photographs of dogs we'd placed, reprints of gruesome articles about the puppy mills that mass-produce the dogs sold in pet shops, and the numerous and varied items donated to our silent auction, not to be confused with the post-banquet live auction to be held on Saturday night. How many auctions? Two. One silent: ours. Rescue's. One live: Saturday night's, when Alaskan Malamute Rescue would be allowed to include ten valuable items among the scores donated to raise funds for our national breed club. And Sherri Ann's lamp would certainly number among Rescue's ten valuable items on Saturday night.

The lamp's height, from the bottom of the base to the top of the hand-painted shade, must almost precisely have equaled the length of Saint Hubert's stole: thirty-six inches. The stole, however, a two-inch band of silk and gold, must have been a cloud in the hand, whereas the lamp base alone, a massive slab of polished pink granite, felt like the rock that it was. Also, had the gold threads of Saint Hubert's stole been interwoven with the silk to depict row upon row of miniature auric Scotties or, perhaps, the image of a single stretched-out dachshund, history would have bequeathed us a sketch of the canine motif, and I myself might even have been wearing a miraculous-stole T-shirt with the pattern flowing across my breasts.

The lamp, in contrast, was about as representational as a lamp can get. It took the form of a massive ceramic Alaskan malamute atop the pink granite slab. Extruding from the middle of its back was a shiny brass post on which perched a shade of skinlike material that bore a red, white, and black painting of a sled dog team and, in bold scarlet letters with a black exclamation point, the word "Iditarod!"

Sherri Ann pointed a puffy hand at the thick gray-and-white fur glued all over the body of the ceramic dog, and declared, "That's Comet's!"

The lamp's full weight shifted from Sherri Ann's hands to mine. Awakened to its reliquary value, I took special care not to drop it. Northpole's Comet was a famous show dog, a long-dead legend, an Alaskan malamute, of course; and, in Sherri Ann's eyes, her gift to Alaskan Malamute Rescue was a sort of inverted shrine lovingly fashioned not merely to display but to illuminate what was no trivial keepsake of Comet, but furry tufts of his venerated remains. The holy human dead also get spread about. They have to, really. It's a matter of supply and demand. Saints and martyrs being lamentably scarce, they don't leave enough to go around, and what there is get divvied up: a skull here, a hand there, a tooth, a lock of hair, disjointed bones and scraps reverently dispersed in what isn't exactly a watering of the spiritual soup, but is nonetheless a transparent effort to make a transcendent little go a long way.

"It takes a three-way bulb," said Sherri Ann.

CHAPTER 2

I was speechless. Sherri Ann said, "Look, I *was* going to give this to Freida, and if you people for some reason don't *appreciate*—"

"Oh, we do!" I exclaimed hastily. "We're really very grateful."

At the risk of revealing myself as thankless, I'll add that the purity of Sherri Ann's motivation in donating the relic to Alaskan Malamute Rescue instead of our breed club was, I thought, heavily contaminated by revenge. As every one of the hundred or so people in the exhibition area knew, Sherri Ann Printz, the chair of the previous year's national, had arrived at the show to discover that this year's chair, Freida Reilly, had chosen a previously unannounced theme: *Putting the SPECIAL Back in SPECIALTY!* In and around the show ring, a lot of things get dropped: gum wrappers, paper coffee cups, scraps of sandwiches, bits of the liver used to bait the dogs. Insults? Let fall, yes. Seldom by accident. And if you happen to be a stranger to the dog fancy, let me explain right now that unless you're a lifelong hermit, you'll understand the competition and politics as well as any insider does. Little League competition? Church politics? The PTA! Stranger, you're right at home here.

Sherri Ann cleared her throat. "When," she demanded, "is Betty getting back here?"

"Any minute," I said. Then I introduced myself. "I'm Holly Winter."

There was no reason why Sherri Ann Printz should have known who I was. I write a column for *Dog's Life* magazine, but even if Sherri Ann subscribed, she didn't necessarily read it. Furthermore, I wasn't a breeder, and I had only two, malamutes. Rowdy, my male, finished his championship easily, and I was still showing him now and then, but only in the Northeast. My cousin Leah was just starting to show my bitch, Kimi, in breed. Leah and I concentrate on obedience, but in Sherri Ann's view, conformation—competition for championship points and beyond—was all that mattered; obedience trials barely existed.

But I knew who Sherri Ann Printz was. Everyone did. She'd had malamutes for decades. Only a few years earlier, the *Malamute Quarterly* had published a two-part interview with her. She lived in Minnesota. Her kennel name wasn't her fault; she'd been brainwashed by the cult. Failing deprogramming, she'd had no real choice: last name, Printz, therefore Pawprintz Kennels. Sherri Ann had bred a lot of top show dogs, including the favorite to go Best of Breed on Saturday afternoon under Judge James Hunnewell, a dog called Bear—officially, Pawprintz Honor Guard—a big, heavy-boned dog named by Sherri Ann's husband, Victor Printz, U.S.M.C., retired, who, according to rumor, had never been heard to utter an intelligible word to a human being, but was reputed to murmur and grunt to his wife's dogs and to christen all of them: Tripoli, Montezuma, Few Good Men.

So, if Sherri Ann thought that I was no one—no one in

malamutes—she was right. Rejecting my suggestion that she wait for someone who counted—and Betty Burley did count—Sherri Ann departed to watch the judging and missed by only a minute or two the return of Betty, who was carrying two cups of that substance without which a dog show isn't a dog show, namely, horrible coffee. Somewhere in South America, I'm convinced, dwells an anti-dog cousin of Juan Valdez who meticulously selects the most shriveled little beans from the most sickly, runty bushes, mixes his harvest with fistfuls of manure, and ships it to the U.S., where it's tested for staleness, and then sold exclusively for brewing and consumption at dog shows.

After handing me a cup and sipping from her own, Betty also passed along a bit of something that's as universal at dog shows as bad coffee: gossip. In this case, though, the news was anything but the usual light hearsay. "Elsa Van Dine was *murdered* last night!" I had the impression that the late Elsa Van Dine had once been a Personage in malamutes. "In *Providence!*" Betty added. She made the city sound as shocking as the crime itself.

The combination of murder and Providence reminded me of something ugly I'd heard from my nextdoor neighbor, Kevin Dennehy, who's a Cambridge police lieutenant. Looking up from a newspaper article about murder-for-hire, my cousin Leah had asked Kevin how much you had to pay to get someone killed. "It all depends," Kevin had replied matter-of-factly. "In Providence, you can get a bat job for sixty dollars." In reply to Leah's baffled look, Kevin had expanded: "Baseball bat."

"The poor thing," Betty went on, "flew in to New York and rented a car, and on her way here, she stopped off with relatives in Providence. And last night, when she went out to her car for something, she was robbed and murdered! Right there on the street! Her wedding ring and her diamond engagement ring were pulled right off her finger. Poor thing! She died of massive head injuries."

Before I could ask exactly who Elsa Van Dine was—had been—Betty aimed a finger at the lamp. "Don't tell me! Sherri Ann Printz. And she made it herself."

I first met Betty Burley when we'd been seated next to each other at a dog club banquet. Even before we exchanged introductions, a flash of recognition informed me that I was encountering a rare case of duplicate reincarnation. Staring into Betty's weirdly familiar almond-shaped brown eyes, I saw the soul of an Alaskan malamute, and not just any malamute, but my own Kimi. The physical resemblance, however, ended with those duplicate eyes; Kimi is young, big, well-muscled, and dark, with the facial markings that make up a full mask: a black cap, a bar down her muzzle, and goggles around her eyes. A tiny, frail-looking woman in her midseventies, Betty Burley never even wore a hat, never mind a cap or a mask, and she used glasses only for reading. Nonetheless, whenever Betty entered my kitchen, I felt compelled to check the counters for food she might steal. In Betty's presence, I'd find myself fishing through my pockets for liver treats, and I'd discover on the tip of my tongue such unspeakable commands as "Off!" "Leave it!" and an emphatic "Watch me!"

"Dear God," sighed Betty, eyes on the lamp, "since when did Sherri Ann start supporting Rescue?" She spoke loudly enough to be easily overheard by the people looking over the collection of silent-auction items arranged on our table. Saturday night's live auction would bring in big money. The objects in our comparatively humble silent auction included a pair of metal dog bowls, a set of malamute refrigerator magnets, a copper aspic mold in the shape of a fish, two pounds of Vienna roast coffee beans, a case of beer that it was probably illegal for us to auction in Massachusetts, and—

my favorite—a framed mirror with malamutes painted all over the glass, designed, I guess, to let you see yourself as your own dogs.

"She was going to give the lamp to Freida," I said quietly, "but she changed her mind. I assume it was that 'Putting the SPECIAL Back . . . '"

Betty eyed the lamp. "What it was—is—is troublemaking."

"That's Comet's fur," I said defensively.

"She hasn't glued it on right," Betty pointed out. "It's falling off."

In fact, stray clumps of fur were loose, as if the stress of finding himself stacked on pink granite and transformed into a light fixture had induced the poor dog to blow coat.

"Did Sherri Ann ever own Comet?" I asked.

"No. Comet had three or four different owners. Actually, poor Elsa Van Dine was one of them. But Sherri Ann certainly wasn't. Some of her dogs do go back to Comet, though." With an un-Kimi-like expression of resignation, Betty said, "Well, if that really is Comet's fur, I suppose we'll have to save it for Saturday night. You don't care for the ugly thing, and I wouldn't give it house room, but someone will just love it."

From her overstuffed tote bag, Betty removed a manila folder and added a note about Sherri Ann's lamp to her list of donations. At Betty's request, I started to move the lamp from its temporary place among the silent-auction items to the long, narrow table that ran along the wall at the back of our booth, where we were displaying the ten special donations reserved for the Saturday post-banquet live auction.

"Don't drop it!" Betty warned me. "If it lands on your foot, it'll crush it, and then where will I be?"

Betty had started checking animal shelters for abandoned malamutes thirty or forty years ago. She was one of the pioneers of the breed rescue movement, which is an effort to tackle the otherwise overwhelming problem of needy and abandoned dogs by dividing the responsibility. It's hard to understand why dog people would have devalued kindness to animals and rejected the simple, practical idea that we should take care of our own, but Betty spent decades being ridiculed for wasting her time and money on what people called "trash dogs." She sometimes found it hard to believe that support was growing. If the lamp had smashed my foot, Yvonne, Nancy, Isabelle, Gary, or one of the other rescue people would have filled in for me. But Betty remained sensitive.

A woman who'd been examining the album of rescue dogs moved along the table. Picking up a book—*Frozen Future*, a book about Antarctica—she asked, "How much is this?"

"It's a silent auction," I explained for the thousandth time. "You look at the piece of paper, the one there, and you see how much the last person bid for it. And if you're willing to pay more, you write your name and the amount on the next line. And then on Saturday afternoon after Best of Breed, you come back and see if you're the highest bidder."

Ever the proselytizer, Betty Burley pounced on the woman and offered her a pamphlet about Alaskan Malamute Rescue. Then Yvonne Johnson appeared and took over for me so that I could make the rounds of the vendors. The booth that especially interested me was run by R.T.I., Reproductive Technologies, Inc., a company that specialized in ovulation timing and semen preservation.

Yes, indeed. I had to see a man about some frozen sperm.

CHAPTER 3

"The bitch that Lois calls Angel is actually quite decent." Pam Ritchie eyed the young—and by implication, far from decent—male that another New England breeder, Lois Metzler, was at that moment gaiting across the ring.

With apparent astonishment, Tiny DaSilva gasped, "Do *you* think so?"

"Yes, I *do*," Pam snapped. "For those lines."

Finding the R.T.I. booth staffed only by a sign that read BACK SOON, I'd spotted Pam and Tiny and decided to catch some of the judging. Fond of my jugular, I'd avoided even the appearance of partiality by moving one of the hotel-supplied chairs to a position behind and directly between Pam and Tiny, whose knees almost brushed the baby gate.

Tiny gave a loud snort. Lowering the volume, she mumbled, "Ball of fluff on toothpicks!"

Everything about Pam, from her big-boned build to the distinctive shape of her head to a familiar and characteristic expression in her eyes, suggested an origin in the lines that had produced Tiny's dogs; and if Tiny had been a malamute, she'd have been one of Pam Ritchie's own breeding, a pure Kotzebue, a descendant of the malamutes bred by Milton and Eva B. Seeley at the old Chinook Kennels, which supplied the dogs for the Byrd expeditions. But the colors were wrong, the coats incorrect: Pam had a mane of unacceptably fluffy curls in non-malamute chestnut. If Tiny had shampooed out the blue tint and let her blunt cut grow, she could have entered herself, I guess, but as it was, the evidence of cosmetic tinkering was unmistakable, and she was obviously out of coat.

Appearances mislead. Despite the incessant exchanges of growls, Pam and Tiny often traveled to and from shows together. At meetings, they invariably sat next to each other. A few months earlier, Pam had had a miscarriage while her husband was away on business, and Tiny had nursed her and taken care of her dogs. Observing what often seemed like an imminent and bloody scrap, a stranger wouldn't have known that Pam and Tiny were self-chosen kennelmates linked by the sturdy chains of dogs.

"Well, I'll tell you something." Pam gestured toward Lois's dog. "Doris likes him. He's just her type."

Tiny narrowed her eyes. "With that tail?"

"You watch and see," Pam told her. "Some of Lois's dogs go back to Doris's, you know. Or maybe you've forgotten."

Tiny, twenty or thirty years older than Pam, exclaimed, "*Forgotten?* What makes you think that I'm getting forgetful all of a sudden? And in case you're forgetting something you don't know to begin with, let me tell you that James Hunnewell's not going to like that dog any better than Doris does. Among other things, Hunnewell never put up a black-and-white dog in his life, and he's not going to start now."

My hopes rose. Rowdy and Kimi are not black and white, but dark wolf gray.

After a pause, Pam added, "Although I, for one, have yet to see any real proof that the man is still alive."

"Don't be ridiculous!" Tiny said. "Hunnewell's name was on the eligible list, wasn't it?"

Each of the various competitions, including the independent area specialty scheduled for Sunday (another all-malamute show entirely separate from the national), had *a* judge. *The* judge of the national specialty itself, however, was James Hunnewell, whose victory in the poll of our entire national breed club membership had come as a gigantic surprise for the simple reason that he'd been out of dogs for so long that everyone had assumed he was dead. No one I'd talked to had admitted to voting for Hunnewell in the judging poll. Everyone in New England blamed the result on people in other areas of the country, where, I suspect, everyone was blaming *us*. In strict confidence, the woman who'd tallied the vote had told me that she'd been so amazed at the result that she'd recounted the ballots three separate times before reaching the conclusion that we had elected a deceased judge. Imagine: In the next U.S. presidential race, the surprise victor turns out to be Calvin Coolidge. Astounded, are you? None too delighted? Thought he was dead? Well, there you have the election of James Hunnewell.

"I still can't understand it," Pam said.

"Splintered vote," I volunteered. "Or name recognition. That's what Janet Switzer thinks. Hunnewell's name is in all the breed books."

Janet is Rowdy's breeder and one of my mentors. "And if they'd known Hunnewell," she'd continued, "they'd have scooped up the little piece of fecal matter and deposited him in the Doggie Dooley where he belongs."

James Hunnewell had drawn a surprisingly large entry: Since no one had even seen him for a long time, few exhibitors harbored resentments about losses under him or had any memories at all about how he'd conducted himself in his ring. Janet had advised me to enter. "The old coot's got to be on his last legs," remarked Janet, who isn't on her own first. "Who knows? He might kick the bucket any day, and you could luck out with a substitute judge."

Faith Barlow, Rowdy's handler, had taken Hunnewell's election as a personal challenge. "There's not a judge on earth that can intimidate me," she'd bragged. "There are a few I won't show under on principle, but otherwise, if it stands in the ring and hands out ribbons, I'll show under it; and if it growls at me, I'll growl back."

Betty Burley, though, had angrily refused to enter under James Hunnewell and had urged me to do the same. Betty's attitude, I thought, must date to some ancient injury or insult, a nasty remark that Hunnewell had made twenty or thirty years ago, an unkind word about her dogs, perhaps, or a mean-spirited comment about Betty's early rescue efforts.

I ignored Betty's advice and entered both dogs. Kimi was just beginning her career in conformation. I entered her in Open bitches. She'd be handled by my cousin Leah. I entered Rowdy, my champion, in Best of Breed. He'd be handled by Faith Barlow. Neither of my dogs would be in the ring until Saturday. Consequently, I had all day tomorrow to observe how Judge James Hunnewell treated those who'd complimented him by paying entry fees for his opinion of their dogs. If I didn't want my teenage cousin in his ring, I could pull Kimi or, over Leah's protests, no doubt, find another handler. Faith could take care of herself. I took her at more than her word: If Hunnewell bit her, she'd bite back.

CHAPTER 4 🔍

According to myth, the New England colonists fled the British Isles in search of religious freedom. In truth, they were extradited—summarily booted out of the homeland of dog worship following a little-known incident, an act of heresy, if you will, that took place at the famous Canterbury Cathedral. There a rebellious clique of Brewsters, Bradfords, Carvers, and Winslows refused to join their fellow worshipers in what would otherwise have been the unequivocally fervent rendering of "All Creatures Great and Small." As everyone knows, the involuntary expatriates first sought refuge in Holland. In the course of a barge tour of Amsterdam, however, one of their number—a Standish, I believe—uttered a very loud and extremely rude remark about a Keeshond, thus causing the previously hospitable Dutch to toss the future colonists over the dikes and into the cold seas of the Atlantic, where they drifted for many months before finally washing up on shore in the vicinity of a large rock on which many of them deservedly cracked their heads. Fable? Fact: The New England colonists

attached dire theological significance to the backward
spelling of *d-o-g*. The black mass: the litany backward. The
dog: the creature of Satan.

What leads me to the topic of the New England colonies
is not the hotel's decor, which was Hawaiian, but my con-
viction that somewhere on Maui, the Milestone chain has
erected a hotel and conference facility structurally identical
to the one in Danville, Massachusetts, but adorned with Ye
Olde New England materials and motifs. The building itself is, I believe, the same as this one: the two-story motel-
hotel at one end, the exhibition hall at the other, with the
space between devoted to a large lobby, a bar, two restaurants, a variety of meeting, assembly, and banquet rooms,
and the center consisting of a cavernous mock atrium that
does not open to the sky and contains some droopy-looking
trees that obviously wish it did and many others that, being plastic, don't care. Through the center of the atrium at
the Maui Milestone flows a miniature artificial trout stream
spanned by a tiny replica of a genuine New England covered bridge. Unwary guests trip on the legs of spinning
wheels, regain their balance, set down drinks on cobbler's
bench tables, and order refills from service personnel
garbed for a grammar-school reenactment of the First
Thanksgiving.

The Milestone chain being a microcosm of a balanced
universe, here in New England the equally cavernous
atrium, the Lagoon, was, as its name suggested, a sort of
South Seas grotto, the focal point of which was a tropical
lava-rock waterfall overhung by artificial coconut palms and
set near a plastic-mahogany bar shaped like an outrigger ca-
noe. The walls, papered in what I think was grass cloth,
were festooned with exotic-looking paddles, feather head-
dresses, bunches of fake bananas, and so many ukeleles that
if strummed in unison their strings could have drowned out
the music being piped into the lobby: a Muzak version of

"As Time Goes By" with the synthesizer set to the sound of Hawaiian guitars.

My room, however, was luxurious, and even if it hadn't been, the Danville Milestone possessed the one advantage that offsets anything from outrigger bars and ukeleles to bathrooms with rusty baseboards and no hot water: It allowed dogs!

Such was the gist of the violent complaint currently being lodged with the hotel manager by a red-faced man who brandished a clenched fist at the innocent-looking black announcement board built into the wall of the hotel lobby. The white plastic letters stuck into the grooves spelled out:

Thursday, October 31
THE DANVILLE MILESTONE HOTEL
AND CONFERENCE FACILITY

Aloha!

Alaskan Malamute National Specialty—Oahu Room
Luncheon and Meeting—Wahiawa Room

Lofgren-Jenkinson Wedding Party
Bachelor's Dinner—Kailua Room
Bride's Dinner—Wahiawa Room

"Crystal plans her wedding," boomed the man, "a full goddamn year in advance! She checks out restaurants, she visits historical houses, she goes to hotels, museums—and she picks *this* place! And her mother comes and sees it, and then she drags Greg out here, and they drag *me* out here, and frankly, all this South Seas shit puts me off, but, hey, they're going to Hawaii for their honeymoon, and Crystal's crazy about the idea . . . And this is the middle of *last* winter! Booked in advance! For *three* goddamn days! We got two dinners tonight, and we got the rehearsal tomorrow,

and we got the rehearsal dinner, and then we got the wedding breakfast, and then we got the wedding and the reception, and NOW! Five minutes ago! Now, we pull in, and
what do we find? This place booked *ten* months ahead of
time, and you, you sneaky little son of a bitch, did not see fit
to inform us that Crystal and Greg's *dream* wedding was
gonna happen in the middle of a fucking *dog show!*"

I found the sentiment as shocking as the language. *To
have and to hold from this day forward, for better for worse, for
richer for poorer, in sickness and in health, to love and to cherish,
till death us do part?* You'll never convince a real dog person
that those words were written about a human relationship.

"Daddy, please! Mummy, make him stop!" The bride-to-
be, Crystal, wore numerous layers of loose-waisted, flowing
garments. Even so, it was obvious that at any moment, her
father might have reason to regret his present loud display
of temper. In terms of experience at whelping boxes, our national specialty was as good as a convention of midwives,
and when it came to familiarity with multiple births, far,
far, better.

Daddy did not stop. And Mummy, a midforties, non-
pregnant Crystal, with the same pert features and the same
long blond hair, didn't make him.

The manager was heroic. "Now, Mr. Jenkinson, let me
assure you that there will be no conflict whatsoever. The
two, er, events are scheduled for entirely separate and distinct facilities; and dogs are never under any circumstance
permitted in the undesignated areas of this hotel." As he
spoke, he must have been employing some nonverbal tech-
nique he'd mastered in the Milestone's management-trainee
program, which, I became convinced, was staffed by Scot-
tish shepherds, because, as effectively as a Border collie, the
manager cut the bridal party out of the crowd in the lobby
and herded together in a far corner the six members of the
nuptial flock: Crystal, her parents, another couple about

their age, and a young man who looked so frighteningly like a Ken doll that if Crystal's condition had not suggested otherwise, I'd have wondered whether anatomy would permit him to consummate the marriage.

As if preparing to flee the pen, Crystal lurked on the periphery of the group with her back toward the others. Catching sight of the only genuinely four-legged creature in the lobby, she stamped a foot and announced to everyone and no one that she, for one, didn't mind at all, because she, for one, *liked* dogs.

"Greg? Greg! Greg, look!" She tapped life-size bride-groom Ken on the shoulder. "That's what *I want!*" Pointing to a malamute bitch so dirty that I'd have been ashamed to take her to the local park, the bride-and-mother-to-be announced, "*I* want a husky! Greg? Greg, that's what we should've asked for! We should've asked for a baby puppy!"

Greg began to move his lips, but before sound emerged, his mother, as she obviously was (Ken in drag), intervened. "Crystal, dear, you're forgetting that Gregory is allergic to dogs." As if pausing to permit a thought to travel across Crystal's mind, she let five or ten seconds elapse before adding, "And cats."

Folding his arms across his chest, Greg mumbled. I caught only one word. The syllables were distinct and prolonged: *Mommmm-meeeee*.

Had the celebrants at my own rites been united not by a passion for dogs but by a mania for vipers, for instance, or stamps, coins, antiques, first editions, the French language, or the topic of alien abduction, the crowd in the lobby might have thinned. As it was, what held me held the other dog people. Crystal's adamant *I want?* Mr. Jenkinson's raised hackles? The challenge to another male, the dominant individual's swift restoration of order, the maternal protectiveness, the whine of the young male . . . Oh, and the unplanned breeding, too. Dog people all, we'd seen and heard it before.

Some of those in the lobby, of course, had business there: People waited in line to check in. The man with the dirty malamute wasn't in line and didn't have a suitcase. His name came to me: Tim Oliver. And his reputation: sleazy. I couldn't remember whether we'd met or whether he'd just been pointed out to me. Perhaps in the hope of being mistaken for an American Kennel Club judge, Tim Oliver wore a navy blazer, but judges are usually tidy, and they don't go around shedding dandruff flakes all over our nice clean dogs.

As I was wondering whether to say hello to Oliver, the hotel door opened and in strode Duke Sylvia. He was a big, tall man who handled mostly Working Group breeds, a lot of Akitas and Danes, Siberians, Samoyeds, malamutes, boxers now and then; and mainly to show off, I'd always thought, also handled an unusually wide variety of other breeds when he got the chance—ridgebacks, bulldogs, and once in a while a toy, a Maltese, or a papillon. Duke was an ungodly gifted handler, one of the best I'd ever seen. Put Mario Andretti behind the wheel of an old VW bug, and maybe it becomes a Maseratti. Hand Duke a dog's lead, you got a whole new animal. People swore that one time, on a bet, Duke Sylvia not only walked into the Pomeranian ring with a long-haired ginger cat, but won, too. The story must have been apocryphal. Watching Duke handle, you could still believe it. That's how good he was.

Duke didn't have a dog with him now, just a leather suitcase in one hand and a metal tack box in the other. Although he was what my father calls "a regular guy," he was also what my grandmother calls "a dandy." He wore starched shirts, flashy ties, jackets fresh from the dry cleaner's, creased pants, polished shoes, and heavy male jewelry: big rings, tie tacks, lapel pins, an ID bracelet, and a wristwatch with a wide metal band. His age? Over forty. Under sixty? He had thick gold-yellow hair streaked with white, like the mane of an aging lion, but treated with some kind of grooming product, maybe one of those conditioners that promise to eliminate tangles, mats, snarls, and static electricity while simultaneously moisturizing dry skin and imparting a pleasant nondoggy odor. As advertised, the effect was more controlled than greasy, and Duke's hair matched the rest of him. He had broad features. Like a lion's, his head was too big for his body.

There was, however, nothing growly about Duke's personality. On the contrary, he was an affable guy with an endearing ability, unusual in our cult, to remember the names not only of dogs but, remarkably enough, of people, too.

"Holly Winter!" he called out. "Saw your dad a few weeks back. Good to see him out and about again. Hey, Timmy, how you doing? You heard about Elsa? Damned shame." Duke didn't look particularly upset. He could have been remarking on the peaceful and natural demise of an elderly pet.

Tim Oliver echoed Duke: "Damned shame." Matching platitude with platitude, he added, "Nowhere's safe these days." Tim—Timmy, as the oldtimers called him—had soft, unformed features, as if a childhood illness or a genetic quirk had prematurely halted his facial development. His hair was lank, his face flat, his ears large. The diminutive, *Timmy*, I thought, flagged a folk diagnosis of what a doctor might have recognized as a subtle syndrome with trivial consequences.

When Duke had finished greeting six or eight other people by name and exchanging remarks with all of them about Elsa Van Dine's murder and the damned shame of random violence, I started to approach him with a request for a favor. The Showcase of Rescue Dogs was set for seven o'clock that night. I wanted to persuade Duke to handle one of the dogs.

Before I could slip in the request, however, Timmy Oliver snagged Duke and launched into a monologue about the merits of his bitch, whose name, as I overheard it, was Xerox, but, as Timmy went on to say, was spelled *Z-Rocks*. According to Timmy, Z-Rocks had easily finished her championship at a young age, was the bitch he'd been waiting for all his life, and—in a stage whisper—exactly James Hunnewell's type. Duke took Timmy's bid for approval with his usual air of calm amiability. I followed Duke's eyes as they played over Z-Rocks, who, viewed as a show dog, seemed to me perfectly decent, but not outstanding. Also, her coat was in disgraceful shape.

"And wait till you see her move!" Tim exclaimed.

Wait was what we didn't have to do. Abruptly tightening the lead in his hand, Timmy Oliver went charging across the lobby with the astonished Z-Rocks doing her best to maintain a proper show gait despite the obstacle-ridden conditions of the odd ring in which she suddenly found herself. Directly ahead lay the invisible pen into which the Border collie manager had herded his distressed nuptial flock. To avoid a collision, Timmy came to a startled halt, and Z-Rocks, displaying a show dog's nose for where power lay, dutifully posed herself before Crystal, who cried, "Oh, you beautiful husky! I just love you!"

Faced with rebellion in the pen and the presence of a wolflike creature just outside it, the manager lost control in a fashion entirely uncharacteristic of his breed. Raising an arm, he pointed directly at the father of the bride. "*Your* daughter," he boomed, "was fully informed of the other event that would take place this weekend. She and I discussed it at length and in detail, and she voiced no objection whatsoever."

Silence fell in the lobby.

"Crystal," bellowed Mr. Jenkinson, "is that true?"

"It does sort of ring a bell," Crystal admitted.

"A wedding bell," I whispered to Duke and to Freida Reilly, our show chair, who'd appeared at his side. "It's a bridal party," I continued. "They didn't know about, uh, us."

To the extent that a national specialty is any one person's show, it is the chair's. Within seconds, Freida Reilly had assessed the situation and was taking action. Freida had been trained by experts: Alaskan malamutes and AA. Pointing at Z-Rocks, Freida addressed Timmy Oliver in tones that suggested the implementation of an intensive rehabilitation program in which the participant is kicked down a flight of twelve steps onto a concrete landing: "Timmy Oliver, you get her out of this lobby, and from now on, you keep her out of the areas of this hotel where dogs aren't allowed. *Out!*" An ornate enamel malamute pinned to Freida's heaving bosom appeared ready to leap off and, if necessary, enforce her order.

Having dealt with Oliver, Freida, who looked exhausted, turned to the manager and the bridal party, and spoke calm words of conciliation. Everyone was here to have a good time, Freida said; no one had any interest in spoiling the fun for anyone else. Freida was a tactful politician as well as a superb organizer. She left unspoken the countercharge that their noisy, smelly wedding was going to ruin our lovely dog show.

CHAPTER 5

At quarter of seven that evening, Betty Burley and I waited nervously for the start of our Showcase of Rescue Dogs. I'd written the script that would be read as our ten dogs were paraded around the ring, spotlighted, and presented with the same awards—white sashes—that would later go to the stars of the breed. The script was supposed to be sappy enough to bring tears to people's eyes but not mawkish enough to bring their dinners back up to their mouths—and let me admit that even for a professional writer, attaining that precise degree of melodrama is far from easy. The ring was festooned with tiny white lights, and in the center was a white trellis that looked as if it belonged in a rose garden, but was surrounded by pots of yellow chrysanthemums. The lights and flowers were for the show-dog event to follow, not for our little showcase.

"Elsa Van Dine, poor thing," Betty informed me, "sent Freida an extremely generous donation specifically for flowers. Little did Elsa ever imagine . . . !"

"That she'd be sending them to her own funeral," I finished.

"That's a bit of an overstatement, Holly," Betty replied. "This is hardly Elsa's funeral." As if reconsidering the entire matter of Elsa and her generosity, she added, "And, of course, Elsa did not send *us* so much as a halfpenny or whatever it is they use over there now."

Fifteen or twenty years earlier, I'd learned, the late Elsa Van Dine had married an English marquis, moved to Great Britain, and dropped out of dogs. Betty, Duke, and her other old friends, however, hadn't seen her since she moved abroad and continued to use the name they'd known her by.

"And Elsa was a *very* wealthy woman in her own right," Betty said, adding rather spitefully, "for all the good it did her. In fact, I can't help wondering whether Elsa hadn't gone and rented some sort of flashy convertible, or whether she might have been wearing a *mink* coat or something else that attracted this mugger." She sighed. "'Massive head injuries.' That's what Freida told me. Elsa would have hated that. She was a pretty girl. Very vain. Oh, well, at least it must have been over quickly."

"Betty," I whispered, "there's Sherri Ann Printz over there. This would be a good time to go and say a quick thanks for the lamp."

Sherri Ann was near the gate to the ring. She stood in a group that included our chair, Freida Reilly, who was about to walk in and take her place in the center.

"With *Freida* right there!" Betty exclaimed. "Never! That is exactly what Sherri Ann has in mind, setting me up to create bad feeling with Freida. Nothing would please Sherri Ann more than to listen to me rub it in Freida's nose that Rescue got the lamp that Sherri Ann promised her. I will *not* give Sherri Ann the satisfaction!"

According to rumor, what was called the "bad blood" between Sherri Ann Printz and Freida Reilly had originated a year or two earlier in what would've struck anyone outside the world of dog breeding as a *nothing* incident. Freida had wanted to breed one of her bitches to Sherri Ann's Bear, Ch. Pawprintz Honor Guard. When Sherri Ann said no, Freida took the refusal as a gross insult to her canine lines and to her own reputation as a responsible, ethical breeder. Suppose that you're traditional Chinese parents, okay? And an arranged marriage is proposed between your wonderful daughter and the splendid son of another estimable family. And his parents quash the deal. The implication? You're not good enough. Neither is your kid. This was like that. Only far worse.

Betty eyed the lamp, which was still with the antique wolf prints and the other valuable donations. Lowering her voice to a level audible to a mere twenty or thirty people, she confided, "Tacky thing! Lowers the whole tone of the booth!" Although I'd never heard Betty express any admiration for Bear, it occurred to me that she, too, might have wanted to use him at stud and, like Freida, been flatly turned down.

The overhead lights blinked and dimmed. The announcer's amplified voice boomed: "Ladies and gentlemen, welcome to the Showcase of Rescue Dogs." To take advantage of the power of first impressions, we'd given the number-one spot to what's called a "quality dog," an obvious blue blood. The "ahs" and "oohs" rose above the announcer's voice. Second was a sweet little female who'd been rescued from the puppy mill; third, a red-and-white male who'd been found with a metal training collar deeply embedded in the festering flesh of his neck. Our fourth, Helen, and the boy who handled her drew cheers.

When Duke Sylvia led in the fifth dog, I thought for a second that sly old Duke had decided all on his own to boost the image of rescue dogs by slipping in a substitute for the one he'd agreed to handle for a timid adopter. The dog,

Cubby, was one I'd placed with a woman named Jeanine,
who was too shy to handle him herself. Three months before
Jeanine had adopted Cubby, a man had broken into her
apartment. She'd tried and failed to fight off the attack. Although the rapist was caught, Jeanine had remained terrified of aggression. She'd asked me for a big, gentle dog.
Cubby was immense, a rangy, gangly creature with long,
thin legs, a gigantic barrel chest, light eyes, propeller ears,
and so many other faults that he might as well have had
puppy mill via pet shop tattooed across his forehead. But he
was as gentle as he was homely. He didn't look gentle,
though, and he was really, really big. I'd omitted Jeanine's
story from my script, of course. I'd also had to leave out the
other interesting feature of Cubby's history. Turned in by a
man who'd bought him at a pet shop, Cubby had come with
AKC papers. I'd run his pedigree—in other words, traced
his family tree. As Cubby's appearance suggested, most of
his ancestors had been owned and bred by operators of
wholesale commercial kennels in Missouri and Arkansas, in
other words, by the people we aren't supposed to call puppy
millers in case they take offense and sue us. Four generations
back, though, I'd found a dog with the kennel named Pawprintz, a male bred by Sherri Ann Printz and, according to
the Alaskan malamute stud book register, owned by a G. H.
Thacker. G. H. Thacker was, I'd figured out while running
other pet-shop pedigrees, a USDA-licensed puppy farmer in
Missouri, a woman named Gladys H. Thacker.

In writing Cubby's part of the script, I'd had to omit
Cubby's true role in Jeanine's life, and I certainly wouldn't
have humiliated Sherri Ann Printz by informing the assem-
bled membership of our national breed club that a Pawprintz dog had somehow ended up in a puppy mill. Sherri
Ann would have been totally disgraced. Suppose you're a
pooh-bah in the Daughters of the American Revolution,
and there you are at the national D.A.R. convention when

over the loudspeaker booms the announcement that your
eldest daughter is a white slave in a brothel in Thailand, and
that you're the one who sold her into bondage. No, no! Consequently, I worried that my deletion of the unmentionable
would focus attention on the dog's unfortunate looks. At the
end of the afternoon's rehearsal for the showcase, however,
Duke had taken possession of Cubby and vanished with him
into the grooming tent. There, the Michelangelo of fur, he'd
applied grooming mousses, sprays, gels, combs, brushes,
and a powerful force dryer to sculpt a new animal out of
Cubby's hair. In so doing, he'd freed the dog from the coat.
The transformation was superficial, of course; even Duke
Sylvia couldn't get great movement out of faulty anatomy.
But Cubby moved as well as Cubby could move. To my left,
Jeanine was clinging to Betty Burley and sobbing hard. In
those few seconds, I fell in love with Duke Sylvia.

The sixth and seventh dogs had what are ordinary stories
in Rescue: abandoned in shelters, saved from gas chambers.
The eighth dog, Frosty, another obvious blue blood of un-
known origin, drew silence, then noisy murmurs of speculation. Frosty's looks maddeningly proclaimed an origin in a
show kennel, any of dozens, without specifying which one.
Ninth was Juneau, who'd been turned in after she'd repeatedly broken loose, located an astonishing number of henhouses and duck ponds, and done what malamutes do.

We'd saved Czar for last. Old and frail, he gamely tot-
tered around the ring at the side of his owner, Lorraine. As
Lorraine and Czar approached Freida to receive his sash and
plaque, the announcer read my commentary. "Anyone familiar with the history of the Alaskan malamute," he announced, "has heard stories of legendary lead dogs that
unerringly followed the trail home through blinding bliz-
zards. Ice-encrusted eyes frozen shut, those legendary dogs
used what remained to them: their wonderful noses, their
keen ears, their mental maps, the intelligence of this breed,

the unmatched will to survive. In Czar, we see the living
history of the Alaskan malamute. Because of bilateral detached retinas, Czar is completely blind; he spends all day,
every day, as his own sightless lead dog."

Too sappy? A lot of tissues. No airsickness bags. And no
one, I thought, had guessed upon seeing him that Czar was
blind. How did Czar end up with detached retinas? Another
ordinary story: turned loose on a highway, hit by a car. Happens all the time.

CHAPTER 6 🐾

As the showcase ended, at least four show people interrogated me about Frosty's origins and remarked that he looked an awful lot like Sherri Ann Printz's dogs. He looked like a lot of people's dogs, I replied. No one wondered aloud about Cubby's ancestry; no one saw Sherri Ann's Pawprintz lines in *his* background.

Betty and I had been so busy that we'd forgotten to eat. We agreed to meet at the smaller of the hotel's two restaurants, the Liliu Grill. She was involved in an intense discussion with the owners of one of the rescue dogs. She was going to walk the people to their car. My bladder was as full as my stomach was empty. On my way to the restaurant, I stopped in the public ladies' room.

Serving as the principal toilet facility available to female patrons of the big restaurant in the Lagoon and to other women who weren't staying at the hotel, the ladies' room was only slightly smaller than the hotel lobby, with dozens of little chairs set at equal intervals along miles of countertop, so you could sit down to reapply your mascara; acres of mirror, so you could get your lipstick on straight and make sure your slip wasn't showing; a dozen sinks, so you could have a choice of where to wash your hands; and a couch covered in beige vinyl, so you'd have somewhere to faint while waiting your turn at the stalls, of which there were four. And were all four occupied? Hah! Only a man would ask. I took my place at the end of the line of three young women, the first of whom, Crystal, was chatting to the other two, who must have been guests at the bride's dinner. Crystal wore what looked like a gigantic baby dress, a smocked pink garment decorated with ruffles and lace. Her friends were thin and wore black. All three held drinks.

"And," Crystal was telling her buddies, "I go, 'Geez, Greg, a puppy! Whyn't we think of that?' and Mrs. Lofgren pipes up, 'Now, now, Crystal, dear'—she hates me; she just really hates me—'you're forgetting that my baby boy Greggie's allergic to *everything*, especially you!' And—"

"Crystal, she did not!" shrieked one of the friends. "She didn't say 'especially you.'" After a pause, the friend added, "Did she?"

"No," admitted Crystal, "but that's what she meant. You should see how she looks at me! She gives me the evil eye. She must spend half her life watching *Rosemary's Baby*, for God's sake. Wait'll she finds out it's twins! She's gonna go totally ballistic. The first thing that's gonna come out of her mouth is, 'What! You mean, my Gregory did it *twice!*'"

Crystal and her friends burst into screams that abated only when one of the stall doors opened. Handing her glass to one of the friends, Crystal said, "Hold this for me?"

The friend took the glass, sniffed it, and said, "Crystal, really! You know, you aren't supposed to—"

Crystal's voice came from behind the closed door. "Oh, yeah? Well, no doctor's telling me I can't celebrate my own wedding, okay? And don't you dare tell—"

The other two stalls freed up simultaneously. Crystal's

friends abandoned the three drinks on one of the counters and took their turns. I considered upending Crystal's glass over one of the sinks and substituting tap water. Before I could act, however, she emerged from the stall. I entered. While I was inside, she told her friends about the husky in the lobby and all the other beautiful huskies, except that they weren't really huskies, but malamutes, and what she really, really wanted for her most special wedding present was a beautiful little malamute puppy. Her friends told her that she was out of her mind. Besides, they said, she'd never talk Greg into it.

"Oh, yeah?" Crystal replied. "How much you wanna bet?"

The smug note in her voice made me uneasy. Leaving the stall, I took a place at the sink next to the one where Crystal was, of all things, brushing her teeth. Unable to keep my own mouth shut, I said, "You know, I couldn't help over-hearing. I thought you should know that there aren't any puppies for sale here. You aren't allowed to sell puppies at a show."

Crystal's self-satisfied expression made me wonder whether she'd already written someone a check. "That's show *grounds*," she informed me. "Otherwise, it's *nobody's* business but your own."

Show grounds? Crystal, who couldn't tell a malamute from a Siberian, seemed a strange source of the dog person's phrase. Odder yet was her understanding of the American Kennel Club's sharp distinction between secular terrain and the hallowed precincts of a show site. As I fluffed up my hair in front of a stretch of mirror, I pondered the matter. While I was touching up my lipstick, Crystal flounced out, drink in hand, and her friends followed. I'd just zipped my cos-metics bag when the door to the ladies' room opened to ad-mit Cubby's adopter, Jeanine, who wasn't just weeping, as she'd been when her dog was in the ring, but sobbing hard.

With her was a woman who just had to be her sister. Both
were tall and lean, with long, straight black hair, fine features, extraordinarily large hands, and long fingers tipped
by nails tinted a shade of rose-brown that picked up the
color of Jeanine's rather drab suit and the flower print of her
companion's silk scarf. Catching sight of me, Jeanine covered her face with those immense, elegant hands. I immediately asked what on earth was wrong.

Her companion answered for her. "We had an unfortunate little experience. I'm Jeanine's sister, Arlette."

We shook hands. "Holly Winter. I placed Cubby with
Jeanine. Jeanine, can you tell me what happened?"

"Jeanine," Arlette said firmly, "you know, this does not
have to be a big huge deal. Get it through your head: This
was *not* an attack. It was just some ignorant people who
didn't even know who we were, okay? So would you go and
wash your face in cold water? And blow your nose and pull
yourself together."

As Jeanine moved obediently toward a washbasin, I
again asked what had happened.

"It's nothing," Arlette answered. "We were on our way
back to the car. With Cubby. We're parked at the opposite
end of the hotel, because when we drove in this afternoon,
we noticed there was a field there, and it seemed like a good
place to let Cubby do his thing. So we left the car there.
Anyway, just now, when we'd almost got to the car, there
were some people talking and—"

Jeanine lifted her wet face from the sink to wail: "Men."

"Deep voices," her sister explained. "It was very dark.
The lighting out there really isn't adequate. Anyway, all
that happened was that we overheard a couple of phrases
that got Jeanine all upset. And for *no* good reason! Have you
got that, Jeanine? For *no* good reason!"

Jeanine took a seat on one of the dainty little white chairs
arrayed along the counter in front of the long mirror. The

ladies' room didn't supply paper towels, just machines for drying your hands, so she was blotting her face with tissues from her purse. I caught her eye in the mirror. "Jeanine," I said gently, "could you tell me what they said? Obviously, it was something painful. I want to know what it was."

"It was about *B-B-Betty's mongrels*," she stammered.

"The killer phrase," Arlette added, "was 'trash dogs.' But they were *not* referring—"

Jeanine abandoned repairs on her face to snarl: "Oh, yes they were! And we did *not* just overhear them, Arlette! They saw us, they saw Cubby, and they said that *deliberately!* And they did it just to be mean."

I said, "I hate to tell you, Arlette, but it's possible that Jeanine is right. Look, in any group of people, there are a few stinkers. And the ones we've got here tend to be super-competitive show people who don't actually know anything about dogs. To cover up their own ignorance, most of what they do is go around saying other people's dogs are trash. They say it about show dogs all the time. Especially the ones that beat theirs. But the rescue dogs make easy targets."

One of the toilets flushed loudly. As the stall door opened, Jeanine startled the poor woman who emerged by exclaiming, "*Cubby* is *not* trash!" Belatedly, she lowered her voice. "I know he's not a show dog. You told me that when you gave him to me, that he's a pet, that he's no show dog. But he is not *trash!*"

"Of course he's not." To my mind, no dog is trash, but it seemed an inopportune moment to say so.

"What *trash* means," Arlette added, "is assholes like those guys out in the parking lot, okay? *That's* trash for you, Jeanine. So just forget it. Hey, Cubby's all alone in the car out there, and we've got a long drive ahead. Let's just forget it and go home."

Jeanine looked a lot better now. With her own spirits improved, she turned her thoughts to someone else. Rising from her seat, she said, "You know, Holly, when we were out there, Betty was out there, too. She was walking with some people to a car. I hope she didn't hear what they said. I hope the other people didn't hear either."

"I hope not," I agreed. "But please don't worry about Betty. She's a lot tougher than she looks." I paused. "But if she didn't hear, I think we won't tell her, okay? I'll tell her eventually, but if it's all right with you, I think for now we just won't mention it."

Jeanine concurred. As it turned out, she and Arlette didn't see Betty again that night, anyway. We took a short-cut through the Lagoon, which rang with the raucous laughter of young men gathered around the outrigger bar, where Greg's bachelor party was in progress. I tried to get a description of the voices Jeanine and Arlette had heard in the darkness. Jeanine was positive that both speakers were men. Arlette said that at least one could have been a woman with a deep voice. Neither speaker had had a foreign accent or a regional drawl. One voice might have been hoarse. There had been nothing to see except shapes in the dark. When we reached the lobby, Betty wasn't in sight. Jeanine, Arlette, and I shared a big hug.

"Thank you, Holly," Jeanine said. "You know, what really got to me wasn't *what* they said. It was the pointless cruelty of saying it at all."

"I know," I told her. "That's what got to me, too."

Although the Liliu Grill was located just off the lobby, I stood perfectly still for a few seconds to try to steel myself for whatever Betty's reaction might be if she'd overheard the voices or somehow learned of the incident. She'd be enraged, of course. But whether she'd be in a hot mood of hell-bent revenge or a cold state of murder-on-ice, I couldn't predict. It was also possible that like me, she'd keep the matter to herself.

In fact, when I entered the grill and located Betty, I

couldn't tell whether she knew or not. She was perched on the edge of a chair too high for her peering with Kimi-like intensity at a menu too big for her small hands. "Now what," she demanded, "would you say that Norwegian salmon Delmonico might be?"

I took a seat. "Cream sauce, maybe?"

Outraged, Betty said, "Well, I find it hard to believe that anyone would drown a nice piece of salmon in *cream* sauce!"

I couldn't resist the impulse to try to mollify her. "Maybe it's smoked salmon on toast," I suggested. "That would be good."

"I should hope so," she snapped. "It's certainly expensive enough."

Before Betty had time to take further offense at the grill's offerings, a waiter appeared and took orders for drinks, and my cousin Leah, who'd been checking on my dogs, arrived. Leah, a Harvard freshman, had driven to Danville with me the day before. First thing in the morning, she'd handled Kimi in obedience. Immediately afterward, she'd borrowed my car and headed back to Cambridge, where she'd taken two exams, one in chemistry, one in Latin, before turning around and returning to Danville. Despite her accomplishments, Leah's a good kid. She doesn't go around swathed in crimson with *Veritas* plastered across her ample bosom. In fact, her wardrobe is so overwhelmingly and exclusively black that if it weren't for her cheerful countenance and gleeful mass of long red-gold curls, you'd mistake her for a raiment major at a mortuary college. She started talking nonstop before she'd even sat down. "I have a message for both of you, actually, two messages from two people who *both* said that when I found you I had to tell you right away that there's a rumor going around about *someone* selling puppies, and you won't believe it, but *both* of these people wanted to know what Rescue was going to do about it!"

"That's not our business," I said. "It's the rep's."

Rep: AKC rep, representative of the American Kennel Club.

"That's what I told them," Leah informed me.

"There's no rep here," Betty said.

I was surprised. "Really? Why not?"

"I don't know," Betty said. "There doesn't have to be one." She shrugged. "Anyway, if someone's selling puppies, it's Freida's business, not ours. There's nothing we can do about it."

"Who's it supposed to be?" I asked, intrigued. "Who is it who's selling puppies?"

"No one knows," my cousin replied. "Maybe it's just a rumor, anyway."

The waiter returned. I ordered a second Johnnie Walker and a seafood casserole. The fare at the Liliu Grill was bafflingly un-Hawaiian; pineapple appeared on the menu only in conjunction with a slice of baked ham, and coconut was completely absent. Leah chose steak with Béarnaise sauce— pure butter—and a diet soft drink that I wouldn't give to a dog. Without finding out what "Delmonico" meant, Betty asked for the salmon. When the waiter left, we debriefed the showcase.

"It *is* too bad that we didn't have a reporter there," said Betty, buttering a cinnamon roll. "Or better yet, TV." She trained her intense gaze on me. It occurred to me that maybe she knew exactly what had happened out in the parking lot and was wondering whether I did, too.

"Yvonne tried," I said. "If we were a little closer to Boston, we might've gotten someone, but I guess no one thought it was worthwhile schlepping all the way out here. I hope the video turned out all right."

The judging of the conformation classes, including the nonregular classes like Brace and Team, was professionally taped and edited by a company that produced videos, which you could mail order. On the grounds that the few people

deranged enough to enter a malamute in a so-called obedience event should be allowed to blot the experience from
memory as soon as possible, the company did not bother to
tape the trial. A fearless obedience fanatic, however, an otherwise nice guy named Jim Kuehl, videoed the obedience at
all our national specialties. Jim had even gone so far as to
produce an underground classic, a tape of bloopers that
showed malamutes zipping madly around obedience rings,
leaping over baby gates, and crashing into handlers. We'd
also amateur-taped the Showcase of Rescue Dogs.

"I hope so," Leah said, "so you can play it tomorrow instead of all that gory—"

I kicked her under the table. One of Betty's tapes was
about family pets stolen and sold to research laboratories.
The video of puppy mills was so revolting that some of the
people who'd caught sight of it on the monitor at the rescue
booth had been unable to take in what they were seeing. Innocent and mystified, they'd peered at the screen and asked,
"What *is* that?" I'd found replies difficult to formulate. *A
chicken-wire cage crammed with the corpses of puppies*, I could
have said, or *A broker who's killing a dog while those two people
wait to buy the meat*.

"People need to see that," Betty told Leah crisply.

Although Betty was right, some of the other rescue people had lured me into a harmless conspiracy aimed at substituting tapes that would attract people to the rescue booth
for the ones that they needed to see. Jim Kuehl was letting
us borrow his tape of obedience bloopers, and we'd also
lined up some films of long-ago shows. According to the
plan, I was one of the people designated to eject Betty's cas-
settes and slip in the appealing ones.

Consequently, instead of minimizing my chances of success by focusing Betty on the subject of videos, I said
brightly, "Betty! Who's that woman over there? The one at
the corner table. She looks familiar."

So familiar that I even remembered her name—Michele Muldoon, Mikki as she was called—and had a good idea of why she'd chosen to eat alone. Her appearance, however, was so striking that I might well have chosen her in an uncalculated pick. She was a beautiful woman whose swept-back white hair was shot with fading red and whose face retained what I always assure Leah will be wrinkle-disguising freckles. I'd never met Mikki Muldoon, who came from the West. But I had frequently seen her picture in ads in the *Malamute Quarterly*, and had read and heard stories about her. She was a popular judge with what I'd been told was a flamboyant manner. As the judge, she appeared on the left in the show photos, usually with her feet hidden behind a large basket or pot of flowers, and maybe a pile of trophies—tote bags, tea sets, glass punch bowls, commemorative clocks—and always an announcement board with letters reading something like BEST OF WINNERS, PRAIRIE SCHOONER KENNEL CLUB. Truly, you'd assume from show photos that AKC judges share some grotesque pediatric disorder or a predilection for the kinds of ludicrous shoes that exhibitors wouldn't want wrecking otherwise impressive pictures of big wins. Anyway, on the right, the smiling handler invariably stood behind the dog, who, being a show dog, usually looked suitably showy. "Highly respected breeder/judge Mrs. Michele Muldoon," as the ad copy often read, looked like every other judge in every other ad, except in one way: Instead of proffering the ribbon to the dog or the handler, she always looked ready to pin it on her own breast.

"That's Mikki Muldoon," said Betty as our food arrived. "You know, she really should've had this assignment. She finished second in the poll. She deserves it. That's what she's doing eating all by herself. Just in case."

Judges, I might mention, do not fraternize with exhibitors before completing their assignments. They don't have to imprison themselves in their hotel rooms, but they do maintain their distance.

Leah, who must have been studying an out-of-date book, looked up from her steak. "But that doesn't mean she automatically gets—"

Betty's malamute eyes darted from Leah's food to her face. "Now it does. They changed the rule. Mikki finished second, so if she's here, she gets the assignment."

"Has anyone *seen* Hunnewell?" I asked. "Do we even know he's here? Maybe he isn't, and that's why—"

"Oh, he's here," Betty said grimly. "Duke saw him checking in."

I said the same thing that everyone always said about Duke: "What an incredible handler he is!"

Equally unimpressed with Duke Sylvia and the salmon she'd ordered—creamed and, from the looks of it, canned, too—Betty edged toward my seafood casserole. "Hah! Hunnewell's not going to look twice at that dog of his. Duke told me so himself."

"But I thought—" Leah began.

Like Kimi anticipating the command to jump, Betty leaped to explain that Duke had not only been around long enough to remember James Hunnewell's likes and dislikes, but was a genius at assessing judges' preferences.

As coolly as I could, I asked what Hunnewell liked. Duke Sylvia's dog was a big gray male, Mal-O-Mine Ironman, that he co-owned with a breeder named Lillian Ingersoll, who was missing the national because she'd broken her shoulder so badly that she'd had to have surgery and was still wearing a clumsy, awkward cast, which, I might comment, couldn't possibly have been any more clumsy and awkward than Lillian herself. Hence her injuries. And her reliance on Duke Sylvia. But back to Ironman, who, to judge from the photos I'd seen, needed Duke as much as Lillian did. Or let's say that Ironman was totally different from Rowdy and that he was just not my type. And if Ironman wasn't Hunnewell's type? Maybe Rowdy was.

CHAPTER 7 🔍

"So what *is* Hunnewell's type?" I asked.

Looking like a skeptical Buddha, Betty said, "Well, ask Sherri Ann, and she'll tell you it's her Bear. The truth is, the dogs that were Hunnewell's type all died a long time ago. Comet was probably the last dog that Hunnewell thought was decent, and Comet died . . . I don't know. Fifteen years ago." Perking up, she merrily remarked, "Of course, that's what's got Freida worried sick."

Having picked out and eaten all the lobster, I was working on the shrimp, which were tough enough to justify the full name of the dish: *Old Tyme Seafood Casserole*. I swallowed. "What is?"

Shoving ahead of Betty in the conversational queue, Leah said, "That Hunnewell's going to withhold all the ribbons!" Unnecessarily, she added, "For want of merit! Wouldn't that be exciting!"

Atlantic City: When the beauty queens have finished strutting and parading, the great moment arrives. The judges' decision? That each contestant is more hideous and less talented than the last. No Miss America this year! Not even a runner-up.

I glared at Leah. "That would be humiliating to everyone here! It would be a nightmare for Freida and everyone else who's worked so hard on this show."

Leah was, as usual, unchastened. "Seriously, can a judge do that?"

Betty said grimly, "AKC wouldn't like it, but when it comes to the merits of dogs, the judge's decisions are final. Period."

Her hopes restored, Leah was bright-eyed. "Does that ever really happen? That the judge withholds *everything?*"

Neither Betty nor I could remember a single instance. If Leah had had a tail, she'd have wagged it. She could hardly wait to witness history.

"Leah," I said severely, "*your* attitude—"

"Is human," Betty finished. "Lay off her."

"Fine," I agreed. "Let her find out for herself. But, Leah, I'm warning you: You walk into that ring with Kimi on Saturday morning, and you're not going to think it's so hilarious if—"

"*I,*" Betty interjected, "hope that she does! Because nothing would please *me* more than to see someone having fun! Leah, thank you. And whatever happens on Saturday, you just remember that all it is, is one person's opinion on one day, and not a darned thing more."

Timmy Oliver had snuck up on us while Betty was preaching. "Well spoken, Betty!" he now applauded. Uninvited, he pulled out the fourth chair at our table and, evidently mistaking it for a horse, perhaps of the rocking variety, turned it around and straddled it. When he reached across the table to grab the basket of rolls, I half expected him to feed his pretend pony. Instead, after grubbing around with his dirty hands, he selected a cinnamon bun and, using a knife lifted from Betty's plate, slathered it with butter, bit, and chewed. With his mouth open, too. I might mention that the restaurant was comfortably cool; it was a grill in name only and didn't have a hot open kitchen or any other heat source to account for the flush and sweat on Tim Oliver's face.

"It's a lesson *you* might do well to remember," Betty told him. "One person's opinion on one day."

Tim Oliver smiled. His upper and lower incisors met in a viselike bite that had forced him to grind his front teeth until he'd worn the edges even. "Exactly," he told Betty. "Good sport or none at all."

Tim's subtle overemphasis of the phrase "good sport," in combination with his ingratiating manner and general air of sleaze, convinced me that he was going to hit Betty up for what I'd ordinarily call a favor. The word that actually came to mind was "succor." For the next five minutes, I listened to him go on with obnoxious enthusiasm about Z-Rock's chances under Hunnewell and his own prospects in distributing a dietary supplement for dogs called Pro-Vita No-Blo Sho-Kote. I came close to asking Timmy whether the secret ingredient he kept mentioning actually was snake oil. Leah had inched her chair back from the table and was gazing silently at Mikki Muldoon. I kept waiting for Timmy to try to enlist Betty, and possibly me, in a Pro-Vita No-Blo Sho-Kote pyramid scheme, but what he finally got around to oozing was the request that Betty tell the hotel that his camper was hers so he could leave it in the parking lot all night. As we'd been repeatedly informed, motor homes were allowed in the parking lot only if they belonged to people registered at the hotel. They were absolutely not to be used for sleeping. A few people, I thought, broke the rule. That morning, I'd noticed four or five of the big, long campers parked unobtrusively at the far end of the lot, but so far as I knew, the management hadn't staged any midnight raids.

"Oh, for heaven's sake, Timmy," Betty told him, "go to the campground! It's only ten minutes from here. If they catch you sleeping out there and your camper's listed on my room card, they'll come banging on my door in the middle of the night expecting *me* to let you in!"

Tim Oliver wasted another few minutes wheedling and whining, but Betty held firm. His scheme having failed, he departed. Between bites of the scallops I'd rejected, Betty predicted that Timmy would find someone else to lie for him. I listened in silence. Although I had no reason to believe that Tim was one of the people whose words had caused Jeanine such pain, he struck me as exactly the kind of person who'd go around talking about "Betty's mongrels" and "trash dogs." If Betty had heard the phrases, however, she obviously had not identified either voice as Timmy's. On the contrary, it seemed that Betty was his defender. Although I kept my opinion of him to myself, Betty tried to change it. "You didn't know Timmy when he was a kid," she said. "He needed a lot of help, and everyone watched out for him and gave him a hand. Elsa Van Dine, among others. Elsa really took him under her wing." With the universal affection of the dog fancy for junior handlers, Betty added sadly, "When Elsa took to someone, she could really be very generous, and Timmy wasn't so full of himself then. He wasn't a bad kid at all."

When the waiter offered coffee, Betty refused, but Leah and I accepted, and all three of us ordered the same dessert: chocolate mousse. Leah and I commiserated about Rowdy's and Kimi's rotten performances in obedience that morning. We comforted ourselves: Of the seventeen dogs in the trial, only four had qualified. If we'd washed out? Well, so had the bitch I'd considered Rowdy's serious competition, Vanderval's Tundra Eagle, C.D.X., whose score I will tactfully not report lest anyone ask, "Oh, and what was Rowdy's?"

Betty stood up. "I am beat," she announced. She looked

it. Furthermore, she hadn't finished her own chocolate
mousse, never mind anyone else's. Like Kimi stealing a
hunk of raw beef, however, she snatched the check, refused
to give it back, and even said what Kimi virtually says,
namely, "This is *my* treat!"

Leaving the grill, we followed a maze of corridors and
stairwells, both up and down, and eventually dropped Betty
outside her room and continued to our own, which was at
the exact opposite end of the hotel from the exhibition hall
and the outdoor grooming tent, but conveniently near the
stairs to an exit to the back parking lot. Our room was much
larger than I'd expected, with a couch, armchairs, side tables, a large-screen TV, a desk, two king-size beds, and lots
of floor space left for Rowdy's and Kimi's crates. The Hawaiian theme so overwhelmingly prevalent in the public areas
was mercifully absent. The room was clean, beige, and
bland, with nontropical bedspreads and framed prints of
distinctly non-Polynesian chickadees and cardinals. The
windows overlooked the rear parking lot and a stretch of
New England field with woods at its far end. Furthermore,
until Leah cluttered up the bathroom with enough cosmetics to do the makeup for the entire cast of all three *Star Wars*
movies, it was a model for what I'd love to have at home:
big sink, long counter, unstained tub, white tile, and new
grout.

Except for their forays in the obedience ring and a couple
of bathroom trips, Rowdy and Kimi, who are used to vigor-
ous daily exercise, had had the kind of crated day that animal-
rights extremists imagine as the show dog's life sentence.

"Hey, buddies! Let's go!" I opened the crates. "Leah, they
need to go out. Besides, uh, something ugly happened. I
need to talk about it. Come on!"

Leah was reluctant. Our room fascinated her. My cousin
had a pop-culturally deprived childhood: no public school,
no white bread, no comic books, no sitcoms, just year after

year of Montessori, seven-grain loaves, and *Rebecca of Sunnybrook Farm*. Chauffeured from eurythmics to Suzuki to conversational French, she barely knew she was American at all. Her parents' idea of fun was to sit around the dining-room table correcting the proofs of her professor father's latest book. Instead of traveling to Disney World, her family visited the birthplaces of obscure composers and made pilgrimages to the graves of minor poets. Leah got dragged on so many tours of Olde Sturbridge Village and Plimoth Plantation that the phrase *You are now entering . . .* sends her into a violent paroxysm of yawning even when there's not a spinning wheel or a Hadley chest in sight. More to the point, she always got stuck on foldout cots at quaint country inns where the rooms were hot in the summer and cold in the winter, and where the bathroom was a converted closet with a metal shower stall and a prominent notice explaining that as part of the management's commitment to saving the planet, the hot-water supply was rigged to give out in three minutes. After a childhood in the black-and-white world of academe, Leah had only recently been snatched up, whirled around, and precipitously deposited in the Technicolor Oz of middle-class comfort. Harvard she took for granted; it was just home, only with more books and worse food. This hotel wowed her.

"Leah," I insisted, "I do not enjoy walking them together when it's dark out and there are so many other dogs around. And there is no reason why I should have to make two trips." I take care of all of our dog expenses, including entry fees and travel costs. That's fair. The dogs are mine alone. I don't trust co-ownership, which, in the AKC legal system, permits either owner to do just about anything except actually sell the dog without the other owner's knowledge or permission. Not that Leah would sneak around breeding Rowdy and raking in stud fees, of course. It's not Leah I distrust. It's the whole arrangement.

As we descended the stairs and crossed the parking lot with the dogs, I gave Leah a full report of everything Jeanine and Arlette had told me. When I repeated the denigrating phrases, I kept my voice low, but I had to persuade Leah to subdue her exclamations of outrage.

"These bastards couldn't have known Jeanine's history, of course," I commented. "And I'm not even all that sure that it's relevant, anyway. You don't have to have been raped to be supersensitive to cruelty."

"But, Holly, these people didn't care one way or the other! People like that don't give a shit whose feelings they hurt just as long as they hurt someone's."

I agreed. "And damn!" I added. "The adopters were *our* guests. Great hospitality we offered!"

"But now that it's happened, what are you going to do about it?"

"For the moment, nothing, really. Just not overreact. That's why I don't want Betty to know. I'm afraid she'll fly off the handle, and I really think that creating a big hullabaloo about it would be counterproductive. The point here is to promote a *positive* image, and a major fuss would be so *negative*. Also, this was just two rotten apples, and I don't want the good people to feel as though they're being blamed. The whole feeling was so warm; I hate to spoil that."

"But you can't just do *nothing!*"

"Oh, I'll write about it, I guess. Not that it'll do any good," I added morosely.

"The pen and the sword and all that."

"Right now, Leah, if I knew who those two people were, I'd greatly prefer the sword." Then I switched to a happier subject by pointing to a row of five or six campers and trailers parked along the edge of the field like giant sled dogs hitched in single file. "When we get rich," I said, "that's what we're going to have—a little house on wheels."

"Bristling with luxuries," Leah agreed. "Kimi, leave it! Would you please refrain from consuming things that are not food! Or we won't give you a ride in our lusciously decadent camper. You'll be stuck home eating garbage and . . . Hey, isn't it illegal for those to be here?"

"Only if you sleep in them."

Unexpectedly money-conscious, my cousin said, "So people don't sponge off the hotel."

On the grass at the edge of the blacktop, Rowdy squatted and produced. Ms. Responsible Dog Owner that I am, I pulled a plastic clean-up bag from my pocket and scooped up after him. As I deposited the waste in a nearby trash barrel, I said, "Also so they don't start their generators at six A.M. and wake up the paying guests."

Strolling past the enviable campers, Leah and I played at choosing ours. In the dim parking lot, all looked—and probably were—the usual dog-show-camper beige. A sort of stretch-camper the length of three limos was so intimidating that neither of us wanted to drive it. We rejected another: two people, two dogs, too small.

"I wonder if what's-his-name's is here." Leah has beautiful enunciation. Highly educated people can be very embarrassing.

"Shh!" I hustled Rowdy away from the campers and onto the grass at the edge of the field. "Tim Oliver. Probably. It's possible that he's talked Betty into telling the hotel that his camper is hers. She's more softhearted than you might think. Oliver might've called her room or just showed up there and given her some story about how he doesn't have the money to pay the campground because he spent it all on vet bills."

"You know, Holly, he's just the kind of little shit who'd get off on making sure someone like Jeanine heard him say 'trash dogs.' And then turn around and suck up to Betty."

"Actually, I had the same thought myself. Rowdy, hurry up! This is a n-i-i-i-ce place to go! Hurry up!"

Rowdy anointed the wall of a little white shed that was apparently used to store recreational equipment. I thought it was the same place he'd marked that morning. Whether because of the killing of Elsa Van Dine or my own anger about Jeanine's pain, Rowdy's harmless leg-lifting made me wonder about murderers who revisit the scenes of their crimes. Do they, too, get some kind of incomprehensible satisfaction from making sure that their scent is fresh?

CHAPTER 8

As we returned to the hotel, Leah remarked that she was thirsty. "There's a Coke machine right near our room. And an ice machine. Room service would be a lot more fun," I acknowledged, "but even as it is—"

"This is costing you a fortune because you're paying for me."

"You're handling Kimi for me. You're working for expenses. I'm lucky you don't charge me."

Unexpectedly, she asked, "Have you ever thought about writing your memoirs? You could probably make a fortune."

"My *what!*"

"Memoirs. Romantic memoirs. You could call it *Women Who Run with Vets.*"

"Leah, I do not 'run with' vets!" I thought the matter over. "As far as I can remember, Steve is the first one."

"You could just make up the others. Or pretend that they were vets even though they weren't."

"Sure," I said, "just tack D.V.M. onto their names, and—"

"Not *all* of them," said Leah, as if there had been thousands. "And at least one ought to be an M.R.C.V.S., like Mr. Herriot." Ascending the hotel stairs inspired Leah to literary heights. "I know! Look, you have to change their real names anyway, so they wouldn't be embarrassed or sue you or whatever. So as long as you're doing that anyway, you call him James. So your readers would naturally assume——"

I halted at the top of the stairs. Rowdy sat. "That what? That I'd had an affair with James Herriot? Leah——"

"It's important to let readers draw their own conclusions. Why should you do all the work? You wouldn't *say* Herriot. You'd just say *James*," Leah pronounced emphatically.

As if in answer to a summons, an elderly man stuck a lizardlike head out of the open archway to the room that housed the vending machines. His head and, as I soon observed, his body as well weren't lizardlike in some vague, generic sense. Rather, he bore an astonishing resemblance to a pet horny toad—a horned lizard—that a childhood friend of mine had bought in Arizona as a living souvenir and had brought home to Maine. There the little reptile entered a permanent state of dormancy and spent year after year in suspended animation on a bed of dry sand in a glass aquarium. Oddly devoted to the creature, my friend provided food and water that the animal never touched. Every day or so, she gently lifted the spiny body out of the artificial desert to make sure that the lizard was still alive. Well, yes, as Dorothy Parker asked when told that Calvin Coolidge had died, *How could they tell?* My friend blew lovingly in the horny toad's face. Maybe Coolidge didn't blink anymore.

Without bothering with the preliminaries, our human lizard loudly announced that the ice machine, like half the other damned things in this world, was not working.

"It was working okay last night," I informed him. "Have you tried kicking it?"

After unlocking the door to our room to admit Leah,

Rowdy, and Kimi, I got the change purse from my shoulder bag and the ice bucket from the bathroom. When I returned to the corridor, the man stood in the open archway in a cloud of what proved to be tobacco smoke and not, as I first feared, the vapor emitted by a broken ice machine. A hand with thickened joints, splayed fingers, and scaly skin clutched an unfiltered cigarette.

Dripping ash on the lapels of a navy blazer, the man lurched, stumbled forward, and bumped into the ice machine. He was short, wide, and flat, with turned-out feet, a mottled complexion, and no hair. I tried to remember whether the horny toad had had lips. The man's were like thin purple strips of raw liver. He raised the hand that wasn't depositing ash on the carpet. Pinched between two fingers was a quarter. In a wheezy voice, he said, "Can't for the life of me get this thing in! All it does is fall back on the floor." With that, he made what was evidently a repeat attempt to force the coin into a narrow ventilation slot. The quarter, of course, dropped to the carpet.

Bending to retrieve the coin, I failed to think of a tactful way to break the news that ice was free. As I straightened, the man gestured to the soft-drink machine. "And that one," he reported, "doesn't work a damned bit better." To demonstrate, he snatched the quarter from my hand, inserted it in the correct slot, and pressed the big button for Coca-Cola. I wondered how many years it had been since a Coke cost twenty-five cents. He probably expected a green bottle.

Dog people, I might point out, are unusually experienced in providing for the needs of elders, both human and canine. Many people stay active in dogs into their eighties and beyond. Even if they feel like vegetating, they can't, because their dogs won't let them, and neither will we. At advanced ages, dogless people suffer from luxury: There's nothing they have to do; no one relies on them; and the future consists of one final certainty. At a minimum, however, a dog has to be walked, and if there's one thing that a dog does even more reliably than go out, come back in, eat, sleep, and love, it's need, need, need. As to the future, when your almost-champion needs only one major win to finish, now is not the time to quit. That *now* coincides with your ninetieth birthday is incidental. And when our senior human citizens are no longer able to participate in the sport, instead of leaving them in peace, we insist on driving them to shows and training classes, and dragging them out to club dinners. Elder abuse! And the entire dog fancy is guilty.

In a tone too loud and bright, I said, "I'm afraid you have to add a few more quarters." After a fit of liquid coughing, the stranger fished through his pockets, produced another coin, and inserted that one, too. I stepped neatly in front of him, opened my change purse, poured quarters into the slot, and pressed the button. With a grinding, metallic shriek, the machine delivered itself of a pop-top can. "There you go!" I announced. "Do you have an ice bucket?"

Like the horny toad, he blinked.

"That's okay. I have one," I said, as if I always toted a spare. Zipping around, I shoved our ice bucket into the compartment of the machine and pushed the button. When I turned around, the man was examining the side of the soft-drink machine.

"You wouldn't happen to know"—he paused to produce another deep, wet cough—"whether there's an opener here somewhere?"

"You pull on the top. It's a, uh, new thing. I'll show you."

As I opened the can of Coke, the man ground the remains of his cigarette on the ice machine and dropped the butt in a plastic-lined trash barrel. Then he pulled out a pack of cigarettes and the kind of gold flip-top lighter I hadn't seen for years. He offered the pack to me. I shook my head. He lit up. I looked around in search of a smoke detector and located one on the ceiling near what looked like the nozzle of a sprinkler system. By now, I thought, the alarm should have been sounding, and the man and I should have been sharing a cold shower. What I could smell was, of course, just smoke and more smoke, but I could almost see the discarded cigarette butt begin to smolder in the trash barrel. Deciding that the alarm and sprinkler system might actually be defective, I told the man that he was all set now. And I bolted.

Unless I doused that barrel, I'd lie awake worrying. The plan was to return with a bottle of water I'd brought from home in case the change from Cambridge to Danville water bothered the dogs. I could sacrifice the water; neither dog had a sensitive gut. At the door to my room, however, I discovered that I'd left the key inside. It wasn't one of those plastic slabs, but a metal key attached to a big tab. I could almost see it lying next to my shoulder bag. As I was knocking and calling to Leah, Pam Ritchie came striding down the corridor waving a sheaf of papers at me. She wore what looked like an old-fashioned prom dress, a three-quarter-length rose-colored gown with shoulder straps as thin as the spiked heels of her dyed-to-match shoes. Crystal had not, of course, suddenly drafted Pam to fill in for an absent bridesmaid. Pam was on her way to or from the Parade of Veterans and Titleholders, which called for evening dress. If I'm ever forced to handle a malamute while wearing formal attire, I'll choose a floor-length gown and running shoes. Also, good coverage. When a malamute pulls, your pecs flex hard enough to snap any spaghetti strap. Topless handling is a fad that has yet to entrance the fancy.

"Isn't that your room?" Pam demanded. "I was bringing this to you." She thrust the papers at me.

"I'm locked out. My cousin must be in the bathroom or something. Oh, the stud book! Thank you."

"I'm sorry it took me so long. November 1990 through June '93. Is that it?"

I nodded. Like Nixon's White House tapes, my copy of the Alaskan malamute stud book had had a significant gap: Until now, I hadn't been able to look up the sire, dam, breeder, and owner of any dog with a registration published in the missing months.

"This'll do it," I told her. As a sort of extra thanks, I added how much I admired the old sign from the Chinook Kennels that she'd donated to the breed club auction. Pam replied that she was glad that someone appreciated it because, these days, a lot of people in malamutes didn't even seem to know that Eva B. ("Short") Seeley was the matriarch of our breed or that the dogs from her Chinook Kennels had gone with Admiral Byrd. As Pam was speaking, the lizard-like man, smoking yet another cigarette, appeared from the vending-machine room and, to my astonishment, uttered a series of succinct and obscene remarks about Mrs. Seeley that I am too grateful to her to repeat. If it hadn't been for Short Seeley, Rowdy and Kimi wouldn't exist. I owe her a retrospective and unpayable debt. She had a wonderful eye for a dog.

Before the man had finished vilifying her, the outraged Pam was aggressively defending her memory: "If Short were alive today, you wouldn't dare say any of that! But now the poor woman isn't around . . ."

In response to the altercation, Rowdy and Kimi were breathing loudly on the other side of the door. They didn't intend to do anything; they just didn't want to miss the fun. Claws scratched. I banged on the door. "Leah! Leah, open the door!" Rowdy began *woo*ing.

". . . know-it-all bitch . . ." I couldn't tell whether the

man meant Short Seeley or Pam Ritchie. From Pam's viewpoint, it didn't matter.

As Pam was sputtering about Short Seeley's sacred memory and demanding to know just who the man thought he was, Freida Reilly arose from the stairwell like a *deus ex machina*. "Holly, get in there and make those dogs shut up," our show chair ordered crisply. "And *you*," she told Pam, "disappear." Swooping down on the lizard, Freida snatched his can of Coke and the ice bucket into which he was dribbling ash. "Please accept our most *profuse* apologies for this misunderstanding," she gushed. And away she swept him.

Ten minutes later, when I'd carried out my plan of drenching the trash barrel, Leah and I were analyzing the episode. Actually, we were just talking about it, but Cambridge is finally starting to get to me. Before long, I'll be deconstructing narratives. Anyway, Leah was sprawled on her bed drinking a diet version of what I used to call tonic, a New England term dating, no doubt, to the era when Coke really was and the pause really, really refreshed; and I was cross-legged on the floor scratching Rowdy's white chest and administering to myself the tonic of my adulthood, cognac, which I'd poured into a bathroom glass from the flask in my first-aid kit, the only medicine therein meant exclusively for human emergencies.

"I'm not handling," I said. "He didn't get all that good a look at you, and he didn't really look at the dogs. The only one it really affects is Pam."

Leah replied by asking for some of my cognac.

"Only if you don't mix it with anything," I said. Anyone who wants to be young again has forgotten the concoctions that youth pours down the throats of its victims.

"Ice?" she requested.

"Oh, all right." He probably had seen her. And her hair is very distinctive. "Freida says he drank on the plane," I said for the second time. "He hates flying."

"You told me," Leah said. "Why was he so pissed at Eva Seeley?"

Pissed. Her language! For this she goes to Harvard.

"At a guess," I answered, "sometime or other, Mrs. Seeley told him his dogs weren't malamutes. I gather that she did that—if malamutes weren't from her lines, then she thought they weren't malamutes, and she didn't mind saying so. Naturally, people weren't thrilled."

"I'll bet she would've *loved* Rowdy and Kimi!" Leah said.

"Mrs. Seeley isn't judging," I reminded Leah. "James Hunnewell is. She's dead. And he's still half alive."

Oh, yes. James. James Hunnewell.

CHAPTER 9

But I was wrong. James Hunnewell's body was found early the next morning. Hunnewell had been smashed on the head with what, in a triumph of honesty over literary aspiration, I shall describe as a blunt instrument. I am, however, relieved to report that despite the proximity of hundreds of keen-nosed dogs, the corpse was discovered by—of all things—a human being, in fact, by an ex-lover of mine named Finn Adams, whom I'll introduce only by falling back on the truism that we all make mistakes.

But Judge James Hunnewell was dead! Murdered! Isn't death, especially violent death, exactly what chichés are for? *He lost his life*, as if it were a folding umbrella he'd absentmindedly left on the seat of a cab, or a glove he'd accidentally dropped, or a forgotten jacket borrowed by a friend who, suddenly remembering, might yet bring it back. *His time ran out?* Death as meter maid! The indignity! As if a cemetery were a grassy parking lot with rows of stones depicting fluttering tickets and stylized Denver boots. "SCOFF-LAW!" shouts each epitaph, which also lists the ticket number, the issue date, and the time of the violation, but not, of course, the amount due, the ultimate price having obviously been paid in full. *He expired?* It could be worse: *Ignoring appeal procedures, he was towed away.* Grotesque? That's the point: that James Hunnewell's time did *not* just run out.

I shall postpone for the moment the matter of the blunt instrument and the mistakes we all make by noting that at six-thirty on Friday morning, some fool in one of the campers at the edge of the back lot decided not to let sleeping dogs lie and, indeed, to awaken everyone but the proverbial dead, in this case James Hunnewell. Leah rolled over, swore, and pulled the hotel's plush blanket over her head. When I'd fallen asleep at ten or so the previous night, she'd just started watching *Back to the Future*. At a guess, she'd been up until midnight, maybe later. Neither of our dogs was in the ring until Saturday; Leah was free to keep on sleeping for the next twenty-four hours. To prevent the dogs from leaping on her bed and licking her awake, she'd crated them, but at six thirty-five that Friday morning, Kimi's metal crate was clanking, and Rowdy was breathing in a meaningful way.

So, ten minutes later I was standing bleary-eyed and messy-haired on the blacktop between my Bronco and Betty Burley's van while the dogs gulped down their carefully measured portions of the defrosted Fresh Frozen Bil Jac I'd been keeping on ice in a cooler in the car. Great stuff. For what it costs me to feed these dogs, I could live on lobster. Since neither of the dogs exhibits the self-sacrificing attitude toward the other that I strive to model, Kimi was breakfasting inside the Bronco, and Rowdy was using the blacktop as a tablecloth. Kimi's head was still in her dish. Rowdy was scouring his with his tongue.

"All done, big boy?" I bent over. When I lifted Rowdy's empty dish, he kept licking it. As I held it for him, my eyes drifted and then froze. On the macadam just under the rear of Betty's van lay, of all things, Comet's reliquary, the Alaskan malamute lamp—pink granite base, brass rod, shedding dog, Iditarod shade and all—Sherri Ann Printz's donation to Rescue's auction. After the showcase, I realized, Betty and I had both neglected to gather up the valuable items reserved for Saturday night's live auction. At some point, Betty must have remembered our lapse and returned to the booth to remove the Inuit carving, the jewelry, the antique wolf prints, and Sherri Ann's lamp. The framed prints were bulky, heavy, and fragile. The lamp, of course, sat on granite. It would've required a six-armed Amazon to carry the entire load at once. Betty was in her seventies. At a guess, she weighed barely a hundred pounds. Instead of making repeated journeys through the exhibition hall, the corridors, the lobby, and the maze of hallways and staircases that led to her room, and instead of asking for help, she must have made a single trip with her van, returned it to its original spot next to my Bronco, and carried some or all of the items the short distance to her room.

What I didn't understand was why the damned lamp was *underneath* Betty's van. Her aging memory? It was usually better than mine. Forty years her junior, I'd entirely forgotten the valuables until now. No, Betty loathed that lamp, and she resented Sherri Ann's use of Rescue in her bid for a seat on the board of our national breed club, a campaign that was heavily focused on beating Freida Reilly. In all arenas, political ambition baffles me. If the United States was populated exclusively by people like me, the race for the White House would be a sprint in the opposite direction, and presidential debates would be fights about who'd have to get stuck with the job this time. But glory isn't wasted on everyone. In vying for the honor of election to the board, Sherri Ann and Freida both wanted the support of the pro-Rescue faction of the club, and Betty took violent exception to what she saw as Sherri Ann's hypocritical effort to seduce our vote with her lamp.

With Rowdy and Kimi barricading the narrow space between Betty's van and my Bronco, I grabbed an old dog blanket that I keep in the car, and slipped it under the van and over the lamp. Taking special care not to damage the lamp, I pulled it across the blacktop, lifted it up into my car, and settled it on the floor where the passenger's feet belong. I hid the lamp under the blanket, locked the car door, and took the dogs for a quick walk, during which, I might add, they failed to find the body of James Hunnewell. Maybe they sniffed in some special way, but after all, they're dogs; they always sniff. If they pulled on their leashes, what do you expect? They're Alaskan malamutes. But I may have missed some subtle sign. I was preoccupied. We were not engaged in a cover-up, I decided. Betty or I might well have locked the lamp in my car for safekeeping; we just hadn't happened to do so. Well, now we had. All I'd done, really, was to change history. A half hour later, when I'd showered and dressed for the day and was following the tortuous route to the Lagoon, where breakfast was served, it occurred to me that during the Watergate affair, the conspirators had probably expressed the same sentiment. Betty Burley, however, was no Richard Nixon.

Despite the tropical vegetation, both organic and plastic, and the plethora of ukeleles, feathers, and paddles on the walls of the Lagoon, the only Hawaiian foods on the breakfast buffet table were several bananas that rested atop a mound of apples and the chunks of canned pineapple in the big steel bowl of otherwise fresh fruit salad. Bearing a plate heaped with scrambled eggs, sliced cantaloupe, and two pancakes, I joined Betty at a small table where she sat alone sipping coffee and nibbling on a triangle of whole wheat toast. Its mate rested on Betty's otherwise empty and clean plate. I am what horticulturists call "a heavy feeder," a sort of human peony. Betty usually was, too. This morning, however, she didn't even glance at my plate. I wondered, of course, whether she'd found out about the insult to our rescue dogs that had caused Jeanine such grief.

"Is that all you're having?" I asked. "Are you all right?"

Betty didn't look sick or tired. Her dark eyes weren't bloodshot or droopy, and her face was as animated as Kimi's. "I didn't sleep very well." Her tone suggested that her insomnia was my fault. "I was fretting about Sherri Ann and Freida and that miserable lamp. It has occurred to me that *inflicting* it on us was an act of hostility."

Except in practical matters like moving dog-shaped lamps, I am incapable of dealing with dog politics until a few hours after breakfast. I ate and listened.

Betty said that Sherri Ann Printz had never done a thing to support Rescue and that Victor Printz hadn't either. Betty was incensed. "How I *detest* being the object of political machinations!"

In neutral tones, I remarked that to Sherri Ann's credit she was fussy about who used her dogs at stud.

"Freida! Hah! In that instance, Sherri Ann was *not* being particular. She was deliberately trying to slight Freida! And nothing more!"

To divert Betty, I told her about finding the lamp. She was indignant. *"Under?"*

"Resting on its side. Under. Underneath." As if there'd been some ambiguity, I said, "Beneath the rear of your van."

She sat back in her chair and scowled. "Well, what on earth was it doing *there?*"

"Betty, I assumed that you——"

"Oh, I got it from the booth. Of course I did. I remembered. Well, I finally did. I'd already got into bed, and when I finally remembered, I was sorely tempted to stay there, but all I could think was, 'Well, if you don't go and get those things, everyone's going to know what an old fool you are!'"

As I'd guessed, instead of asking for help, Betty had moved her van from its spot next to my Bronco to the un- loading area near the exhibition hall.

"It took me three trips," she reported. "I got my tote bag and that damned lamp first. Then I went back for the prints. Then I packed the rest in a cardboard box. And I covered the tables with bed sheets—the things for the silent auction. Now I know that that's not perfectly secure, with us only one booth away from that great big door, but—"

"We can't move all of it every night," I assured her.

"And then I drove back, and I parked right in the same place, next to you." She hesitated. In a low voice, she added, "And then I was a lazy old fool after all."

"Betty—"

"I carried the box up to my room. And I didn't go back. But that van was locked, and the windows were up. Every door was locked! I checked every one." Involuntarily, it seemed, Betty had grabbed a fork and was now pounding her armed fist on the table. "This is Freida's doing!" she whispered venomously. "I can feel it in my bones! That woman cannot bear to watch Sherri Ann get the edge on her, and she's delighted to make us look bad, too." Midthump, she dropped the fork, grabbed her purse and her tote bag, rose, and said, "Damn! The wolf prints! The frames alone are worth . . . I'll be right back!" Coming to a halt, she interrupted herself. "In the meantime," she whis- pered in my ear, "this is best left—"

"Not a word," I vowed. "Do you want me to go with you?"

"No! The less fuss, the better."

Before Betty had taken a step, though, Freida Reilly came stomping up to the table to demand whether either of us had seen James Hunnewell. As befits a show chair, Freida wore a well-tailored CEO-style gray wool suit with a medium-length knife-pleated skirt. Her silky-looking white blouse had a built-in scarf that wrapped itself around her neck before slithering into her bosom. Her makeup was careful, if a bit heavy; her red nails matched her mouth; and her overall look was so perfectly lacquered that I wondered whether, having devoted great effort to her appearance, she'd closed her eyes and preserved her perfection by misting herself right down to her spiked heels and pointy toes with an entire can of ultra-hold hair spray. Her show chair badge was pinned to one lapel, a big pewter malamute to the other. Two of the big fellow's just-like-Daddy pups bit so deeply into Freida's earlobes that I hoped she was up on her tetanus shots.

Betty checked her watch. With not a hint of the accusation she'd just voiced about Freida's role in the lamp's odd appearance under her van, she asked, "What time is it?" Answering her own question, she said, "Seven-thirty. Judging's at nine, isn't it? Hunnewell's probably still asleep."

Freida sourly replied that she'd rung James Hunnewell's room twice, banged on his door three times, and failed to get what she described, and I quote, as "any sign of life."

"Well, Freida, delegate someone to go and roust him out!" advised Betty, who had moved the auction items all by herself. "Maybe he's not in his room. Maybe he's wandering around somewhere."

Freida bristled. The pewter pups on her earlobes trembled. "Naturally, I have people looking, but after all these years, there aren't all that many of us who know what he looks like."

A gigantic horny toad, I longed to say. Instead, I picked up my check, excused myself, paid, and dashed to the nearby ladies' room, where investigation confirmed that Mother Nature had once again adjusted my menstrual cycle to make my period coincide with a big dog show. I will swear that She consults the *AKC Events Calendar.* I could practically hear her: *Hm, Alaskan Malamute National Specialty, October thirtieth, so let's see, obedience on the thirty-first, we'll hit her with PMS for that, and on Friday morning . . .*

As I sat in the cubicle digging around in the little cosmetics bag in my purse, the metal door of the next stall slammed shut, and a lock slid in place. Someone got violently sick. The toilet flushed. Dogs, fine. I stroke their heaving ribs and whisper sweet moral lessons about eating steel-wool pads and paying the consequences. But people are hard to help. Morning sickness? Crystal, I thought.

Again, I was wrong. A few minutes later, while I was washing my hands at one of the dozen sinks, out of the cubicle emerged a green-faced Mikki Muldoon, who had finished second in the judging poll, second to James Hunnewell. Ignoring me—I was a stranger to her, anyway—Mrs. Muldoon made her way to one of the basins, turned on both faucets, and, without using soap, rubbed her hands together as if trying to warm her fingers. As I combed my hair and daubed on lip gloss, she produced a makeup kit from her pocketbook. Just as Crystal had done, she brushed her teeth. Then she began to restore color to her face.

Five minutes later, when I was crossing the lobby and heading toward Betty's van, Duke Sylvia told me that James Hunnewell was dead. My thought was of Mikki Muldoon, who was a decade beyond Crystal's kind of morning sickness. Nerves? After all, with Hunnewell permanently out of the picture, she was now about to judge a national specialty.

Had she known? And if so, how?

CHAPTER 10 🐾

As Duke Sylvia told me about the demise of James Hunnewell, he could have been remarking about how many autumn leaves had fallen overnight. "Fellow from R.T.I. found him," Duke informed me. Arms folded across his chest, Duke leaned comfortably against a wall of the hotel lobby.

Infected by Duke's placidity, I said, "Oh, I was looking for the R.T.I. guy yesterday. I wanted to ask him about . . ." I stopped myself. If we'd been attending a service at an open grave, Duke wouldn't have considered a discussion of Rowdy's sperm in the least out of line. I cleared my throat. "He was looking for him?"

"Who?"

"The guy from R.T.I. He was trying to find Mr. Hunnewell?"

Duke shook his head. "Just happened on him. Right out in back here, in back of the hotel. At the end of the parking lot, there's a baseball field, recreation area, and there's a little storage shed."

"What on earth was James Hunnewell doing out there?"

Duke shrugged. And when I asked what should have been my first question—what Hunnewell had died of—Duke said he didn't know. He made the obvious guess. "His lungs must've finally quit. Freida's shaken up." Duke made Freida Reilly's distress sound as distant and foreign as a volcanic eruption on some South Sea island he'd never visited and never would. "Once Freida calms down, she'll be relieved. James would've botched the judging. He'd've done an awful job."

Over the next hour, in the lobby, the parking lot, the corridors, the grooming tent, and the exhibition area, everyone seemed to agree: We were better off without James Hunnewell passing judgment on our dogs. But relief turned to astonishment when the word spread that instead of passing peacefully to the ultimate Judgment, Judge James Hunnewell had been bludgeoned to death. Busy at the rescue booth, I, however, must have been one of the last to hear the word "murder."

When Betty Burley arrived at the booth bearing the heavy lamp, I knew only what Duke had told me. "The parking lot is crawling with police," Betty complained. She sounded like a fastidious homemaker describing a dishwasher invaded by ants. She thrust the lamp at me. "Here, take this thing, will you? My arms are aching. I had to carry it all the way here. When I saw which way the wind was blowing, instead of moving it to my van, I marched right into the hotel and straight to my room, and then I went back and got the wolf prints."

"Which way *is* the wind blowing?" I asked.

"Well, now they've got the whole area cordoned off—that whole end of the parking lot—so if I hadn't hustled out there and whisked everything away, for all I know, they wouldn't have let me move it at all! And hideous as this thing is, it's arousing a lot of interest."

As she spoke, one of our rescue people, a guy named Gary Galvin, arrived with the prints. The heavy antique frames were handsome, but the subjects made me uncomfortable, mainly, I think, because I saw them as rather silly allegories. In one, a lonely looking wolf was howling at a faceless moon: *Rescue Lifts a Lone Voice in an Uncaring Wilderness.* The other was a grisly depiction of a wolf attempting to disembowel an elk that was kicking and fighting back: *Compassion Battles Politics, the Outcome Undecided.* Or maybe *Freida Reilly and Sherri Ann Printz Do Battle for a Seat on the Board.* A woman named Isabelle, who trailed after Gary, was carrying the cardboard box that contained the Inuit sculpture, the jewelry, and the other small valuables. The first to arrive at the rescue booth, I'd gently unshrouded the silent-auction items, made sure they were matched with the correct bid sheets, and otherwise readied the display to present what Betty Burley was always calling "a positive image of rescue." I'd felt so much like a Barbara Pym character, an excellent woman making herself useful at a church jumble sale, that I'd half expected someone to come up and offer me the first in a series of endless cups of tea. Now, as Betty rearranged the table I'd tidied up, Gary slipped me two videotapes. "One's last night's showcase," he said. "Betty can't object to that. And the other's the obedience bloopers."

"Betty will have a fit," I whispered. "Gary, Betty says the whole back of the parking lot is cordoned off and . . . Do you have any idea what's going on? Someone told me that Hunnewell was dead, but . . ."

Even if no one had informed me of Hunnewell's demise, the presence of a substitute judge in one of the two baby-gated rings would have alerted me that something was wrong. In one ring, all was as it should have been: Today's sweepstakes judging—another innocent gambling game— was already under way. In the second ring, the one that should have belonged to Judge James Hunnewell, the competition for championship points—*the* show—was due to start. In preparation, Judge Mikki Muldoon was dutifully pacing up and down: The condition of the ring is the judge's responsibility. Maybe the Pope, too, is obligated to check the Vatican's streets for potholes. Within the ring, the judge's authority is as absolute as his. Authority dies with death. *The judge is dead*, I thought. *Long live the judge.*

Before Gary could answer my query about what was going on, Betty asked me the same question I'd just asked him, but her tone was the one I use to accuse the dogs of crimes I've actually watched them commit. "Holly Winter," Betty demanded, "what is going on here?"

Instead of pointing to the substitute videotapes, however, she banged her tote bag and a photograph album down on the table. We had two albums. One was a big, fat maroon binder overstuffed with snapshots and stories about malamutes rescued all over the country. The other—the one Betty slammed down—was a slim beige volume devoted exclusively to the dogs who'd appeared in last night's showcase. The separate album for the showcase dogs had been Betty's idea, and it was Betty who'd put it together. I'd looked through the big album, but I already knew about the showcase dogs. In straightening out the booth, I'd lined the beige album up next to the fat maroon one. Otherwise, I hadn't touched it. I reached the obvious conclusion: Betty had learned that in Jeanine's presence someone had called our rescue dogs "trash." Furthermore, Betty knew that I'd kept the episode from her.

Before I could confess, however, Betty raged: "You had absolutely no business removing Cubby's pedigree or that page of the stud book or anything else!"

Cubby, I remind you, was Jeanine's dog. As I've said, Jeanine's reason for adopting a big dog wasn't something she'd have wanted boomed over a sound system. But Betty was talking about the second piece of information I'd suppressed. Cubby, who'd been bought at a pet shop, had been turned in to Rescue with AKC papers. As I mentioned earlier, in running his pedigree, I'd found that way back there in Cubby's unfortunate family tree of puppy-mill dogs was an ancestor bred by Sherri Ann Printz, a dog that bore her kennel name. The dog had been registered as Pawprintz Attic Emprer and owned by Gladys H. Thacker, who, as I've mentioned, farmed puppies in the state of Missouri. According to the stud book, she'd had malamutes for decades. After I'd taken Cubby in and placed him with Jeanine, I'd sent a full report to Betty, who'd threatened to include Cubby's pedigree in our showcase album. Until now, I'd assumed she'd been joking. I seldom raise my voice, even at people. "You did not! Damn it! I never meant—"

Betty interrupted. I fell silent. In the hierarchy of Rescue, she outranked me. "If people don't see it, they just go on thinking that those poor dogs being bred to death in the puppy mills have nothing whatsoever to do with *their* dogs. May I point out that *you* were the one who proposed that we take out an ad in the *Quarterly* and start publishing these pedigrees? And if memory serves me, Cubby was exactly the dog you had in mind."

A regular feature of the *Malamute Quarterly* is what's known as the centerfold: a celebration of a famous malamute, including an article written by the dog's breeder or owner, photographs, of course, and a pedigree. What I'd proposed, strictly in jest, was a corresponding centerfold of rescue, with Cubby as a sort of Playdog Rescue Bunny, mainly because, as his pedigree revealed, his Pawprintz ancestor had been sired by the legendary Northpole's Comet.

I was ripping. "Betty, you knew then and you know perfectly well now: It was strictly a joke. When I sent you that pedigree and the page of the stud book with that dog's registration, it was understood that the information was totally confidential. I did not intend to humiliate anyone, and you had no business putting that stuff out here where everyone could see it!"

"As a matter of fact," Betty responded tartly, "that material was not in the album. It was in *my* private tote bag, which you had no business with, Holly Winter. For your information, I intended to give Cubby's pedigree to Jeanine, and I also had several others that I intended to give to other people. But in the rush, I forgot."

"Betty, I did *not* remove those pages! I never even looked in your bag."

Isabelle intervened. In a near whisper, she interjected, "If the two of you don't cool it, you're going to find yourselves starring on tonight's evening news."

The TV reporters and camera crews had arrived in the exhibition hall in plenty of time to capture the arrival of the police; and since the media people happened to be there anyway, they performed the incidental task of informing us of the murder of James Hunnewell. It was a Channel 5 interviewer who told me that Hunnewell had been bludgeoned to death. Her name was Alex Travis. I'd seen her on TV. She looked almost the same in person—no fatter, no thinner, very young, with sleek black hair and perfect skin, her lipstick and blush a little redder than on TV so her color wouldn't wash out on camera. According to Alex Travis, James Hunnewell had been murdered last night. His bed hadn't been slept in. His body had been cold. Alex Travis was the one who used the phrase "blunt instrument" and who told me that whatever it was, it hadn't been found.

I strongly suspected otherwise.

CHAPTER 11 🔍

In the thirties, dogs were big news. Other socialites just threw parties, but Geraldine Rockefeller Dodge gave fantastic dog shows at her New Jersey estate, Giralda. Mrs. M. Hartley Dodge wasn't the only Rockefeller prominent in the dog fancy, and *The New York Times* faithfully reported on the Morris and Essex shows and lots of others as well. In the thirties, Admiral Byrd was news. So were sled dog racing, the Chinook Kennels, breeds newly recognized by the AKC, show results, everything.

So on this November day, the murder of Judge James Hunnewell transported us back to the future, forward to the past: cameras, yes, but video cameras; brilliant halogen lights; and umbrella-shaped devices with undersides of shiny metallic foil, parasols devised to bounce limelight off clouds with silver linings. In the aisles around the rings, in the parking lot, in the grooming tent, the dogs preened for cameras, *whroo-whroo*ed into microphones, and rose up to rest gentle, mammoth snowshoe paws on the shoulders of startled, flattered reporters here to cover a homicide.

Basking in the reflected light of one of the silver-lined umbrellas, Betty Burley grabbed the opportunity to make an ardent pitch for the wonderful, friendly, healthy, young rescue malamutes who awaited loving adoptive homes. I should have done the same, but my face was still stinging from Betty's verbal slap. Instead, I wandered around exchanging rumors, eavesdropping on conversations, watching the judging, and otherwise doing pretty much what I'd have done if James Hunnewell had still been breathing.

The arrival of the police had put an end to the worry that they'd halt the judging and maybe even force the cancellation of the national. Hunnewell's room was sealed off immediately, and so was the area around the shed. Scrutinizing the entire hotel and its grounds, as well as the myriad of vans, campers, and cars, not to mention the hundreds of dogs and people, was a task no homicide team wanted to tackle. It would have meant summoning zillions of technicians to collect monumental amounts of evidence, all of which would have had to be processed and analyzed, and almost all of which would undoubtedly have been utterly irrelevant to the murder. People would have protested; search warrants might have been a problem. The course the police followed, as I see it now, was a sensible one meant to protect the evidence and maintain the availability of witnesses. If they'd closed down the hotel, for instance, what would they have done with us? The hundreds of hotel guests could hardly have been forced to camp out or to rent rooms elsewhere; with the show canceled, the dog people would've all gone home. Could we have been locked inside? Not for long. And no one, I imagine, wanted to smell the consequences of depriving the dogs of access to the outdoors. Furthermore, antagonizing *all* potential witnesses would have been a poor strategy for getting people to talk.

The air in the exhibition hall was thicker with theories than it was with dog hair. Nepotism: According to Pam

Ritchie, who said she'd heard it from Freida Reilly, the police couldn't close us down without ruining the wedding, and our national had been unintentionally saved by Crystal's father, who had a brother high up in the attorney general's office. Tiny DaSilva disagreed: the groom's father, not the bride's, and not a brother in the attorney general's office, either, but a fraternity brother in the state police. In what I thought was an effort to present herself as the kind of fiscally minded person who'd make a splendid member of our breed club's board, Sherri Ann Printz argued for strict economic determinism: The hotel brought money to Danville. Shut it down, and who'd ever book here again? Then there was the show-precinct debate: Had Hunnewell's body been found on or off show grounds? Freida Reilly and a few other exceptionally devout worshipers at the shrine of AKC were apparently unable to conceive of circumstances in which the distinction didn't matter. Freida may even have believed that if the hallowed ground of a show were desecrated by bloodshed, AKC was obliged to dispatch a high priest rep to reconsecrate the sanctuary; otherwise, like mock marriages, the awards wouldn't count.

I watched and listened as a mousy-looking little breeder with a resplendent name—Celeste LaFlamme—casually told a police officer about a quirk of Mikki Muldoon's that was universally taken for granted. I hate to speak ill of any dog, but if tomorrow's competition had been for Worst of Breed instead of Best, Celeste's dogs would have been the only ones to make the final cut. Every malamute of Celeste's breeding had a pinched expression, a narrow front, feeble little legs, splayed feet, and wary-looking, hooded eyes. In other words, Celeste's dogs looked astonishingly like Celeste herself, who didn't belong at a national any more than they did. And here Celeste was informing the police about highly esteemed Judge Mikki Muldoon's little quirk, which was that Mrs. Muldoon always carried a handgun and that it was always loaded.

Perhaps Mikki Muldoon didn't understand just how strict a handgun law we have here in Massachusetts. The handsome young police officer certainly did, but obviously formed the same opinion of Celeste that everyone held of her dogs—namely, that she was unsound. Glancing at Judge Muldoon, then back at Celeste, the policeman wore the expression you see on the faces of kind, sane people listening to first-person accounts of UFO abductions.

And, of course, Hunnewell hadn't been shot.

The manner of James Hunnewell's demise, in fact, suggested a copycat crime. Rumor even had it that Hunnewell's murder had been inspired by the slaying of poor Elsa Van Dine, who'd been bludgeoned on a street in Providence. The precise nature of the blunt instrument was another favored topic of intense speculation. Examined from a murderous point of view, the exhibition hall was packed with bludgeons. The vendors selling sledding equipment were asked to account for all their snow books. In viewing the wooden walking sticks, iron weather vanes, and handcrafted wall plaques for sale and on display, the police got a crash course titled Five Thousand and One Ways to Depict Malamutes. In the absence of any one likely weapon, the authorities seized none. Excitement spread when one of the trophies went missing, a big malamute-shaped pewter doorstop on a heavy base, but it was soon returned by its donor, Pam Ritchie, who was offering it in Mrs. Seeley's memory and who had briefly removed it from the trophy table and taken it outdoors so someone could admire its craftsmanship in good light. I remain convinced that under impossible circumstances the police were as diligent as possible. Elaine Barrasso, the president of our national breed club, told someone who told someone who told me that Greg and

Crystal's wedding presents, which were on display at a sort of nuptial trophy table in a special room of the hotel, also received a thorough going-over.

And so did we. I gave my name, room number, permanent address, and license-plate number to a state police detective named Peter Kariotis. I told him that, yes, I'd seen James Hunnewell last night. I'd helped him use the Coke machine and get ice. Like the reporters, Detective Kariotis couldn't seem to grasp that, no, the dog show didn't exactly have "a winner," but that, yes, in a way it did: Best of Breed. Leah and I both donated our fingerprints. One of the two ice buckets found in Hunnewell's room was from our bathroom. Leah might have touched it. My prints must have been all over it and also on the can of Coke I'd helped Hunnewell to buy. Freida Reilly and her son, Karl, gave their prints, too. Freida had been in Hunnewell's room. Karl had carried Hunnewell's luggage when he'd picked him up at the airport.

To a remarkable extent, however, the atmosphere was disconcertingly normal, at least normal for a post-homicide dog show. In the grooming tent, the powerful dryers roared and blasted away at dogs who weathered the storms of this strange new Arctic. As gregarious and curious as our dogs, we always socialize and speculate; and like show people everywhere, we invariably help the show chair out by making sure that she fulfills her principal responsibility, which is to take the blame for everything. "I am fully aware of just how hard it is to manage the millions of little details that go into making a show a success," Sherri Ann Printz commented to me. "After all, I did it myself just last year. And last year's national went off without a hitch. Not that any of this is Freida's fault! Or that I'm tooting my own horn. Let's just say that I stand on my record."

Not everyone blamed Freida Reilly. On the contrary, instead of blaming Freida, at least one person gave her credit.

As I sat watching the judging with Janet Switzer, Rowdy's breeder and the alpha figure in my life, Janet told me, "The truth is, the old expletive deleted probably wouldn't have held up for two days, anyway. He might've dropped dead in the ring all on his own. Hunnewell was in no shape to judge. He should've resigned; he should've removed his name from the eligible list years ago." After an uncharacteristic pause, she added grimly, "Instead of leaving poor Freida to do it for him."

CHAPTER 12 🐾

Remember all those Old Testament *begats*? Men begat men. Cush begat Nimrod; Arphaxad begat Salah, who begat Eber; Terah begat Abram, Nahor, and Haran. Haran begat Lot, whose father, in violation of Jewish custom, wanted to call him Haran, Jr., but whose mother, an overlooked pioneer in the feminist movement, sensibly held out for a name that the other kids wouldn't make fun of. "You, Haran," she snorted, "can take your patriarchal tradition and shove it! I, for one, take it with a grain of salt!" Thus was cast and forecast poor Lot's lot.

In the beginning, though, God held a monopoly on the begetting industry. God alone created. Adam and Eve probably wanted to; they just didn't understand the mechanics until a venomous industrial-espionage agent slipped the secret plans to Eve, who is justly famous as the world's first union organizer and the founder of the happy free-enterprise system we enjoy today.

In *Genesis*, people first had to figure out how begetting was done. Only after that did they get busy creating new life: Cain and Abel. If therein lies a natural order, we at the national violated it. Among us, violent death came first. Thereafter, in innocent near-ignorance of how the deed was done, we mated motive to motive. Suspicion begat suspicion. It was fruitful. It multiplied.

Freida Reilly had a motive as obvious as Cain's, although rather different from his. As I recall, all Cain wanted was a little r-e-s-p-e-c-t, whereas what Freida craved was success. This show was Freida's. If Hunnewell had botched the judging, the failure would have been hers. The gain was hers: Mikki Muldoon's judging was smooth and efficient. The gain was Mikki Muldoon's, too. Judging a national specialty? A prestigious assignment, one she'd prepared herself to accept. So everyone suspected Freida, who, as rumor had it, suspected Mikki, but who was also said to have raised questions about the culpability of some member of the wedding party, whether out of genuine suspicion or loyalty to Mikki no one knew.

Betty Burley, who always suspected everyone, even me, of greater dedication to winning with malamutes than to rescuing them, raised questions about Sherri Ann Printz, whose Bear was supposed to be the favorite under Judge Hunnewell, but was definitely not so supposed by Betty Burley. Now that Hunnewell was dead, Betty vehemently asserted that Hunnewell would have shamed everyone by withholding the ribbons and thus announcing that the entire entry lacked merit—Betty insisted that she'd said so last night.

I, by the way, did not merely suspect Sherri Ann Printz of stealing Cubby's pedigree and the stud book page from Betty's tote bag; how Sherri Ann had known that those papers were in Betty's tote, I wasn't sure, but I had no doubt whatsoever that it was Sherri Ann who'd taken them. In Sherri Ann's position, I might have protected my reputation just as I was sure she'd done. Although I didn't know whether Betty had even asked to use Sherri Ann's Bear at stud, I nonetheless suspected Sherri Ann of having insulted Betty by refusing. Whether Victor Printz suspected anyone remained a mystery to everyone except the Pawprintz dogs. They were the only creatures who seemed to comprehend a syllable of Victor's disjointed mumbling.

Bear's true chances under Hunnewell? In predicting the would-have-been opinions of a deceased judge, the forecasters had the benefit of never being proven wrong. Sherri Ann Printz graciously accepted the condolences of supporters who were absolutely certain that Bear was just Hunnewell's type, a shoo-in for Best of Breed. *Rotten luck*, they told her. She agreed: *Rotten luck*. If Bear's boosters and Sherri Ann's supporters were correct, the expression was grossly inadequate. In dogs, rotten luck is missing the judging at a little local match because of a flat tire. It's watching your half-trained pup scramble to his feet on what was supposed to be the down-stay exercise (lie down and stay down) because of some damned toddler with an ice cream cone. Furthermore, Best of Breed at a national specialty isn't just *an* honor, one more big win; it is *the* honor, the ultimate win within the breed. Consequently, discovering that your top contender for Best of Breed at a national has suddenly become just one more competitor is not rotten luck. It's a damned disaster.

If Sherri Ann really believed that Bear would have won under Hunnewell, she must have suspected Duke Sylvia, whose name Betty Burley also let drop. "I know you think a lot of him, Holly," Betty told me, "but you haven't been around as long as I have, and there's plenty about Duke Sylvia that you just don't know." What I *did* know was that Mal-O-Mine Ironman, the big male that Duke co-owned, was supposed to be a strong contender under Mikki Muldoon. While I'm on the subject of Duke Sylvia, let me pass along my impression that in a sense Duke alone held himself above suspicion. Duke had such quiet confidence in his own handling and in Ironman, I thought, that it wouldn't have fazed him to discover that the change had been from James Hunnewell to Mikki Muldoon to the Great Last Judge. As to who had murdered James Hunnewell, Duke Sylvia rose above suspicion by becoming the one person at the national who really didn't seem to care at all.

Sherri Ann Printz publicly lamented the loss of Bear's now-certain victory. With considerably less modesty than Sherri Ann displayed, Timmy Oliver, too, grieved for the honor that Hunnewell would most certainly have bestowed upon Z-Rocks. It seemed to me, though, that Sherri Ann rejoiced in the stolen glory a little more than she lamented its loss; and that she considered the man, James Hunnewell, no loss at all. Timmy Oliver's face, however, bore the rawness of recent sorrow.

I have digressed. What begat my "begat"s was not suspicion, but Timmy Oliver's sad, anxious look. Had I ever seen him in daylight before? At an outdoor show, perhaps, where almost certainly, my attention had been fixed exclusively on the dogs. Today, just outside the exhibition hall, my gaze wandered. I blamed the weather, which was startlingly clear and bright, as if God had finally gotten around to washing our windows. What I saw in Timmy was a life history of incompleteness: coitus interruptus, premature birth, and delivery by a hurried obstetrician who'd rushed off elsewhere leaving the umbilical cord half-tied. Today, only the collar and sleeves of Tim's shirt had been pressed. His hair was longer on one side than on the other, as if he'd bolted out of the barbershop midway through his last haircut or been abandoned in favor of an important customer. His razor had missed a thin patch on his left cheek, and he'd certainly fled the breakfast table before wiping his mouth.

"I don't know whose generator it was," he told Freida Reilly, "but it wasn't mine, and I'm fed up with this crap of everyone saying it was. The damned thing woke me up, too, and I'm pissed about it, just like everybody else."

Freida, accompanied by a brace of broad-shouldered men, had cornered Tim in an angle of the building just outside the big, wide door. Our show chair pointed the red nail of her right index finger straight at his belt. I almost expected her to make a loud *bang-bang*. She didn't. What she said was, "You're pissed? Pissed? First of all, Timmy Oliver, let me tell you that I do not appreciate having that kind of gutter language directed at me. And second, if someone else has been accusing you of anything, that's not my problem, because all I did was ask you one simple question, which was whether it was your generator, and if it wasn't, all you had to do was to say no. But did you just say no? You did not! What you did was, you got yourself all in a huff, and you know what that makes me wonder? I see somebody puff up like that and start sputtering all about how it was all somebody else's fault, and I have to ask myself in all honesty if I'm not dealing with someone who's got something to hide." Her arms folded against her chest, she glared at him. Her pewter malamute jewelry almost seemed to mirror the expression.

"Honest to God, Freida, it woke me up, too."

Undaunted, Freida demanded to know where Tim had spent last night, but before he had time to respond, she accused him of staying in his camper.

"Jesus, Freida, I tried to get a room, but they're all booked up, and I couldn't find anyone to room with. Ask anyone! I must've asked a dozen people. Ask Duke! But, hey, you know, I wasn't the only one, and I didn't have a choice, and, you know, it's not like I—"

"Enough! I have heard all I want to hear," Freida sliced in. "Just a word to the wise, Tim. One more violation, and you are no longer welcome at this show. And you know what I am talking about, because I warned you once before.

I am referring to the poor filthy bitch I saw you with this morning, and what I am doing is, I am dashing any hopes you may have of getting her into a bathtub in this hotel and giving her the good scrubbing she needs before she's fit to be taken out into the light of day, never mind into the ring! Don't do it! And one more word to the wise, Timmy, and this is a very quiet word, and it is based on extensive conversations that I have had with certain members of the wedding party that is struggling just like me to make things work in spite of everything, and that one word is *puppies*, and the one thing I have to say to you on that subject is, *not on show grounds!*" With that admonition, Freida and her deputies wheeled around and marched into the hall.

His face red, Timmy Oliver turned to me, only, I think, because I happened to be right there. I'd overheard the confrontation because I'd been playing mugwump between the end of the breed club's booth and the outdoors. I hadn't been lurking around in search of a fellow victim of public accusation; I'd just been coveting the old sign.

"Jesus," Tim said. "Jesus, this is a shock. You know, I was one of the last friends James had."

"I didn't know he was a friend of yours." In the background, I could hear Betty Burley's voice, as animated and opinionated as usual. "I sort of had the impression that, uh, he'd been out of dogs for such a long time . . ."

Tim's face was flushed an increasingly unhealthy color. "Yeah, well, James didn't like the direction the breed was going in."

"A lot of people don't," I said. Name any breed of dog, and there'll be a lot of people who don't like the direction it's going in.

"Yeah, well, James really didn't like it, and shit, here I am with this bitch that he was goddamn crazy about, and . . . Shit!" Oliver gave the pavement a hard kick. As his knee bent, the cuff of his trousers rose a little, revealing a sock that had slid down around his ankle. He delivered a second fierce kick to the asphalt. "Z-Rocks was a goddamn sure thing."

"At a dog show," I said, "there is no such animal."

CHAPTER 13

The glossy brochures spread out at the Reproductive Technologies, Inc., booth had a paradoxically ill-bred habit of posing intimate questions:

IS YOUR STUD OVERBOOKED?
WORRIED ABOUT POOR-QUALITY EJACULATE?
MANUAL STIMULATION? OR AN ESTRUS TEASER BITCH?

Compromised libido, membrane fragility, intrauterine deposition, vaginal smears, ancillary aids—kinky, that one?—and an orgasmic-sounding phenomenon called the *L-H surge*: It all felt alarmingly human. WITH R.T.I., WHEN SHE'S READY, HIS COUNT IS ALWAYS UP! Good God! *The trauma of freezing*! And *chilled* semen? Couldn't it at least be warmed to room temperature? But Reproductive Technologies, Inc., was for dogs, not people. No matter what the query or the problem, the answer was always the same: *R.T.I.*, where, as a red-and-

gold satin banner proclaimed, FOOLING MOTHER NATURE IS
OUR ONLY BUSINESS!

And a lucrative one it apparently was. Here were no
hand-scrawled signs taped to the concrete wall, no home-
made posters, no paper tablecloths, no piles of bargain-
photocopied handouts, none of the hallmarks of the amateur
vendors whose promotional efforts announce, if read between the lines: *We're new at this!* Here, fabric screens in
royal blue formed the backdrop for a little stage richly set
with props: chairs with upholstered seats; a portable com-
puter; giant blown-up photos of handsome men and beautiful women in white coats—scientists, yes, concerned
scientists; even larger pictures of litter after big litter of
thriving purebred puppies; a long, cloth-covered table offering shiny booklets and discreetly boxed kits containing . . .
No, don't ask.

Standing behind the table was my ex-lover Finn Adams,
who clutched in his hands a pair of sanitary panties for
bitches in season. The fabric was pink-and-white polka dot.
The edging was lace. I hadn't seen Finn since the summer
before I left for college. He'd been a tall, lean kid with sun-
bleached curls and an impressive tan. My first impression
now was that something dreadful had happened to him.
Then I decided what: time.

Finn knew me right away. Fiddling with the Velcro on
the doggy lingerie, he said, "Holly Winter."

"Finn, for God's sake," I said. "Put that down!"

Why, if he had to be here, couldn't he have been a carver
of wooden malamutes, a dog food salesman, a vendor of ceramic statuettes, a dealer in polar books, an AKC rep, or an
anything else that had nothing to do with sex? But, no, after all this time, the love of my young life had to be
fondling canine underpants!

"Of all the dog shows in all the world . . ." he said.

I tried to remember whether we'd seen *Casablanca* together. We couldn't have. We'd never watched television; home video hadn't been invented yet; and midcoast Maine wasn't exactly Brattle Square, Cambridge. Had we ever even gone to the movies? I couldn't remember what, if anything, we'd seen. I sure knew what it should have been: *Seduced and Abandoned*.

As lightly as I could, I said, "Oh, is this your show? I had the impression that it was mine, too." I glanced at Rowdy, who was with me because I'd felt guilty about leaving him stuck in his crate. Also, I'd missed him. If Rowdy had been less gorgeous and sweet than he is, I'd still have been glad to have him with me, but probably a little less delighted than I was at the moment. I hoped that Finn had a malamute, too. I hoped Finn's dog had a mean disposition: you know, the kind that makes a dog turn on its owner.

Finn said, "You were supposed to send me your college address."

"You were supposed to send me yours. *You* were changing dorms, remember?"

I didn't want to look in Finn's eyes. I was holding a brochure. I skimmed a paragraph about sexual rest.

"I must've written you ten letters, Holly. I always wondered what happened to you."

I, in contrast, had known through the years exactly what had become of Finn. Either he was a Wall Street type like his father, an investment banker or a bond trader with a big house on Long Island, a pied-à-terre in the East Sixties, and a thin blond wife who'd majored in art history at Wellesley or Smith and would eventually hit the glass ceiling of her career in mothering their towheaded children; or he was spending his life cruising around the world—Fiji, Madagascar, Cape Horn, Punta Arenas—in a Hinckley yacht even bigger than the one his parents had had. We'd met through his parents. Rather, through our mothers. His bought a puppy from mine, a golden, a pet sold on a spay-neuter contract, but a nice dog.

Remembering that dog, I asked, "What ever happened to Barry?" Finn's parents were political conservatives. It used to be against AKC policy to use the name of a famous person, living or recently dead, in registering a dog, but considering the breed, you can see how "Goldwater" slipped through.

Finn's face looked strange. Really strange. "He just died a few years ago."

I was amazed. "Good God, he must have been—"

Finn looked up at the ceiling, as if Barry's ghost might drift by and be summoned downward. "I didn't see him near the end. He was with my parents. They, uh, moved to Brazil."

Except to the extent that Brazil has a long Atlantic coastline and birds to be examined through binoculars and looked up in a Peterson field guide, Mr. and Mrs. Adams were possibly the least Brazilian people I could imagine, not that I've ever been to Brazil, but so far as I know, it has a tropical climate and a melting-pot citizenry given to Mardi Gras celebrations that make the ones in New Orleans seem as cold, Yankee, and noncelebratory as Finn's parents. As I remembered them, these were people who would've felt more at home at the North Pole than on the sunny beaches of Ipanema. But the North Pole is a difficult place to vanish into, I guess. Miles of permafrost. Very exposed. I had the horrible sensation that entirely against my will I was about to remind Finn of his parents' fate by uttering the word "junk" or "bond" or maybe both in the same sentence. I couldn't think of anything that might prompt me to start blabbing about litter, Chinese boats, investments, or adhesives. Even so.

"Brazil," I said. "Oh. And you work for R.T.I."

That summer, Finn's parents had been renting a house in

Port Clyde, but spent most of their time on their boat. My family lived nearby, in Owls Head. My father still does. We didn't spend most of our time in the house, either; we spent it in the kennels. Finn and I didn't exactly have a town-gown relationship. It was more tail-sail. Unless his family owned a conglomerate that owned a parent company that owned R.T.I., I now reasoned, Finn's ship had gone out, and he'd had to take shelter in a dog house.

"Yeah. A second cousin of mine got me into it. I was in California until a couple of months ago. Then I got transferred." Finn was cheerful enough. The language of canine reproduction was easier than Portuguese, I suppose, and he didn't seem to be working very hard. At this show at least, he'd been away from his booth most of the time. "Of course, I travel a lot." Then he told me all about the car he drove. I can't remember what kind it was. He described the route he'd followed to get from a New Jersey show site to Danville. And then the highways he planned to take after he left. My first retake on Finn had been abysmally correct: Something horrible had happened to him. But I'd been wrong about what. The terrible change was the last one I'd ever have imagined: If he'd joined a motorcycle gang, become a Roman Catholic bishop, or pursued a career in worm farming, I'd have been less astounded than I was by the incredible truth, which was that he'd gotten really boring; and when I say *boring*, I don't mean slightly tedious or a little dull, but radically stupefying. Amazing! That summer, the sight of him had turned me to liquid. Now, all these years later, I was still producing fluid: copious tears of passionate *boredom*.

I eventually squeezed in a word about what I was doing at the R.T.I. booth in the first place. Mistake! I heard everything I already knew about fresh chilled and frozen semen. Although I'd displayed no interest in an international breeding, Finn went on and on about avoiding problems with customs and quarantine. Maybe Rowdy was gratified to hear that large dogs usually produce more semen than small dogs. I wasn't; I'd read it somewhere. How long did it take Finn to get around to long-term storage? Well you might ask! Frozen semen is expected to stay good for ten thousand years, the approximate length of time that it took Finn to tell me so. As to the preservation itself, the semen was evaluated, and if it passed inspection, extended with a buffer solution, and then counted, diluted, and frozen in liquid nitrogen in individually labeled straws. Yes, *straws*, ten to twenty per ejaculate, more than enough to put you off milkshakes for the rest of your life.

To my extreme annoyance, instead of cooperatively whining to be taken outside or drowning Finn out with a series of *woo-woo-woos*, Rowdy remained silent and attentive throughout the monologue, which eventually led through legal aspects of the ownership of frozen semen—an asset just like any other, Finn said, no different from a house or a car—to R.T.I.'s claim to unmatched superiority in complying with AKC regulations about record keeping. Not that the topics were unimportant. I mean, no matter how much of a real dog person you are, your stud's semen still isn't the kind of thing you tuck in the back of your freezer with the orange juice and the TV dinners. Even if you could get the temperature down to minus one ninety-six Celsius, what would you do in a power failure? With a banquet's worth of unexpectedly defrosted food, you can always invite a few hundred neighbors to dinner, but with thawed-out sperm, you aren't going to throw a spur-of-the-moment potluck orgy for bitches in season. And the labeling and record keeping mattered, too. You don't go to the bother and expense of immortalizing your stud so that ten, twenty, or a hundred years from now, you or whoever buys or inherits and uses his semen gets a surprise litter of mal-a-poos or Dober-mutes.

Finn was droning on. I cut in. "I guess I still need to think it over. My main hesitation is"—I perched on the verge of heresy—"that, uh, am I ever really going to use it? Rowdy is a typey dog, he's sound, and he really has a classic Kotzebue head, but what I keep hearing about frozen semen is that it hardly ever gets used. What I've heard is that when the technology first became available, in the sixties, and then when AKC approved it, in the early eighties, there was a lot of initial enthusiasm, and a lot of breeders did it without realizing that, uh, the popularity of types would, uh, change over time."

As Finn's had with me, my face burned. I had as little desire to hurt Finn as I had desire *for* him. He must have written me ten letters? My mother, I realized, had committed a federal offense. I suddenly knew how. I'd been home for Thanksgiving when my mother had presented the half-grown puppy, a littermate of Barry's, to Mildred Fielders, who delivered our mail. Who'd clearly been bought off. I felt so sorry for my teenage self that I wished that my mother and Mildred Fielders were still alive so I could send them to a penitentiary for conspiring to tamper with the U.S. Mail. My mother had objected quite strongly to Finn Adams. Until now, I'd almost forgotten her principal complaint. Her only objection to Finn, she maintained, was that the boy was intolerably uninteresting.

She'd had no right to interfere with my mail. But I could have gotten pregnant. I could have married him! I felt suddenly light: elevated, levitated, elated, joyous. What a wonderful life I'd had since I'd last seen Finn Adams! What a lucky person I was! My nights with Steve, my days with Rowdy and Kimi, my house rocking with the booming pitter-patter of malamutes crashing off the walls.

So, I wasn't angry at Finn. Far from it. I felt a sort of senseless gratitude to him for vanishing from my life, which had been vastly better than his, I thought. Lacking the golden glow of sunny curls and family money to begin with, I'd had little to lose. I felt thankful that my eccentric father was still embarrassing me by being around instead of humiliating me by having had to flee to Brazil for financial wrongdoing. Also, my father had always been mortifying; I was used to it. I felt really sorry for Finn. The popularity of types changes mightily over time. But I shouldn't have said so.

To cover up my blunder, I blundered on. "So," I said, "I don't believe in breeding for sentimental reasons." A coughing fit seized me. After clearing my throat, I said, "I mean, before I decide, I have to be sure that it makes objective sense, that at some point in the distant future, the semen would be worth using. Not that it would be *junk*—far from it—but I don't want to do it just because I'm *bonded* with my dog—"

Rowdy examined me with large, empathic eyes. So far as I could tell, though, Finn entirely missed what Rowdy immediately grasped. Steve Delaney wouldn't have noticed, either. So what? I pity men who love women who don't have dogs like mine. Rowdy and Kimi are brilliant and intuitive. They offer me boundless entertainment and unconditional worship. They occupy my time and attention. They are excellent company. Steve is my lover. He doesn't have to be my dog, too.

Anyway, whether densely or tactfully, Finn ignored my faux pas and said something that rendered me speechless.

"You're thinking about the distant future," he said. "This morning, right outside here, I went for a walk, and what I came across was the body of the guy who was supposed to judge today. Think about it, Holly. Your dog could die *tomorrow*. So could I. So could you."

CHAPTER 14

If I weren't so cowardly, I'd have made a great cop. When I'd made the claim a few weeks earlier to my neighbor Kevin Dennehy, who actually is a cop, Kevin had suffered what our therapist friend Rita diagnosed as an hysterical seizure, meaning, as I understood it, that the problem was in Kevin's head, not mine. Rita brought him out of the attack by lying: She said I was joking: I'd make a rotten cop. Kevin believed her. That's Cambridge: always a mental health professional at hand to pour snake oil on the waters of turbulent truth.

But I would have. For example, if I'd been Detective Peter Kariotis, *I'd* have known *I* was lying or, if not exactly lying, not spilling the full truth. Observing a fishy look in my own eyes, a tightness about the mouth, and a rigidity in my Yankee jaw, Detective Holly Winter would have made a swift verbal pounce. "Just what," I'd have demanded, "did you find on the blacktop under Betty Burley's van? And what did you do with it? And why?"

But before I abandon the topic of fishiness, let me summarize what Finn had to say about finding the corpse of James Hunnewell. Summarize is precisely what Finn didn't do. On the contrary, he went on and on about his reasons for taking a walk, his estimation of the air temperature, the excessive warmth of the windbreaker he'd been wearing, and the makes and models of the ambulances, emergency vehicles, and police cruisers that had subsequently arrived. I'd found Finn boring when he'd delivered his sales pitch about reproductive artifice, but he was even more staggeringly boring when he prattled on about unnatural death. Rita would have interpreted Finn's obsessive dwelling on tedious detail as symptoms of anxiety; she'd probably have decided that Finn was having a post-traumatic stress reaction exacerbated by the unexpected resurgence of an object of libidinal cathexis: Instead of getting freaked out by finding a dead body, Finn got boring, and the reason he got really, really boring was that I made him nervous. Anyway, what I finally managed to extract from him about the murder of James Hunnewell was not much. Hunnewell's head had been crushed. His skin had felt cold to the touch; although death had been obvious, Finn had checked. The body had been propped up against the wall of the shed, under a little open porch. Finn wondered whether Hunnewell was supposed to look like an old guy who'd settled there to watch a game of horseshoes or volleyball in the open field. If so, the odd angle of the neck and, of course, the battered skull spoiled the effect. Hanging around to be questioned, Finn gathered that the body had been moved a short distance, from a spot near the edge of the parking lot. Needless to say, Finn dwelled on how *many* feet.

Leah (mercifully!) interrupted his monologue. I performed introductions. Leah would have made a great cop, too. Within seconds of the time we left the R.T.I. booth, she'd not only guessed about Finn, but was saying, "*Finn!* Holly, even the name . . ."

Embarrassed, I said, "I was only a kid." In what must have hit Leah as blatant self-contradiction, I added, "I was only about your age."

Leah remained unsympathetic, or I thought so. "Burble burble" isn't my idea of a supportive comment. What rankled, though, wasn't the fish imitation, but the realization that my cousin's judgment about men actually was better than mine had been at her age and that she thought less of me now than she had before.

Brooding over my own foolishness, I failed to notice the approach of Detective Peter Kariotis until he spoke my name, and when he did, my first thought was that, yes, now and then I certainly did imagine a universe in which powerful authority figures hovered around waiting to deliver timely little respect-your-elders lectures to know-it-all Harvard freshmen, but that, no, right now I did not require police intervention. My second thought was that the one Detective Kariotis had come for was not Leah, who had presumably told the police everything she knew and who had known nothing whatsoever about the small mystery of the malamute lamp.

In a way, my second thought was correct, except that the lamp wasn't what Detective Kariotis wanted to ask about. He'd seen it, of course, just as in the past few hours he'd seen zillions of other malamute objects—large, small, light, heavy, sharp, and blunt. If I didn't mention it, I told myself, he wouldn't, either. And he didn't. Consequently, I wasn't nervous. Also, I should reveal that I'm perfectly used to being interrogated by the police. Kevin Dennehy is always asking me how I'm doing, and whether it's hot or cold enough for me. I always answer truthfully: "Fine" or "Sure is!" So I pretended that Kariotis was a Greek-American version of Kevin. The tactic worked. Detective Kariotis looked almost as Greek as Kevin looks Irish, and the effort required to achieve the radical ethnic transformation left me no energy to think about lamps. Kevin has red hair and pale freckled skin, and he's a tall, beefy guy. Kariotis was dark and wiry, but his accent eased my task. It wasn't Kevin's heavy Cambridge-Boston, but the vowel sounds were pretty close, and Kariotis treated the right *r*'s as silent letters.

We talked in a room off the corridor that ran between the exhibition hall and the Lagoon. This function room, as I guess it would be called in hotelese, had three or four chairs, a little table, no windows, and zillion-watt fluorescent lighting. Maybe the hotel was courting the mortuary trade. The obvious function of the room was to make people look as if they'd died of anemia.

When Kariotis and I had seated ourselves on opposite sides of the table, he began his interrogation with a question that sounded like a line from an old movie. "Miss Winter," he said blandly, "do you smoke?"

For a second, I thought he must've been studying a hopelessly out-of-date text on interview procedures and was trying to put me at ease by offering me a cigarette.

I blinked. "No."

"When you encountered Mr. Hunnewell last night, did he ask you whether you smoked? Or whether you had any cigarettes?"

"No. He didn't have reason to. He was smoking constantly. He was chain-smoking. He had a pack of cigarettes with him. And a lighter. An old-fashioned gold lighter, the kind you put lighter fluid in, with a sort of flip top." I snapped my fingers. "I just realized something. I didn't know who he was then, but now that I think of it, he probably won the lighter at a show, a dog show. Years ago, ashtrays, lighters, cigarette boxes, all that stuff used to be given as trophies. It seems ridiculous now, but people's dogs used to win them all the time."

"This, uh, pack of cigarettes he had. Did you notice how full it was? Or if it was, uh, almost empty?"

"Uh, I don't know. I don't . . . I'm sorry. I just don't know."

"Did Mr. Hunnewell say anything at all about buying cigarettes? Or, like, uh, when you were helping him with the soft-drink machine and the ice machine, did it seem like he might've been looking around for a cigarette machine?"

"I don't think so. Not that I noticed. And he didn't say anything about cigarettes or smoking or anything, except that he did offer me a cigarette. Mainly, he just . . . I mean, he was smoking, and then he kind of stubbed out the cigarette and threw it in the trash barrel, and he lit another one. I remember because I was worried that the cigarette wasn't out, that it would start a fire. And . . . this probably sounds kind of silly, but . . . he didn't just smoke: He *really* smoked. There was so much smoke that I half expected the smoke alarm to go off. It sort of worried me that it didn't. And just in case his cigarette was still smoldering and the alarm was broken or something—really, so I wouldn't stay awake worrying about it—I went back, after he was gone, and poured water in the trash barrel."

"The last time you saw Mr. Hunnewell was when he was leaving with Mrs. Reilly?"

I tried to read Kariotis's expression. He didn't have one. "Yes," I said.

"And then you entered your room?"

"Yes. And later, I went back out and poured a lot of water in the trash barrel. And I got ice, and I got something to drink. That's what I was doing there to begin with, only I ended up helping him instead. So I went back."

"And what time was that?"

"I have no idea."

"Yes, you do," my interrogator said impassively. "Midnight?"

"No. Nine-thirty, I think. Before ten. Well, it must've been well before ten, because that's . . . I think that's about when I went to sleep."

"And this last time, when you were in the corridor, did you see anyone?"

"Not that I remember. No, I don't think so."

"Did you see or hear anyone or anything during the night? Or in the morning?"

"At, uh, somewhere around six, six-thirty, someone in one of the campers started a generator. That's what woke me up. It woke everyone up, I think. But that's normal. It happens all the time at shows. Other than that, nothing." I did not say that I, like a lot of other people, had assumed that the offending generator was Tim Oliver's.

"You had a dog in your room?"

"Two. And my cousin." I suppressed an irrational impulse to explain that Leah was human.

"At any point, did your dogs bark?"

"Someone must've told you this by now," I said, "but they're malamutes, and most malamutes don't exactly bark. And they're not watch dogs. A few malamutes will rumble or growl if a stranger comes to the door, but a lot of them won't do a thing, except maybe stand there wagging their tails. That's what mine do. They *like* strangers—strange people, anyway. If they'd heard other dogs, they might've made some noise. But malamutes don't go around warning you about anything, because the typical malamute attitude is that no matter what it is, he can handle it. So why get worked up?"

"While we're on the subject of dogs . . ." Kariotis attempted. He pulled out two pieces of paper and asked me to explain what they were. One bore my name: Cubby's pedigree, the one I'd run myself. The other was a page of the stud book register, the page I'd included with the pedigree when I'd sent it to Betty Burley. He asked me to explain exactly what they were.

In my effort to divert him from anything related to the lamp—anything being, of course, Betty Burley—I made a total fool of myself by setting a personal best (maybe a world record) for dog talk. Detective Kariotis showed almost no reaction. When I said the words "stud book," however, even those death-light fluorescents couldn't wash out the red that abruptly coursed into the man's cheeks. Flashing him an innocent smile, I said, "Relax! It's dogs. It's not for eligible bachelors."

The second time he looked interested was when I explained that the stud book listing of Pawprintz Attic Emprer meant that the dog had been bred by S. A. and V. Printz and owned by G. H. Thacker. The pedigree I'd run showed Gladys Thacker's full name at the bottom of the page and the notation "MO A," my shorthand for a USDA Class A dealer, a puppy farmer rather than a broker, in the puppy-mill capital of the United States, Missouri. (Shorthand, indeed! Have I lost you? The USDA, United States Department of Agriculture, licenses operators of wholesale commercial kennels. The Class A dealers, the puppy farmers, breed puppies that they sell to the Class B dealers, the brokers, who resell the puppies to pet shops. And Missouri? According to the USDA's reports, the Show-Me State had 1,084 licensed dealers. Kansas, by comparison, came in a distant second with a mere 448. Why such small numbers? Two reasons. First, at least half of the puppy farmers don't have licenses. Second, lots of the brokers are big time. What does big time mean? There's one broker who's reported to ship 24,000 puppies a year. That's twenty-four *thousand*. And that's big time.)

Fingering the pedigree, I said, "I guess that all this has

something to do with Mr. Hunnewell's murder." I meant Cubby's ancestry, the Printzes, and Gladys Thacker, of course, not the business about smoking. One thing I knew for sure was that James Hunnewell hadn't lived to die of lung cancer.

Detective Kariotis's face remained blank. "The originals of these were found with the body. You got any idea about why?"

I answered truthfully: "No."

Kariotis stared at a spot over my left shoulder. "Gladys Thacker," he said. "She usually comes to these, uh, shows?"

A puppy-mill operator at a national specialty dog show? Like a prostitute at a nuns' convention. Except that good sisters would presumably refrain from casting stones.

"Not that I know of," I replied. "But this is the first malamute national I've been to myself."

"Most of you people here know each other, is that right?"

"Not all. But a lot of people do. And one of the things about a national is that it's a chance to meet people—people you've just heard of, people you've talked to on the phone and haven't met in person before."

"One thing I've observed today," Kariotis remarked impassively, "is that you people talk a lot."

"Really!" I exclaimed. "Do you think so?"

He finally cracked a hint of a smile. "You ever hear any talk," he said, "of any hard feelings here?" He started tapping the pedigree.

I looked at his finger. "Where?" I asked.

"Here," he said, tapping Gladys Thacker's name. "Between Mr. Hunnewell and his sister here. Between him and Gladys Thacker."

My jaw must have dropped.

"The lady'll be here tomorrow," Kariotis continued. "Says she wants to take her brother home with her to Missouri for a Christian burial."

CHAPTER 15

Before my interview with Detective Kariotis, I'd instructed Leah to return Rowdy to our room and to turn herself over to Faith Barlow, who was handling a number of dogs today (besides Rowdy tomorrow) and could probably use help. After the interview, I considered seeking Faith out to beg her to minister to me instead. From the moment I'd spotted that cursed lamp under Betty's van, I'd botched everything. Now I was furious at Betty, disappointed in Finn, ashamed of myself, and enraged at my dead mother's high-handedness. Leah had sized up Finn in a second. At about her age, why hadn't I? Tomorrow, Steve Delaney, my lover and my vet, would be here. I'd told him all about the fascinating Finn who'd abandoned me. If they met? I consoled myself with the thought that I hadn't spoken to Steve today and thus hadn't had the opportunity to foul things up between us. Tomorrow, reformed, I'd speak the simple truth. Better, I'd quote Shakespeare. "I feel like Titania," I'd say, " 'Methought I was enamor'd of an ass.' " For all I knew, though, Steve and Finn would sit in Finn's posh booth happily conferring about impaired motility and artificial vaginas. Today, I would do what I always advised newcomers to do at any dog show: I'd keep my eyes and ears open and my mouth locked shut. I would contemplate the ultimate reality: I would look at dogs.

And, catalog in hand, I did. Right on schedule, Mikki Muldoon had completed her judging of the boys—the males—and started on the girls. Tomorrow morning, she'd begin her day with what was rather ingloriously described as "Remainder of Bitches." Flipping through the catalog, I noticed that Freida and her committee had been quite successful in filling it with paid advertising and pages of boosters and tributes. In Pam Ritchie's ad, a circa 1935 photo of Eva B. Seeley had been cropped and merged with a contemporary picture to present the image of an admiring Mrs. Seeley beaming approval at one of Pam's bitches. The listings on the pages headed "Tributes" offered brief, inexpensive homage to assorted collections of people and dogs. Freida Reilly thanked "Karl Reilly, Ch. Tuffluv's A Plus," as if her son and her stud were one and the same. Rowdy, Kimi, Leah, and I paid tribute to Faith Barlow and Janet Switzer, whom I'd scrupulously listed in alphabetical order. Janet's full-page ad, bordered in black and headed "In Memoriam," showed Janet's great dog, Denali, Rowdy's sire. I wished that judges were allowed to look at catalogs. The photo of Denali would surely have primed Mikki Muldoon for the sight of his son.

When I raised my eyes from the catalog, Mrs. Muldoon was pointing one finger—number one, first place in the twelve- to eighteen-month puppy bitch class—to a lovely female of Pam Ritchie's and a junior handler I recognized as Pam's nephew. Sherri Ann took second with a black-and-white puppy called Pawprintz Amber Waves. Putting the kid first was, I guess, picking the sentimental favorite, but the crowd was pleased, and Sherri Ann hadn't come to a national specialty with her ambitions fixed on a puppy bitch. The dog she gave a damn about was Bear, and the prize she craved above all others was the purple-and-gold rosette for Best of Breed.

I wondered whether James Hunnewell would have put Sherri Ann's bitch first today and whether he'd have liked Bear as much as Sherri Ann evidently believed. Years earlier, when Sherri Ann had sold that Pawprintz dog to Gladys H. Thacker, had Sherri Ann known that the woman was Hunnewell's sister? If so, the family connection must have felt like a high recommendation. The brother, James Hunnewell, held a respected position in the dog fancy. It certainly hadn't occurred to Sherri Ann that his sister operated in the ninth circle of hell: the puppy mills.

Over and over, television, newspaper, and magazine exposés had documented horrendous filth and disease on puppy farms. I'll give one example. At a recently raided operation in the Midwest, the puppy miller maintained what she called her "death barn." That was where she dumped the bodies of dead dogs and puppies. It was also where she took any dog in desperate need of veterinary care. The sick dogs that entered the death barn didn't get veterinary care, of course. They got neither food nor water nor euthanasia. They just stayed locked in the barn until they died. Want to hear more? Gee, why not?

When, if ever, had Sherri Ann found out exactly how James Hunnewell's sister made her shameful living? Could Sherri Ann have made the discovery only recently? In her position, I thought, wisely or foolishly, fairly or unfairly, I'd have blamed James Hunnewell for his sister's sins. *He should have known*, I'd have thought. *He should have warned me. He should never have let this happen*. Was that how Sherri Ann had felt? Had she taken revenge at the first opportunity?

And Betty Burley. When Betty received Cubby's pedigree from me, she'd unquestionably seen that Gladys

Thacker was a licensed dealer, which is to say, no amateur dabbler in the commercial puppy trade, but an official operator, a farmer whose produce consisted not of maize, soybeans, eggs, or milk, but of AKC-registered dogs. Betty had been in malamutes for decades. So had Sherri Ann Printz and James Hunnewell. So, in a very different way, had Gladys H. Thacker. Betty might have known that James Hunnewell and Gladys Thacker were brother and sister. If so, it would have been exactly like Betty to confront both Sherri Ann Printz and James Hunnewell. Could Betty have approached Hunnewell last night? Betty didn't have a dog entered. Nothing in the AKC regulations would have barred her from knocking on his door; and she'd been in the corridors before and after she'd retrieved the lamp from the booth.

My anger came back. If Betty had to be so judgmental, she should've become a judge! And before judging me, she should've heard my side! I hadn't touched her tote bag. And I'd kept my mouth shut about the damned Comet lamp.

Betty could be as ruthless as Kimi, as high-handed as my mother, and as judgmental as God on the Day of Wrath, all at the same time. And that awful lamp meant a great deal to Betty: Cubby, a puppy-mill dog, was descended from a Pawprintz dog, a dog sired by the famed Northpole's Comet. James Hunnewell had owned Comet. The lamp bore Comet's fur. As a weapon in Betty's hands, had the lamp symbolized vengeance for the descent of Comet's glorious genes into the puppy mills, for the suffering of all dogs doomed to lead miserable lives as puppy-mill breeding stock, and for the heartless elitism of breeders and judges who cared only for *quality* dogs and denied responsibility for so-called *trash?* And those voices in the dark parking lot? The voices that jeered at "Betty's mongrels" and "trash dogs"? That parking lot was not far from James Hunnewell's room. Judges, as I've said, need not imprison themselves. Catching the cruel words, Jeanine had worried that Betty, too, might have overheard. Jeanine and Arlette had not recognized the voices. Betty might well have known James Hunnewell's. Jeanine, who loved Cubby, had been wounded. It had not occurred to Jeanine to strike back.

Betty was a tiny woman, and the lamp was heavy, but Hunnewell was small, a diminished man, and Betty had the strength of a lifetime spent handling great big dogs. Like everyone else with years of experience in rescue, Betty had had to euthanize dogs that were a menace to children, dogs that had savaged people, malamutes that were a danger to everyone and a threat to the breed's good name. *Euthanize*: destroy, put to sleep, put down, give the needle. Take to the vet. But last night in the parking lot there hadn't been a vet handy, had there? And she could hardly have rushed James Hunnewell to the nearest animal hospital. If Betty had decided to destroy him, she'd have had to do it herself.

CHAPTER 16 🐾

Stacked in a human show pose—feet frozen, head high—Sherri Ann Printz had the black-and-white Amber Waves at her gold lamé side. In six months, I predicted, the puppy bitch would be chunky and unrefined. Sherri Ann, of course, had already ripened to beefy coarseness. Amber Waves, however, was behaving like a perfect, if far from little, lady. Sherri Ann, in contrast, was engaged in an ill-bred shouting match with Freida Reilly.

"Everyone knew I gave that lamp to Betty!" Sherri Ann screeched. "And I never, ever, not once promised it to you, Freida Reilly, and you damn well know it!"

Freida's early-morning lacquer had developed cracks. It was now four or so in the afternoon. The judging was over for the day. In the ring, the hands-on portion of the judges' education seminar had just started. The participants consisted of six or eight demonstration dogs and the usual dog-world combination of many women and few men. It won't always be this way, you know. Modern science, I am happy to report, is already at work on a solution to the scarcity of men in the dog fancy. In the future, we'll collect, extend, and chill them so they can be conveniently and inexpensively shipped all over the country to be warmed up as needed, just like sperm. As it is now, our human studs are hopelessly overbooked.

The group surrounding Freida Reilly and Sherri Ann Printz at the national breed club's booth, however, showed the underrepresentation of men that we temporarily endure. In addition to Freida, Sherri Ann, and Betty Burley, there were four or five other women. Victor Printz lingered at the edge, as did Tim Oliver. Taking yet another covetous look at the old sign from the Chinook Kennels and poking through a stack of collector's item issues of the *Malamute Quarterly*, I wasn't really part of the crowd.

But back to Freida. Her badge was askew. Her short, tight perm was crushed on one side. The other side puffed out. Her head looked coyly tilted at an uncomfortable angle. Hanging upside down from her lapel was a dainty corsage of white baby's breath and bruised pink rosebuds. The pewter malamute pin was now upside down. In a voice hoarse with overtried patience, she declared, "Sherri Ann, you know as well as I do that a good six months ago you told me all about that lamp, in detail, and when you did, you asked whether I would like it for our auction, and I said yes, we certainly would."

Administering an unwarranted leash correction to the innocent Amber Waves, Sherri Ann fiercely defended herself: "I very well may have happened to *mention* my lamp to you in passing, Freida, but I definitely did not *offer* it to you. In fact, I remember perfectly that at that point, I was thinking of keeping it for *myself*."

As if responding to some inaudible, invisible cue, Sherri Ann and Freida turned in unison to Betty Burley, who stared silently back at both of them.

"And furthermore, Freida," Sherri Ann continued loudly,

"when I donated it to Betty to help save her poor rescue dogs, I did *not* do it *behind* your back, and—"

"You damned well *did!*"

"No, I did not! I made no secret of it. I did it *right* over *here* at Betty's nice little booth, yesterday, right out in the open. Ask *anyone!* And it has been sitting there, on display, at Betty's booth ever since then, as you'd *know* if you'd even so much as gone out of your way to stroll by there!" Anticlimactically, Sherri Ann added, "Which you obviously *have not*." Turning to Betty, Sherri Ann demanded to know whether Freida had even *once* visited the rescue booth.

Taking a tiny step backward, Betty replied that she had no idea.

Freida's eyes narrowed. She nervously fingered one of the pewter puppy earrings. "Well, Betty," she began in a voice like permafrost, "is this the thanks I get for all the support I've offered you? I gave you that booth space, and I *slaved* over the schedule to squeeze in your showcase on the evening that you wanted it. I gave you every single thing you asked for! And *this* is what I get?"

I thought: *Neither you, Freida, nor you, Betty, gets a litter of puppies sired by Sherri Ann's Bear. And that's why you're both so mightily put out with Sherri Ann.*

Betty's lips twitched. "Why, Freida," she replied, her voice oozing dignity and graciousness, "I am absolutely astonished to discover that I have been operating on what is clearly a set of erroneous assumptions. I am particularly amazed to hear that the booth and the showcase are somehow my own personal property! Until this moment, I have assumed that the visible presence of rescue at this national was just as important to everyone else who cares about this breed as it was to me." She finished with the trace of a naughty little smile.

Freida really had been cooperative about the booth and the showcase. She couldn't afford to be otherwise, Betty had maintained. No one running for the board of our national breed club could risk a reputation for opposing rescue.

"I am one hundred percent pro-rescue!" Freida snapped. Her pewter dogs danced. "But you know as well as I do—"

Shrugging her tiny shoulders and addressing a heaven evidently populated by rescued malamutes, Betty bulldozed on. "Money!" she exclaimed, as if she'd just now discovered the invention of currency. "Is that what this is about? About failing to meet the basic survival needs of the rescue dogs because *some* people are afraid that it will be money taken away from trophy funds, and they'll have to go home without a lot of knickknacks and bric-a-brac and gewgaws that supposedly prove—"

Heresy! And hypocrisy. The glass-fronted china cabinets in Betty Burley's dining room were jammed with loot her dogs had won. I must admit, though, that I understood Betty's attitude perfectly. The costly show trophies presented to other people's dogs might well be junk, but by virtue of being won by one of my own dogs, even the most trifling bauble always became an inestimably precious icon.

Freida's face had turned an alarming red. "Betty, you are getting carried—"

"Carried away?" demanded Betty. "Well, if I get picked up and carried away, it'll be the first help of any kind that anyone doing rescue has ever received from a lot of the breeders here!"

An unfamiliar male voice mumbled in an undertone. Peering over my shoulder, I witnessed an historic moment: Victor Printz was uttering comprehensible words to a fellow human being. ". . . more of Betty's Christ damn sob stories," I actually overheard him say. "Don't know what Sherri Ann thought she was doing giving so much as a plugged nickel to her and her bunch of mongrels."

Victor Printz was addressing a distinguished-looking gray-haired woman whose face I'd seen in show photos, but whose name I'd forgotten. She nodded to Victor. "Most of this rescue business is a lot of crap." Her deep, resonant voice brought her name and identity to me: Harriet Lunt, a member of the board of our national breed club and a lawyer who specialized in matters that concerned dogs. She published articles in the dog magazines about co-ownership agreements, stud dog powers of attorney, contracts between breeders and puppy buyers, and all that sort of thing. "I, for one," this cyno-legal eagle continued, "don't mind saying that I don't believe in throwing away *good* money on *trash* dogs."

In my anger at Harriet Lunt, I forgave Betty Burley everything. Two pieces of paper had disappeared, and Betty had blamed me. So what! After years of fighting the vile opposition of people like this snotty Harriet Lunt, Betty had every reason for her incendiary temper. No matter what, Betty was always on the side of the dogs. Therefore I forgave Betty anything.

"I must say, though," Harriet Lunt observed in a tone of condescending resignation, "that sometimes at those god-awful rescue parades, the tear-jerking goes on for hours. At least their little performance last night was blessedly short."

Looking down at the old *Malamute Quarterlys* in my hand, I saw that I'd have to buy the top one. I'd torn the front cover. I'd ruined the bottom one, too. My grip had made crease marks, and the sweat from my hands would leave permanent stains. As proof of my honesty, let me report that I immediately paid for all five issues I was clutching.

Then I swerved around and gave Harriet Lunt the kind of eye-to-eye stare that is dangerous to direct to a strange dog. Furthermore, when I spoke, I smiled very broadly, thus baring my teeth. "Trash dogs, huh?" I said. "Interesting perspective." I added, "My name is Holly Winter. I'm a columnist for *Dog's Life*." That's true. "But right now," I said, meaning as of the last three seconds, "I'm writing a piece for the *Gazette*." *Pure-bred Dogs/American Kennel Gazette*: the official publication of the American Kennel Club, and one with which I have no connection whatsoever except, when I get lucky, as an occasional freelance contributor. "And I couldn't help hearing what you said just now," I chirped, "and when I did, I said to myself, 'Well, now, Holly, isn't this someone with a distinctive point of view that AKC will certainly want represented!' Because, you see," I confided, "with AKC so in favor of breed rescue, making the whole thing so politically correct, it's unusual to hear someone express a divergent opinion." I showed Victor my fangs. "And you, too, of course," I told him. "So, if the two of you don't mind, I'd just love to quote you. What did you say your names were?"

With an indignant toss of her head, Harriet Lunt said that she couldn't imagine what I thought I'd overheard. "I, for one, have always been a very, very strong supporter of rescue," she announced, "and I know for a fact that Victor has been, too."

She gave me her full name and Victor's. I promised to quote her. Now I have. Victor again broke his lifelong silence to inform me—Holly Winter, the eyes and ears of AKC—that his wife, Sherri Ann Printz, a top breeder, had donated a valuable item to Alaskan Malamute Rescue. Said precious donation to be auctioned off on Saturday night. His wife had made it herself. She'd used the hair of a legendary dog, a malamute, Ch. Northpole's Comet, R.O.M.

In her deep courtroom voice, Harriet Lunt added what felt like a contribution to the defense of Sherri Ann Printz. "Sherri Ann is so proud of her beautiful lamp! Last night, at the end of our Parade of Veterans and Titleholders, she took me by the arm and led me right over to the little rescue booth so I could admire it. She can't help showing it off to absolutely everyone. It is truly a work of art."

I wasn't thinking about art, though. Or even about the

lamp. What kept ringing in my ears and through my mind was Harriet Lunt's voice. Jeanine has been sure about those cruel people: *Men*, she'd said damningly. Arlette had corrected her: *Deep voices*. Harriet Lunt's voice was as deep as a man's. She had a resonant voice: a voice that carried. And *trash* was Harriet Lunt's word.

CHAPTER 17

"I could have strangled the pair of them," I raged at Betty Burley. "Simultaneously. One with each hand."

Betty and I were lingering just outside the ring, where the judges' education seminar was continuing. Betty was studying the demonstration dogs. Maybe she was interested. Maybe she was avoiding eye contact with me. I'd reported only what I'd just heard; I hadn't told her about Jeanine. "Victor Printz is an ignoramus," Betty decreed. "But Harriet Lunt is a lawyer. She's an educated woman. She should know better." She sounded troubled.

"Speaking of knowing," I said abruptly, "I want to know what you know about James Hunnewell's sister." The whole sentence came out as a single word: *Iwannaknowwhatyouknowabout JamesHunnewell'ssister.*

"Not a dog in that ring I care for," remarked Betty, who had once spoken admiringly of Rowdy, but only after she'd had two glasses of wine.

"That silver male is very nice," I said.

"*Nice?* Really? Is *that* your idea of nice?"

"Yes," I said. "It's one of them. Betty, James Hunnewell's sister?"

"Will you look at those feet! Poor thing couldn't make it one turn around the block!"

"Gladys Thacker. Gladys H. Thacker. The *H* must be for Hunnewell." My reason for pressing Betty was the piece of surprising information I'd picked up from Detective Kariotis at the end of our interview. "Gladys Thacker's going to be here tomorrow," I reported to Betty. "I heard it from the state police. Well, she's not necessarily coming here to the national, but to Massachusetts. The story is that she's very concerned to see that her brother gets a Christian burial."

"What does she expect? Hindu rites?"

"I have no idea. And who's going to bury him here, anyway? They'll release the body . . . Well, I can't imagine that she'd have to come here and get it."

"Well," said Betty, "we can only hope that this Thacker person has the nerve to turn up. I, for one, will be most interested to have a very lengthy discussion with her."

Betty, I believe, placed no special emphasis on the words "I, for one." My own ears added the emphasis. "Betty," I demanded suspiciously, "did you show Cubby's pedigree to Sherri Ann Printz?"

Without answering the question, Betty huffily said that what Sherri Ann or anyone else may or may not have known, and may or may not have done, was a complete mystery to her. "If you did not go through my tote bag and take that pedigree, and I do believe you, Holly, then I do not know who did." Rocking her head backward in what I took to be the direction of the breed club's booth, she changed the subject, more or less. "A fine show of support I got back there!"

"I'm sorry," I said, "but I was dealing with something else. Remember? Besides, you were taking care of yourself fine without my help."

"I wasn't thinking of you," she said, as if I'd have been

useless, anyway. "I meant everyone else, including Timmy Oliver. You'd think he'd—"

"*You* might," I said. "*I* wouldn't."

"I suppose Timmy is very peeved with me," Betty reflected, "but if he didn't want my honest opinion of that poor bitch of his, he shouldn't have asked. But, no, he just had to go and drag me out and show her to me."

"Z-Rocks," I said, "is perfectly decent, and you know it. She's just not in any condition to be here."

"She is not outstanding," Betty ruthlessly proclaimed. "She is ordinary. And *ordinary* does not go Best of Breed at a national specialty." Betty paused. "Even under James Hunnewell. I don't know what Timmy was thinking."

"Daphne is a much better bitch," I said, naming a frequent competitor at New England shows. "She moves a lot better, and she's always beautifully presented."

"She usually beats your male," Betty observed.

"She usually beats most of the other males, too," I replied sharply.

"If it's any comfort to you, Daphne'll get her comeuppance tomorrow, because Casey's here, and she won't beat him." Casey: Williwaw's Kodiak Cub. I'd seen dozens of photos of the beautiful, top-winning sable dog, but I'd never seen him in the ring. Casey was supposed to be a great competitor, a master showman.

A masculine hoot interrupted any further speculation about Casey and Best of Breed. "Duke! Hey, Duke, come on over and take a look, man! They got your baby pictures here!"

Startled, Betty and I turned around and stared at by far the largest group our rescue booth had ever drawn. At least thirty people were clustered around the booth. I briefly lost my mind. After all our pleas, our sob stories, our reasoned arguments, our cold presentations of fact, our appeals to conscience, finally! This overwhelming show of support. The crowd was utterly staggering.

But Betty was not taken in. She was also not pleased. "Gary Galvin has gone and done it again!"

Yes, the video monitor.

"Don't complain!" I whispered. "They're here! That's progress."

When Betty and I had worked our way close enough in to get a good view of the screen, I realized that what we were watching had been converted to video from a film taken with an old home-movie camera held by an amateur hand. I couldn't begin to guess the date of the show. When it comes to men's clothing, I can tell a zoot suit from white tie, and I know whether Steve is wearing jeans or scrubs, but that's about it. In some vague way, the judge's suit—or maybe he wore a coat and tie?—looked old-fashioned. His hair was short. In contrast, by today's standards, Duke Sylvia's was long, and he had sideburns. But, oh my! Funny whiskers and all, the young Duke Sylvia was smooth. He was as good a handler as his knock-out dog deserved.

"Comet," Betty told me, eyes on the screen.

The dog in the grainy footage was tremendously powerful and consummately agile, as if he'd been sired by a linebacker out of a prima ballerina. Northpole's Comet: He leaped out of the jumpy black-and-white footage with such vigor and style that you could hardly believe he was dead.

The camera lingered on Comet. Then, as if fighting to move away, it jerked along the line of dogs in the long-ago ring.

Even then, whenever this was, Duke had been much too skilled a handler to outdo his superlative dog. Duke moved almost as well as Comet, and that's a compliment to Duke.

"Hey, Duke, when is this?" someone asked.

"Don't know."

"Aw, come on. Who'd you handle him for?"

"Elsa Van Dine," someone said. "Elsa would've loved to see this. Goddamn shame."

"Duke handled him for everyone," contributed someone else. "Himself, among others."

I hadn't known. "Duke, you owned Comet?" I was wildly jealous.

"Co-owned," Duke said. "For a while."

With a whoop and holler, a man I didn't know darted to the monitor and pressed some buttons. "Whoo-ee! Gotcha, Duke! Texas handling! And the kid didn't have a clue."

Texas handling: trying to draw the judge's attention to your dog's good points by running your hand over them. It's no more common in Texas than it is anywhere else. It is my theory, however, that the term originated when the novice handler of a Dandie Dinmont tried the ploy on the Only Law West of the Pecos, the legendary Roy Bean, the Hanging Judge, a terrier man himself. Bean resented the insulting effort to manipulate his opinion and swiftly dealt with the offender in his accustomed fashion—swift hanging. When news of the barbaric incident reached New York, horrified officials at the American Kennel Club dispatched an indignant letter to Judge Bean. The power to *suspend for life*, they explained, was the exclusive prerogative of the board of directors of the AKC. West of the Pecos or not, Judge Bean had acted in gross excess of his authority. In a postscript, the letter pointed out that the phrase ordinarily referred not to stringing up exhibitors in their entirety, but to suspending their AKC privileges. A man of action, the judge shot back the famous two-word reply that now hangs, appropriately enough, in the AKC's offices: *"Same difference."* Just kidding. Have I digressed?

Anyway, even in the old days, Duke Sylvia had been much too polished to practice Texas handling in its crude form. What the old tape captured was a common twist. Here's how it went. The dogs were lined up, and the judge was temporarily out of the picture as the dog just before Comet gaited to the far end of the ring. Comet, I should note, had an outstanding front, a strong chest and big-boned legs that contrasted with the somewhat weaker front of the dog just beyond him, a dog with a junior handler, a kid. Making sure that the junior handler beyond him was watching—and, I assume, that the judge wasn't—sideburned Duke made a quicker-than-the-eye move, a quick flick of his hand to Comet's chest. I followed the rest of the sequence. As the judge went over Comet, Duke's hands went nowhere near his dog, who acted as the ideal co-conspirator in his handler's scheme by projecting the image of the canine know-it-all who can display his own virtues just fine, thank you, with no help from the human nuisance tagging along at the wrong end of the show lead. When the judge approached the next dog, the junior handler did what he'd just seen the master before him do: He ran a hand over his dog's chest, thus simultaneously calling attention to a weak point, insulting the judge, and drawing the judge's wrath. The film was silent. The judge's deadly ire, however, was visible on his enraged face.

The manipulated junior handler: Timmy Oliver. The judge: James Hunnewell.

CHAPTER 18 🐾

In signing up for Friday night's Alaskan malamute luau, we'd been given the standard dog-clubbanquet choice of London broil, chicken cordon bleu, or baked scrod. Upscale is prime rib, chicken Kiev, or broiled swordfish. Downscale is beneath me. I won't join an organization that offers nothing but creamed table scraps and peas on tough patty shells.

By the time Leah and I arrived, the Lagoon was packed with people milling around, sipping drinks, and chatting. In the background, Hawaiian guitar Muzak twanged what I eventually decoded as "Time Is on My Side." I ordered a Scotch for me and a diet cola for. Leah. Soon after a saronged waitress brought the drinks, people began to settle at the tables.

After lingering to watch the old film of Comet, I'd joined Gary and a couple of other rescue people in helping Betty to move the most valuable auction items to her room. Then Leah and I had fed and walked the dogs, taken quick showers, and changed into new black dresses that we'd kept in plastic bags, but had to de-fur anyway. We'd shopped for the dresses together. For the first three hours, Leah had rejected every suggestion I'd made. In her view, every bright solid color made her look like a bridesmaid. Flowing garments were maternity dresses. Anything with a waistline reminded her of Scarlett O'Hara. According to Leah, a gray tweed suit turned me into a dowager. In navy blue, we were flight attendants. When I finally persuaded her to try on a pretty flowered print, she gave the mirror one disgusted glance and cried, "Oh God! *Little House on the Prairie!*" The plain black dress that she eventually picked for herself was so short that only my frazzled exhaustion prevented me from telling her that it made her look like an Olympic figure skater who'd just suffered a death in the family. She costumed me as an Italian widow. On our way to the Lagoon, Leah remarked that we looked extremely sophisticated. "You know, Holly," Leah advised, "men really do like black."

Do they ever! As people began to seat themselves at the big round tables and to dip spoons into the fruit cocktails, Finn Adams approached me in a manner disconcertingly reminiscent of the demeanor of my mother's most enthusiastic stud dog, Bertie. Bertie had to be restrained from leaping the fences to offer his valuable services to all takers free of charge instead of waiting for his carefully planned trysts with our own bitches and the occasional visits of paying guests. As Finn joined us, I devoutly wished Bertie were with me now. Bertie would have hated the whole idea of artificial insemination. Bertie had the perfect gentle, affectionate golden retriever temperament, but if he'd even begun to guess how Finn Adams earned his living, he'd have taken a chunk out of his ankle. Or perhaps elsewhere.

But Bertie was long dead. Leah was no help. When Finn suggested that we have dinner together, Leah smirked. I scanned desperately. At a nearby table sat Duke Sylvia. Next to him were two empty chairs. I threw Duke an imploring glance and held up two fingers. He nodded.

"Sorry," I told Finn, gesturing in Duke's direction, "but we've already promised . . ."

Men really do like black. Duke seemed unusually glad to see me. He rose from his seat and pulled out the chair next to his. Leah took the place next to mine. Beyond her sat Timmy Oliver. Between Timmy and Karl Reilly, Freida's son, was a seat that I assumed was being saved for Karl's wife, Lucille, who turned out to be home with the flu. Pam Ritchie and Tiny DaSilva sat between Karl and Duke. How Duke had contrived to get Timmy seated alone with two empty places on one side and one on the other, I didn't know, but I held Duke responsible. Wherever Duke sat automatically became the head of the table. A waiter showed up with two bottles of wine. After filling our glasses, he left both bottles in front of Duke. Then Finn Adams wandered along and, gesturing to the empty place between Timmy Oliver and Karl Reilly, got Duke's unspoken permission to join us.

At the risk of sounding like the Camille Paglia of dogs, let me admit that I dearly love a true alpha male.

When Finn sat down, he exchanged introductions with Karl Reilly and with Pam and Tiny. He nodded politely to Leah and me and greeted Timmy Oliver, whom he obviously knew. To Duke, he said, "Finn Adams. R.T.I." Duke tipped his big lion's head. I suppose Duke took it for granted that at a dog show, everyone knew who he was. I had the sense that in Finn's case Duke was right.

At dog club banquets, the standard appetizer is fresh fruit cup. Upscale is with sherbet. Ours was without, but each of us did get a garnish of mint leaf. Duke picked up his spoon and ate a melon ball. The the rest of us began. As we passed the baskets of rolls and the plates of butter, everyone agreed that, especially considering the circumstances, Mikki Muldoon was doing a very good job.

"Mikki always runs a tight ship," Duke commented. "She's a real pro."

As if to suggest that Freida Reilly wasn't, Tiny turned to Karl and said, "Your mother looks done in. She must be ready to drop."

I didn't really know Karl Reilly. What gave me a false sense of familiarity was Karl's resemblance to a man who appeared in a lot of obscure-channel TV commercials for a local chain that sold cheap men's suits. Whenever I saw Karl, I found myself expecting him to display his trouser cuffs and utter negative remarks about high-priced stores. Before Karl could respond to Tiny, however, Pam Ritchie said, "Well, of course Freida's showing the strain! Who wouldn't be? It's enough of a job to chair a national to begin with, never mind having your judge murdered. Exactly how do you expect her to look?"

In self-defense, or perhaps in defense of Freida's qualifications for the hotly coveted place on the board, Tiny said, "All I meant was that I, for one, don't envy Freida one bit. All of us owe her a debt of gratitude for coping so magnificently with this terrible situation."

"Of course we do! Karl, I hope your mother knows what a remarkable job everyone thinks she's doing. Among other things, I expected to walk in here and find us stuck with an, uh, undercover cop at every table." Pam's eyes lingered on Finn Adams.

With a trace of his old charm, Finn smiled crookedly and raised his hands in a gesture of surrender.

"Hey, like he says," Timmy Oliver said, "he's from R.T.I. We've been talking a little business. Besides, him and Holly go way back."

I cringed. "Pam," I said, "I swear he's from R.T.I. If there are any cops here, Finn isn't one of them. And if they want to know anything, they don't have to sneak anyone in. There's nothing to stop them from just asking."

As if to prove me right, Karl Reilly shook his head glumly. "The cop I talked to really put me through it." As one waitress removed the remains of his fruit cup and another replaced it with a salad plate, he added, "I'm the one who picked Mr. Hunnewell up at the airport. Favor to my mother. Turned out to be more than I bargained for, and the cops had to hear all about it." The salad in front of me was composed of a bed of shredded iceberg lettuce topped with one leaf of arugula. Karl must've decided that the dark green leaf on his had gotten there by mistake. Or maybe a bug or a strand of hair clung to it. He delicately removed the leaf with his fingers and speared a fork into the lettuce. "Geez, at first I didn't . . . The fact is that my mother'd warned me that Mr. Hunnewell was . . . that he wasn't necessarily Mr. Nice Guy all the time, but whoo! If I'd've known, I'd've told her to let him take a cab."

Lowering her chin to peer censoriously over imaginary eyeglasses, Pam pointed out, "It was much more courteous to have someone meet him personally, you know, Karl. And it's an awfully long ride for a taxi."

"You're telling me," Karl said. "Halfway here, I came close to reaching over and opening the door and giving him a hard shove." Taking a bite of lettuce, he nearly choked. When he stopped coughing, he said hastily, "Not really, but—"

Duke and Timmy started ribbing Karl about waiting until later.

Laughing, Karl said, "With the way that guy smoked, I don't know why anyone bothered. Geez, between Boston and here, he must've gone through two packs of cigarettes. Every time I opened the window, he'd complain he was cold . . ."

Pam dipped her head. "Poor circulation."

"And," Karl went on, "I'd have to shut the window again. And the thing was, he couldn't've been on a plane for a long time, because he didn't know they wouldn't let him smoke, and from what he said, he took it like it was something personal, and so when I picked him up, he was in a wicked foul mood, and he'd had a few drinks, on top of the nicotine fit."

"The police asked me about that," I said. "About how much he smoked, did he offer me a cigarette, which he did, a lot of stuff like that. I can't figure out what it had to do with anything."

"Well, *that* I can tell you," Tiny said triumphantly. "He ran out of cigarettes."

Karl snorted. "Geez, no wonder."

"And," said Tiny, "that's what he was doing out of his room. He called room service, and he called the desk, and he was not very nice about it!"

"And how would you know?" Pam demanded.

"The chambermaid told me," Tiny replied smugly. "The woman at the desk told her supervisor who told another chambermaid who told—"

"Gossip!" Pam decreed.

"No, it is not gossip," Tiny said. "They noticed because he wanted a whole carton of the things, and all the hotel has is a machine over in the bar somewhere, and when Hunnewell heard that, he expected them to send someone out to a store for him! Can you imagine? Eleven o'clock at night or whenever it was, and he expected—"

"I don't know who James Hunnewell thought he was," Pam interrupted, "but after the encounter that Holly and I had with him, I can believe anything! The arrogance! Karl, I'm surprised he didn't try to get your mother to play errand girl for him! Poor Freida, getting stuck with him for a judge! Judge! Hah! That man didn't strike me as being safe out alone. What he'd have done in the ring, I shudder to contemplate. I don't know what he was like years ago, but if he was in his right mind then, he wasn't last night. You should have heard the terrible things he said about Mrs. Seeley!" Pam bowed her head. Her lips moved in what I took to be a silent prayer addressed to the matriarch of our breed.

"You have to admit that Short *was* opinionated," opined Duke.

He might as well have reached over and jabbed his dinner knife into Pam's ribs. Flying half out of her seat, she shrieked, "OPINIONATED! Opinionated? Short Seeley was not opinionated! Short was *right!*" Without Eva B. Seeley, Pam declared, there wouldn't be an Alaskan malamute at all, and if, on occasion, Mrs. Seeley had seen fit to speak *authoritatively*, well, she was, after all, *the* authority, wasn't she? Or did Duke imagine otherwise?

As affable as ever, Duke tried to pacify Pam. What he'd meant, he said cheerfully, was that Mrs. Seeley had been a woman who never shied away from speaking her mind.

"As she had every right to," Pam declared with satisfaction. "Every right." Seizing her fork, she attacked her salad with great ferocity, as if it, too, had somehow desecrated the memory of Eva Seeley.

In a gentlemanly effort to change the subject, Finn Adams remarked that considering what had happened, the hotel was coping pretty well. And we'd certainly lucked out with the weather!

The weather! I ask you!

As Timmy Oliver informed us that it was supposed to pour all day tomorrow, the hotel staff began to remove the salad plates and to dole out our dinners.

"This your first national?" Duke asked Leah.

She said that it was, and that, yes, she was handling my bitch tomorrow, and that, yes, she did intend to relax and have a good time.

"Fun's what it's all about," Duke told her.

With the tape of Comet's old show appearance in mind, I glanced at Timmy Oliver. He nodded in agreement and repeated Duke's words: "Fun's what it's all about."

It occurred to me that if Duke and Timmy happened to be in the ring together tomorrow, Duke could play the same old Texas handling trick, and Timmy Oliver would probably fall for it all over again. Duke wouldn't try it, though. Over the years, he'd gained in subtlety. Besides, he respected Mikki Muldoon.

Digging a fork into my scrod, I saw that I'd gotten swordfish instead. As I was about to say so, Pam Ritchie wondered aloud why she had prime rib. All of us, we found, had been mysteriously upgraded.

"Freida must've taken in more money than she expected," Tiny suggested. "She'd hardly have bothered to ask if we wanted better than we paid for."

Pam, of course, disagreed. "If there'd been a surplus, she'd hardly have—"

"There wasn't," Karl announced. "The hotel's made a mistake. I'd better let my mother know."

When he'd excused himself and left in search of Freida, Leah said boldly that if we'd been served good stuff by accident, we'd better start eating before someone came and took it away. Duke, I noticed, was already digging into his prime rib. I took a quick survey of the plates. Tiny, Pam, Karl, Timmy, and Leah also had beef. As I'd suspected, Duke's was by far the biggest, thickest piece. Leah didn't notice or didn't care. After chewing and swallowing, she said, "This is the first real meat I've had in over a month!"

"Leah's in college," I explained. "She eats cafeteria food."

Finn asked her where she went.

"Harvard," she said.

Silence fell.

Finn said that two of his uncles had gone there. No one else said anything.

Then Duke had the sense to ask Leah what she was going to do after college. When she announced her intention of becoming a veterinarian, everyone started talking again. Timmy Oliver and Finn Adams got involved in an intimate one-to-one discussion of recent advances in sperm preservation—canine, I presume; and Tim made a general pitch for the wonders of Pro-Vita No-Blo Sho-Kote. Having sipped her way through several glasses of wine, Pam confided to everyone within hearing distance of a shotgun blast that, well, strictly between ourselves, we had to admit in all honesty that whoever had murdered our judge had at least had the courtesy not to do it on show grounds.

"What a perfectly awful thing to say!" Tiny looked horrified. "And I'm not even sure it's true. That field is part of the hotel. As far as I know, that means it's show grounds."

"No," Pam insisted, "show grounds means to the end of the parking lot, and obviously, since it would've been just as easy to clunk him over the head *on* show grounds as it was *off*—"

"Who says it's the end of the parking lot?" Tiny challenged. "It must be you, Pam, because it's not AKC."

"It certainly is! That field is definitely not on show grounds. Among other things, the obedience people were training there on Wednesday, and they *can't* train on show grounds."

"Yes," I confirmed, "but I think it was okay to work a dog there unobtrusively on Wednesday, the day before the trial. As far as I know, there's no strict written definition of *show precincts*. How could there be? Show sites are all so different. But you'd really have to ask an AKC rep."

Speaking, for once, with one voice, Pam and Tiny said in unison: "There's no rep here!"

In response to the outburst, a waiter who'd been helping to arrange an elaborate dessert buffet on a long rectangular table behind ours scurried over to ask whether something was wrong.

Dismissing him rather abruptly, Pam complained that she didn't understand the absence of an AKC rep. "It seems to me that it would've been to Freida's advantage to see that there was one."

As I've mentioned, the principal responsibility of a show chair is to take the blame for everything. In accepting the job, Freida had made sure that everyone would know who she was. She'd also gambled on satisfaction with how she'd performed. "There doesn't have to be a rep," I told Pam, "and it certainly wasn't Freida's decision. As far as I know, reps determine their own schedules."

"Well," insisted Tiny, "at a minimum, Freida might've arranged for better security."

Leah joined in. "Isn't security the hotel's responsibility? Especially out in the parking lot?"

None of us really knew. "When clubs give shows," I said, "they have to take out big umbrella policies that cover anything that happens, so it can't be just the responsibility of the site. Clubs can get sued; it does happen."

Leah, the A student, rose in her chair. "Oh my God! I've got it! Holly, that's why his sister is coming here! She's coming to sue—"

"Whose sister?" Tiny's face was avid with curiosity.

"James Hunnewell's," Leah said impatiently. "The police told Holly. Supposedly, his sister was coming to make sure he got a Christian burial, but that doesn't make sense, because she could have his body shipped back to Missouri and give him any kind of burial she wants, so—"

"I don't see what Missouri has to do with anything," Pam said crossly.

"Missouri," Leah told everyone, "is where James Hunnewell's sister lives. Her name is Gladys Thacker, and she lives in Missouri, and she runs a puppy mill."

Before anyone could interrogate Leah about these revelations, a hullabaloo broke out a few table-lengths away from us. Craning my neck, I saw that towering above the otherwise unexceptional collection of puddings, pies, and yet more fruit salads on the dessert buffet was an immense multitiered cake heavily frosted in pale apricot and richly decorated with ornate flowers, both real and confectionery. Jabbing a finger of outrage at the bird-of-paradise blossom perched atop this tropical masterpiece of the pastry-maker's art was a woman I recognized as Crystal's mother. Flanking his wife on the opposite side of the cake was Crystal's father. Completing the tableau were the hotel manager and Freida Reilly. Freida wore a floor-length black skirt and a dressy black jersey top elaborately embroidered in gold with the immense head of guess what breed of dog. She and the manager held themselves formally upright and faced the festive cake from several yards back, as if determined to proclaim themselves attendants at this ceremony, the best man and the matron of honor, perhaps, and not its central figures. Freida and the manager must have been murmuring: Crystal's parents leaned toward them. Then, as if on cue, the father began shouting at the manager, and the mother started yelling at Freida Reilly. I wished that they'd take turns so I could hear them both, but I caught enough to understand the cause of their rage.

". . . screw up the entrees," the father bellowed, "and stick us with your goddamn cheesy London broil for the rehearsal . . ."

And the mother: ". . . *my* Crystal's beautiful, beautiful Hawaiian wedding cake for her . . . and it's too late now, because one of your rotten *dog* people has gone and taken a slice right out of the middle!"

At the word "dog," the father whirled away from the

manager, took a threatening step toward his wife, and, almost punching her with his upraised fist, shouted, "*Dog! Dog! Dog!* You know, Mavis, anyone who listened in on this wedding would think that Crystal was going to marry one of the Christ damn things and present us with—"

Stamping a foot, the wife screamed: "Harold—shut—up!"

"Jesus Christ Almighty, Mavis!" Blasphemy? To my ear, the poor man uttered a plea of genuine anguish.

But the only response Harold got came from his desperate wife, who had flushed a panicked shade of crimson. "Now, Harold, you know as well as I do that—"

Without waiting for her to finish, Harold made a stupendous effort aimed, I think, at salvaging the situation.

Or at least at salvaging the Hawaiian cake. Barging into his wife, the manager, and Freida Reilly, and shoving past several hotel employees who'd gathered, I suppose, in the hope of offering some assistance, Harold stomped up to the cake, loomed over it, spread his arms, got a grip on whatever tray or giant platter supported it, and, with a massive show of muscle, succeeded in dragging the confection forward and raising it upward until it cleared the table. Maybe his fingers slipped on the icing. As the huge cake began to tremble and slide from his grasp, he lunged ahead and, like a desperate parent snatching for a plummeting child, wrapped his arms around the cake and attempted to hold the crumbling mass in a gigantic bear hug. Instead of mercifully dropping with one thud, the cake slowly peeled itself apart layer by layer and chunk by chunk. The icing, as I've said, was a pale apricot color intended, perhaps, to suggest orange blossoms. The interior, however, proved to be dark chocolate. Gobs of cake glued themselves to Harold's suit. The icing must have been exceptionally adhesive. His sleeves bloomed with little sugar flowers. The bird of paradise tarried in the middle of his stomach before dropping pitifully to the floor.

The gasps and laughter were inevitable. Mavis, the mother of the bride, did not join in. In ringing tones, she demanded to know who the hell was responsible for this inexcusable screw-up.

Instead of answering directly, the manager apologized. "An unfortunate miscommunication," I heard him valiantly maintain.

With a look of scorn that would have set lesser men aflame, Mavis exercised the organizational skills that she must have developed in planning the wedding. Rounding up various waiters and waitresses, she held a huddled conference. Then she announced the results to the entire Lagoon: "In the kitchen, *our* beautiful cake was clearly labeled WEDDING. Then it was moved into the corridor, where it sat completely unattended! And while it did, our label was maliciously replaced with a card that read LAGOON!" Her voice quivered. She cleared her throat and glared at the manager. "Maliciously replaced by a heavyset woman who was observed by one of *your* waitresses in the vicinity of *our* cake!" Turning to address us all, she continued, "By a heavyset woman that this *same* waitress had previously observed on the grounds of this hotel walking a *DOG!*"

Which waitress was now apparent. A woman in a sarong was slinking out of the Lagoon. On her face was a big smirk.

"Darlene!" the manager called. "You will get back here this minute and help us straighten out this misunderstanding! Why in God's name didn't you stop this individual, whoever she was, from fiddling with the labels on the cake?"

"I didn't see her *touching* the label," Darlene answered so defiantly that I could hear, see, and smell the lie. "I thought she was just looking at the cake."

"And do you see this woman here? Is she here now?"

Darlene nodded. In response to a request from the manager, she pointed a finger straight at Sherri Ann Printz.

Sherri Ann bounded from her chair. "I damned well went nowhere near that cake!"

"Oh, yes you did!" Freida charged. On her fleshy bosom, the gold malamute seemed to frown. "And I don't know how you did it, but you got the entrees mixed up, too! From the moment you arrived here, you have done nothing but cause trouble, trouble, trouble! You are a jealous, spiteful woman, Sherri Ann! And I have had *all* I intend to take from you!"

With that, Freida stooped, grabbed two huge fistfuls of the sugary glop at Harold Jenkinson's feet, marched over to the Printzes' table, and, with both hands, smeared Crystal's dark chocolate wedding cake, apricot icing, and confectionery flowers all over Sherri Ann's astonished face.

The silence in the Lagoon was absolute.

Excusing myself, I went to the bar, ordered a double Scotch, and drank alone. Downscale really is beneath me.

CHAPTER 19

I awoke at three o'clock, stumbled in the darkness to the bathroom, and hunted through my two cosmetics bags. Reluctantly, I looked in Leah's numerous makeup kits, searched through the beautifying debris strewn around the sink, and checked the travel cases Leah uses for her hair dryer and her rechargeable toothbrush. Inspired, I tiptoed back into the room, got my purse, returned to the bathroom, and, in its bright light, discovered that I'd used the last spare tampon I always carry. Suppressing a sigh, I padded back into the room and eased open the closet door. The dogs stirred. "Shh!" I told them. On my knees, I located my big softsided suitcase and blindly ran my hands over its interior, including the side compartments. I hate to admit that I looked in Leah's handbag, too. Nothing. I'll skip the gory details and report only that the situation was dire.

After making do with the scanty supply of tissues in the bathroom dispenser, I threw on a sweatshirt, jeans, and shoes, and belatedly remembered to take the room key and every piece of change from my purse. I recalled that in addition to miles of mirror and counter, the fainting couch, and the dainty chairs, the big public ladies' room had vending machines. I slipped out into the silent, empty corridor. As I was passing the alcove that housed the soft-drink and ice machines, a sudden liquid rattle sounded to me like the hacking, coughing ghost of a thirsty, cranky James Hunnewell. Before I even peered into the little room, I knew it would be empty of the quick and the dead alike. The only movement was invisible: the hidden motion of a cycle-shifting motor somewhere deep inside the ice machine.

My pace quickened. At the end of the hallway, I descended a flight of twisting stairs. Instead of taking the familiar route through the maze that ultimately led to the lobby, I followed the series of arrows that read TO THE LAGOON. The arrows eventually led me to a door that opened to what I recognized as the grotto end of the dimly lighted Lagoon, a mock-tropical garden with split-leaf philodendrons, narrow flagstone pathways, and patches of fir-bark mulch planted with vines and impatiens. Avoiding the shadowy paths through this South Seas paradise, I followed a sort of sidewalk of artificial-grass carpet that ran along the perimeter, past the numbered doors of guest rooms and big, heavily curtained plate-glass windows intended, I suppose, to compensate for the airless undesirability of the interior rooms of the hotel by offering a bold vista of plastic foliage.

After I turned a corner, guest rooms finally gave way to function rooms. The deserted restaurant appeared. I hurried past it and dashed into the big, brilliantly illuminated ladies' room, where I poured large amounts of small change into the vending machines and supplied myself with enough sanitary protection to last through the next week. Feeling shy about passing through the lobby clutching a bouquet of feminine hygiene products, I decided to retrace my route around the grotto. Despite all the talk about random violence engendered by the recent slaying of Elsa Van

Dine, I was only slightly more wary than I'd ordinarily have been in making my way alone through a sleeping hotel. Although I assumed that Hunnewell's murderer must be someone at the show, probably someone staying at the hotel, my vigilance was the taken-for-granted alertness that prudent women develop. In fact, my mind had drifted to memories of a seventh-grade girls-only minicourse called, of all things, "Growing Up and Liking It," which, despite the name, said nothing about orgasm and everything about cramps and self-adhesive pads.

I had just passed the dark, empty restaurant and entered the tropical-garden area when a series of muted noises emanated from what sounded like the far end of the cavernous Lagoon. A door opening? A soft voice? Someone taking a dog out, I thought. Or maybe another woman in my little plight. If so, I'd generously spare her the trip to the ladies' room. Then a voice again, a deep voice, a man's, I assumed: "Hello?" And only seconds later, a gut-wrenching scream, ungodly loud, that rang through the huge, ridiculous Lagoon, reverberated off the high glass ceiling, and sent me pounding down the carpeted walk toward the source of that ungodly scream. As I rounded the corner at the far end of the Lagoon, the only movement I noticed was the slow, automatic closing of the door through which I'd first entered, but when the door had finished closing itself and had sealed off the bright light of the corridor beyond, on the dark carpet ahead of me a figure moved.

Foolishly rushing on, I slammed my foot into what turned out to be one of the decorative paddles from the Lagoon walls, and in a frantic effort to keep my balance, stretched a hand toward one of the plate-glass windows of a guest room and found myself teetering amid a pile of tampons and carefully packaged sanitary pads as guest-room doors opened and voice after voice demanded to know what was going on. It took me a second to identify the angry, distraught face of the figure sprawled motionless on the carpet at my feet: Harriet Lunt, the lawyer who specialized in dogs, the hypocrite who'd joined Victor Printz in belittling our rescue dogs and who'd suddenly become an ardent supporter of breed rescue when I'd pretended to represent the *Gazette*.

Ignoring the stuff I'd dropped, I hurried to her, helped her to her feet, and asked the inevitable: "Are you all right?"

By then, eight or ten people had emerged from nearby rooms.

"Just my shoulder," Harriet Lunt reported. "My left shoulder." With the fingers of her right hand, she explored the injury. Then she raised her left arm, moved her elbow around, and said, "Probably nothing worse than a bad bruise." She wore the kinds of gigantic foam hair curlers that are banned in Cambridge (they're a symbol of female oppression) and an old-fashioned pink mesh hair net dotted with miniature bows. Her quilted cotton bathrobe was identical to one I'd given my grandmother last Christmas.

As people crowded around to ask what had happened and how Mrs. Lunt was doing, she kept saying that she was shaken up, that was all, and that there was nothing wrong with her shoulder that an ice pack wouldn't fix. Before long, someone appeared with a plastic bag of ice cubes, and a woman I didn't know introduced herself as a doctor and tried to persuade Mrs. Lunt to let her look at the injury. Mrs. Lunt, however, was exclusively interested in finding out whether anyone had seen her assailant. "You were the first one here, weren't you?" she asked me.

I had the sense that she didn't remember me. "Yes, but all I saw was that door over there closing. What happened?"

"I really have no idea," she said. "I was asleep. I heard a tap on the door. That's what woke me up. And I assumed it was Sherri Ann or Victor, because Bear's been having a little trouble with the change in the water, and I told them I had some Lomotil, if they wanted it. They said no, but when I heard that tapping on the door, I thought maybe Bear had gotten worse, and they'd changed their minds." She paused. "Should've," she commented. "Nothing like Lomotil."

"Very effective," I agreed.

"So I threw on my robe and went to the door. But when I opened it, there was no one there. And then I heard . . . I thought I heard someone say my name. So I took a step out and I said 'Hello?' But there was no answer, so I thought I'd imagined it. Or maybe I'd heard somebody's dog. So I turned around to go back in my room, when all of sudden! Out of the blue! Something came crashing down! And I must have spied something out the corner of my eye, because I managed to duck my head and raise up my arm. And that's where he got me: right here. Knocked me to the ground." She wrapped her right hand around the injured shoulder. "What did he get me with?"

"A paddle," I said. "One of those Hawaiian paddles that are hanging on the walls."

"Poor Elsa," sighed Harriet Lunt. "And then James. And now me."

CHAPTER 20

Epithalamium: a marriage song.

The gray, wet day of Crystal and Greg's wedding dawned with the music I'd have chosen myself. One voice rose, then another and another joined the first, caught the tune, and lifted the melody to the rainy sky. How many dogs? Fifty? A hundred? But how many voices? Countless. A full choir of choristers, each singing multiple simultaneous songs, each canine voice soaring in dissonant harmony with itself and all the others. Crescendo! The climax reached, one by one—diminuendo—the voices fell almost to silence until a lone note sounded, then another and another, and the song rose again in this weirdly circumpolar Ode to Joy. For all that happened in those days in Danville, my most vivid memory is of that early-morning howling.

Unloading cardboard boxes of paper products from the back of a delivery van in the parking lot, a guy nodded in my direction and said, "Jesus, don't those damned things ever shut up?"

To my ear, the damned things that never shut up weren't

the dogs, but the forced-air dryers already blasting like horrid mini-hurricanes in the grooming tent where I'd just delivered Rowdy, Kimi, and Leah to Faith Barlow. Over the roar, I'd shouted to Faith about the predawn attack on Harriet Lunt, and Faith had bellowed back that she'd already heard.

After surrendering my dogs and my cousin to Faith, I left the grooming tent. I was heading across the parking lot in search of breakfast when a drenched and dripping Z-Rocks splashed through a puddle, shot to the end of Timmy Oliver's lead, wiggled, shook hard all over, and gave me my second before-breakfast shower of the day. I didn't mind. The old issues of the *Malamute Quarterly* that I'd brought with me to leaf through while I ate were safely stowed in my newest malamute-decorated tote bag. After breakfast, I intended to change into real clothes and spiff myself up. In the meantime, I was wearing my old yellow slicker over jeans and the new national specialty sweatshirt that already sprouted fur. My hair was damp from the light rain, and the dogs had licked off the moisturizer I'd patted on. It's hopeless. Why I bother, I don't know. I should just get out of bed, throw on the clothes that Rowdy and Kimi slept on, reach into my pockets and dust myself with the powdery residue of dried liver, let the dogs cover my face with saliva, and then go outside and roll around in mud. No one but me would know the difference.

So, when Z-Rocks spattered me, I said good morning to her and asked Timmy Oliver whether he'd heard about Harriet Lunt. Harriet herself had told him about the attack, he said. He'd seen her only a minute ago at the hotel entrance. The manager had been trying to talk her into having her shoulder x-rayed, but Harriet had absolutely refused.

"He's probably terrified she'll sue the hotel," I commented. "I wonder if he knows she's a lawyer."

Then Timmy changed the subject to Z-Rocks. Instead of

waiting for me to say something flattering about her,
Timmy took advantage of her plastered-down coat to deliver
himself of so enthusiastic a disquisition about her good
bone, broad skull, admirable angulation, and so forth that I
was tempted to ask whether he intended to show her to
Mikki Muldoon in her present soaked and thus anatomi-
cally revealing condition.

As Timmy went on and on, dwelling on Z-Rock's ideal
this and excellent that, I'm sorry to say I tuned him out until he triumphantly burst forth with a single word: "Comet!"

As dense as ever, I said casually, "Oh, Z-Rocks goes back
to Comet?"

So did thousands of other malamutes: show dogs, pets,
puppy-mill dogs. The presence of an illustrious ancestor in a
family tree is always interesting, but that's about it. Just because you're the direct descendant of Helen of Troy, it
doesn't mean you've got a face to launch a thousand ships.
But in Timmy Oliver's eyes and, according to him, in James
Hunnewell's, Z-Rocks was what Timmy called "a living
legacy," the female reincarnation of the fabulous Northpole's Comet. Z-Rocks, I should say, was not utterly unlike
Comet. Instead of looking like a female replica, though, a
sort of sex-changed Xerox copy—hence her name, I guess—
she was as good as Comet had been outstanding, as decent as
he had been superlative, and she totally lacked Comet's innocent arrogance, the all-eyes-on-me attitude that had kept
my gaze fixed on a grainy black-and-white image of a long-
dead dog whose radiant glory burned across decades.

And James Hunnewell's opinion? What would he really
have thought of Z-Rocks? Obviously, Hunnewell had
known Comet's lines better than I did. Maybe Hunnewell
could have seen something in Z-Rocks that was eluding me.
Whatever *it* was, I thought that Judge Mikki Muldoon
would miss it, too. About Z-Rocks's chances under Mrs.
Muldoon, Timmy Oliver agreed: When I wished him luck,

he smiled and looked sad and said thanks, but Z-Rocks just wasn't Mikki's type. He and Z-Rocks headed for the grooming tent. I wanted breakfast.

The glass-fronted announcement board in the hotel lobby informed me that Greg and Crystal's three o'clock service was sandwiched between a wedding breakfast—scheduled for the Lagoon at twelve-fifteen—and what the notice board called a "Gala Hawaiian Wedding Reception." Since the Lagoon was being set up for the wedding breakfast, the only restaurant open for ordinary breakfast was the grill. I filled a plate at the buffet and, on impulse, helped myself to a loaner copy of a Boston paper. Then I sat by myself in an uncrowded area, where I ate and read. Because of the multitude of reporters who'd questioned everyone at the show yesterday, I expected to find a long article about James Hunnewell's murder in a prominent place in the paper. Instead, it appeared as a small item on the last page of the business section. When Boston papers say *Boston*, Boston is what they mean. I read:

DEATH OF DOG JUDGE
DEEMED MURDER

DANVILLE. Police were summoned early yesterday morning to the grounds of the Danville Milestone Hotel and Conference Facility when a guest of the hotel discovered the body of James Winston Hunnewell, 79, of Kiawah Island, South Carolina. The deceased was to head the panel of judges scheduled to pick the top dog from among the hundreds of beautiful blue-eyed pet huskies gathered here for a multinational dog show. Dog show president Freida J. Reilly, of Portland, Maine, dismissed the suggestion that one of the show dogs was responsible for the death. State and local authorities are pursuing their investigations.

The item was harder to swallow than the lump of half-chewed pecan roll lodged in my throat. It was impossible to say what offended me most—the nasty, senseless piece of anti-dog libel, the ignorant bit about the blue-eyed pet huskies, or the amazing vision of a revolution that had turned conformation judging into a sort of jury system. Opinion is what breed judging is all about, and if there's one topic that gives rise to violent differences of opinion, it's the relative merits of show dogs. The AKC is less likely to spread the judge's authority among a bunch of committee members than the Vatican is to delegate infallibility to a board of Popes. James Hunnewell at the head of a panel of judges? Now that would truly have been a setup for murder.

And speaking of murder, the item, of course, offered less information about James Hunnewell's than I already possessed. Despite the numerous inaccuracies in the piece, I was, however, inclined to believe that Hunnewell had, in fact, been seventy-nine and that he'd lived in Kiawah Island, South Carolina. At any rate, Freida did live in Portland.

About Kiawah Island I knew a little because my friend Rita had spent a week there when her parents had rented a big condo that they'd shared with their children and grandchildren. Rita, being a psychologist, had come back talking mostly about family dynamics, but, then, you could rocket Rita into outer space, and she'd splash down analyzing the structural patterns of astronaut interaction and dropping only an incidental word or two about planets, stars, or black holes, unless, of course, the objects in the cosmos embodied symbolic psychic meaning, as I guess might be the case with black holes. Kiawah Island, I gathered from her, was sort of like Hilton Head, a fancy resort and retirement community with restaurants, beaches, swimming pools, and—here come the black holes—real-live alligators lazing around on golf courses and, on occasion, emerging from gator holes to gulp down small dogs. So, as a retirement spot for a dog person, Kiawah Island was a place with one big advantage—dogs were allowed, at least small dogs—and the corresponding disadvantage that they were vulnerable to being eaten by alligators. But, of course, I didn't know whether James Hunnewell had had—or even wanted—any kind of dog at all. He'd been out of malamutes for years. He could have switched breeds. For all I knew, the presence of dog-eating predators was what had attracted him to Kiawah to begin with.

Kiawah, though, did tell me something solid: James Hunnewell had had money. The business about Rita and the astronauts is true. It's also true that Rita had refrained from tantalizing me with descriptions of a vacation that I couldn't begin to afford. Wondering who'd inherit James Hunnewell's estate, I turned to the death notices, but found nothing under Hunnewell. I didn't need a newspaper, though, to realize that wealthy men leave wills. I put down the paper, ate my breakfast, and toyed with a new idea about why Gladys H. Thacker was coming all the way to Massachusetts to see that her brother got a Christian burial. The new idea was that Gladys H. Thacker was already *here*.

A puppy-mill operator like Gladys Thacker was probably selling puppies for thirty-five, fifty, or a hundred dollars each to a broker who'd get two or three hundred dollars or more apiece for those same pups, and with a quick turnaround. Pet shops would then resell those same pups for between five hundred and a thousand dollars. As I understood it, a lot of the Gladys H. Thackers are small-time operators, farmers and farmers' wives, whose puppy income is strictly supplemental: egg money derived from dogs instead of chickens. A puppy broker could well be a millionaire. Gladys Thacker had probably just traded her roosters and hens for Alaskan malamutes, and moved the dogs into the same old henhouses.

Was Gladys H. Thacker already here? After all, she'd had

a motive to arrive before her brother's death—if, that is, she'd wanted to get here in time to cause it. And the attack on Harriet Lunt? Harriet Lunt was of James Hunnewell's generation. Harriet was a lawyer. Was she *his* lawyer? If Gladys Thacker had had a motive to murder her brother, maybe Harriet Lunt knew what it was.

I remembered what Harriet Lunt had said last night: *Poor Elsa. And then James. And now me.* James Hunnewell, yes. Here at the show site. And Harriet Lunt, of course. But Elsa Van Dine? She had been fatally mugged and robbed of her diamond ring on a street in Providence. *Poor Elsa,* everyone kept lamenting. *Poor Elsa, the victim of* random *violence.*

CHAPTER 21 🐾

Elsa Van Dine's unexpected marriage to the elderly and long-widowed Marquis of Denver was considered a mésalliance. The marquis, you see, did not have malamutes. What he had, in addition to a title, a country seat, and a modest fortune, was life-threatening asthma. The marquis's most virulent attacks had all been triggered by inadvertent contact with dogs. During the rapid kennel dispersion that preceded the moderately young and very beautiful Elsa Van Dine's immigration to Great Britain, the bride-to-be made a big deal of expressing public concern for her fiancé's ailing lungs. In private, however, she confided her reluctance to subject her dogs to the ordeal of a six-month quarantine. Ah, the transparent foolishness of exchanging a pack of gorgeous show dogs with numerous impressive handles to their names for a man who possessed but one! Thus Elsa Van Dine became the Marchioness of Denver. And Ch. Northpole's Comet was sold. Elsa Van Dine, I think, made a very bad bargain. The marquis was one peer among many; Comet was without peer.

The story of Elsa and the marquis I learned from Duke Sylvia while I was hanging around the exhibition hall watching Mikki Muldoon judge what are called Bred-by-Exhibitor bitches, more or less what it sounds like—and nervously awaiting Leah and Kimi's time in the ring. When I'd last checked, Kimi had been standing on the grooming table wagging her tail and looking really lovely, and Leah had finally changed into the dress that I'd sprung on her at the last minute, together with the threat that if she refused to wear it, I'd withhold permission for her to handle Kimi, who is not co-owned, but officially belongs only to me. The flower-patterned dress fit perfectly, just as it had when Leah had made fun of it in the store. It had big pockets for stashing bait. Furthermore, judges prefer the *Little House on the Prairie* look to Leah's usual layers of black on black over black, a style that owes more to Bram Stoker than it does to Laura Ingalls Wilder, and if you had to pick one or the other to handle your bitch, just which one would *you* go for? Reconciled to the dress, Leah had seemed as happy and confident as Kimi. I, of course, was racked by an acute case of vicarious stage fright.

The enviably calm Duke Sylvia was waiting to handle a big, dark Kotzebue bitch entered in American Bred. The assignment wasn't exactly what had brought Duke to the national, but I was willing to bet that later in the day, when he waited to show Ironman in Best of Breed, he'd seem as casual and congenial as he did now. "There was one thing Elsa didn't count on," he remarked, filling me in on Elsa Van Dine. "And that was, when the old guy passed away, she'd get stuck being a dowager." Smiling rather fondly, he added, "I'll bet Elsa didn't like that one damned bit."

"You handled Comet for her?" Feminist linguists have supposedly cured women of this shrinking-tongued habit of letting driveling questions drip from our lips when we ought to be spitting out bold assertions. I apparently suffer from a polemic-resistant case of the ailment. I knew damn well that Duke had handled Comet for every owner the dog had had. Only an hour or so earlier, as I'd finished my coffee, I'd studied the *Malamute Quarterly* centerfold about Comet in one of the old issues that I'd taken with me to breakfast.

Duke nodded.

For no good reason, so did I. "And you handled him, uh . . . when Hadley . . ."

I'd heard about the incident dozens of times, but until I'd read the centerfold piece, I hadn't connected it with Duke or Comet or, for that matter, with Alaskan malamutes. Anyway, J. J. Hadley was Comet's breeder, and when Comet wasn't even two years old, Hadley entered him at the Westminster Kennel Club Dog Show, with Duke handling. This was in the old days, of course, back before Westminster was champions only. Anyway, spectacular dog that he was, Comet not only finished his championship at Westminster, but took Best of Breed. And J. J. Hadley died of surprise. Literally. He had a heart attack right outside the ring. Of course, it was a thrill for anyone to finish a dog there, especially a young dog that took the breed, but it is possible to carry this dog thing too far, and it seemed to me that that was just what J. J. Hadley had done. Hadley's widow, Velma, however, instead of sensibly realizing that breed competition is no sport for the faint of heart, laid the blame on the innocent Comet and on the equally innocent Westminster Kennel Club. Maddened by grief, Velma Hadley promptly sold Comet to Elsa Van Dine and launched her prolonged but ultimately successful campaign to prevent future ringside fatalities like her husband's. Thus it is that the Westminster Kennel Club Dog Show is now limited to champions of record, all because of that silly Velma Hadley. Just kidding. But Velma Hadley really did make a fuss.

So Duke admitted that he'd handled. Comet on the infamous occasion of J. J. Hadley's demise and on numerous other occasions, first for Hadley, of course; then for Elsa Van Dine; then for James Hunnewell and, of all people, Timmy Oliver, who'd co-owned the dog with Hunnewell; and finally, after buying Timmy out, for himself and James Hunnewell.

"So how did Timmy Oliver ever get to own Comet?" I was amazed. Comet was my idea of serious quality. Timmy Oliver certainly was not.

Duke's big, leonine face showed the first negative emotion I'd ever seen it reveal. Exactly what the feeling was, I couldn't identify, but, for once, Duke looked other than pleasant. "Elsa offered. Timmy said yes."

I remembered that Betty had said something about Elsa's taking Timmy under her wing. "And Hunnewell? How did Hunnewell . . . ?"

"Money," Duke said. "Timmy had dibs—Elsa liked him—but he was broke, so he got James to put up the money, promised him co-ownership, and as soon as Elsa signed Comet over to Timmy, Timmy kept his part of the deal. They had a whole elaborate agreement worked out. James paid the purchase price, the vet bills, uh, handler fees, everything. James had possession. Harriet Lunt drew it all up for them. And that was it. Timmy didn't get a thing out of it. Co-owned him in name only. Couldn't say *boo* to Comet without James's written agreement." Duke added with surprising scorn, "God, there was one time there where Timmy had this bitch he wanted to breed to Comet, and James turned him down flat! Poor sucker! Didn't even have stud rights on his own dog."

"That's a pretty unusual arrangement."

"Yeah, well, Comet was an, uh, unusual dog. And, hey, if *you* were going to co-own a dog with Timmy . . . ?"

"Perish the thought!" I exclaimed.

"Yeah, well, James was no dummy. He felt the same way."

"So why didn't James Hunnewell go to Elsa Van Dine in the first place and just buy Comet outright?"

"Elsa didn't care much for James. James could be, uh, abrasive. This judging poll was probably the first popularity contest James ever won in his life." Duke frowned.

"I thought he judged quite a lot."

"He got assignments. People had a lot of respect for his *opinions*. It was *him* they didn't like. With Elsa, it was . . . Elsa was a pretty woman. James used to hit on her. She hated it. She knew he wanted Comet, and the worse he wanted the dog, the more she'd have sold him to someone else. When she found out he got Comet after all, she was ripping mad at Timmy. But by then, it was too late. And she got over it. She always had a soft spot for Timmy."

"That old tape we saw," I said. "That was when Comet belonged to Elsa Van Dine?" The judge had been James Hunnewell, who, for obvious reasons, wouldn't have been permitted to judge a dog he co-owned. "She owned him for what? Four years?"

Duke shrugged. "Give or take."

"So how did Timmy happen to sell to you?" The transaction was none of my business. I felt awkward. The sensation jarred. Ordinarily, Duke Sylvia had the flattering gift of making people feel as though they'd always said the right thing.

But Duke didn't seem to sense my discomfort. "Things got ugly for a while there. One of Timmy's get-rich-quick schemes fell apart, he was dead broke, and of course, no one was stupid enough to loan him a dime. Comet was the only thing he had that was supposedly worth anything, but, like I said, that was in name only—James had total control. According to this contract they had, he could veto any buyer Timmy came up with. And James wasn't about to buy Timmy out. He'd bought Comet once. He'd paid the full purchase price, and he'd paid everything since then. He wasn't going to pay for the same dog twice."

"There might've been someone else who just wanted his name on the dog," I said stupidly. "Someone Hunnewell would've agreed to. People do that. They want the glory. *And* they contribute to the cost."

Duke smiled. "Yeah, well, there was someone."

"Oh, of course! And that's how you ended up co-owning Comet."

"It worked out for everyone. James saved himself a bundle in handler fees. Timmy got some cash. I paid a decent price. Of course, after Timmy got back on his feet, he had second thoughts. You had to feel sorry for him. He never wanted to sell Comet, but he had no real choice." Duke spoke with the easy self-confidence of someone who's never been the object of anyone else's pity.

Loud applause tugged me to the present. The Bred-by-Exhibitor bitches were sailing around Judge Muldoon's ring. I smiled at Duke. "Whatever you paid, I think you got a great deal. I'd have given anything to own Comet."

Duke pulled out a metal comb and started to do a little last-minute work on the bitch. "Christ," he said, "who wouldn't?"

CHAPTER 22

In species after species, from turtles to alligators to human beings, sperm counts are dropping and, with them, the size of male genitalia. According to radical environmentalists, chemical pollution is to blame for a multitude of diverse and alarming signs of feminization: hermaphroditism, retained testicles, shrunken members, unpaired gonads. It's males who are losing their virility, you see; females are staying the same. In Florida's Lake Apopka, for instance, the sexual organs of the female alligators have remained as capacious as ever, while those of their mates have shriveled to a fourth their former size, and, yes, I know that Masters and Johnson shored up a lot of shaky male egos by declaring that size doesn't matter, but let's be honest: What Masters and Johnson had in mind or in hand or in wherever was trivial variation; it wasn't *one-fourth*.

When the news first reached me, I didn't believe it either. I didn't want to. Eventually, though, my defenses broke down, with startling consequences for Rowdy, who found himself flipped onto his back on the kitchen floor so I could take a close-up look and make sure everything was exactly as it had always been, as I'm happy to report that it appeared to be, so far, yes, but for how long? The matter suddenly took a grave and terrifying turn. The reproductive future of turtles, alligators, and human beings I could joke about. But the breed of breeds, pinnacle of dogdom, acme of woofy evolution, howling apex of canine creation, shining quintessence of the utmost in *real* dog, yes, the incomparable Alaskan malamute—extinct?!!

Not if I could help it. So that's why I thought about freezing Rowdy's sperm—not for now, but for the future, for the good of the breed.

"For the good of the breed," said Lisa Tainter, our show secretary, who was crowding up against me to watch the judging and, in addressing Freida Reilly, spoke almost in my ear. Easing away from Lisa, I glanced down and caught sight of a sheaf of R.T.I. leaflets in her hand. "When it comes to the gene pool," Lisa declared, "it's better to be safe than sorry."

Before I say anything else about Lisa, I want to make it clear that, like everyone else at the national, I was grateful to Lisa for serving as show secretary, in which capacity she had done a massive amount of unenviable paperwork without, so far as I knew, creating a single snafu. I also need to say that Lisa is a sweet, kind person and a responsible, ethical breeder. Finally, let me point out that a highly developed interest in Alaska and all things Alaskan is, of course, perfectly common and understandable among fanciers of the Alaskan malamute, many of whom travel to Alaska, collect Eskimo art, and accumulate libraries of old books by early missionaries who made their way from village to village by dog sled. Most of us do not, however, carry our passion to the point of habitually costuming ourselves in the traditional garb of the native people of the forty-ninth state.

But Lisa Tainter was an exception: From the furtrimmed

hood of her skin-side-out parka to the heavily insulated toes of her authentic-looking mukluks, the woman habitually dressed for a hunting trip on frozen tundra and often, in fact, carried a variety of pelts and hides. How Lisa endured life in her portable sauna, I don't know. Her face was usually red, and her forehead and nose were often beaded in sweat. Today must've been moderately comfortable for her. Although the exhibition hall was heated, cold air poured in through the door to the parking lot. Lisa's breed loyalty, however, remained fast throughout changes in the seasons. July and August forced her to abandon the parka—she'd have died of hyperthermia—but she compensated for the loss by adorning herself with numerous bracelets and necklaces fashioned from claws, fangs, bones, and strips of rawhide. Lisa often talked about moving to Fairbanks. She probably wouldn't have been happy there. I think she'd have had social problems. The locals, I'm afraid, would have found her eccentric. We, however, were used to her and saw her as odd only through the startled eyes of strangers who wandered into dog shows, didn't really belong, and after catching sight of Lisa, didn't want to.

Freida Reilly agreed that when it came to the gene pool, it certainly was best to take no chances. "I'm still not sold," she told Lisa. "You know what makes me nervous?"

Sherri Ann Printz, I longed to say. *Wedding cake. Murder.* Freida did not, however, look nervous. On the contrary, venting her pent-up rage on Sherri Ann seemed to have had a beneficially cathartic effect.

Echoing my reflections about extinction, Freida went on: "Frozen semen is forever! It's not like owning a dog. It's a totally separate asset! Among other things, how do you take responsibility for puppies whelped ten thousand years after you're dead?"

My eyes were on Mikki Muldoon's right hand, which swept across a black-and-white bitch's faulty rear. I was so

focused on the judging that even when the hullabaloo broke
out nearby, I ignored it until Lisa Tainter's skin-draped arm
brushed my shoulder. "Holly? Holly, there's a problem here
that maybe you rescue people . . ."

Turning, I saw that whatever the problem was, it centered
on Crystal. The bride's blond hair was elaborately done up in
rows of intricate little braids, twists, and ringlets inter-
twined with strings of tiny pearls, and she wore a volumi-
nous hot-pink maternity sweat suit decorated with sequins
and sparkles that took the form of firecracker explosions on
her belly, as if the fetuses inside were igniting Roman can-
dles. Her head looked as though it had gotten accidentally,
maybe even maliciously, switched with the one from a Just-
My-Size Bride Barbie I'd recently seen at F.A.O. Schwartz.
There was, however, nothing doll-like or radiant about this
bride's expression, which was one of enraged petulance. Crystal had drawn a crowd: Lisa, Freida Reilly, Karl, and a lot of
other people. Stamping one foot on the floor, Crystal made
what I think was a deliberate effort to project her voice.
"When I said I wanted a *puppy*," she complained somewhat
shrilly, "I meant a *little puppy!* I did not mean a big dog, and
the one out there that he wants to sell me is big, and it's
dirty, and it's not even all that cute! That man took my two
hundred dollars! He took it yesterday!" Punctuating her delivery with stomps of her feet, she added: "And I" (*stomp!*)
"want" (*stomp!*) "you" (*stomp!*) "to" (*stomp!*) "MAKE HIM GIVE
IT BACK!" (*Stomp, stomp, stomp!!!*)

Freida Reilly cleared her throat. To no one in particular,
she said quietly, "This should not be happening." She fingered a team of tiny gold sled dogs that pranced across her
breast. Then she took charge. "Karl," she told her son, "go
and find Timmy Oliver for me, and if he's doing something
else, you tell him from me that, no, he isn't, because I want
to see him this minute." Seizing the opportunity to exert
her authority over Sherri Ann Printz, she pointed a finger:

"Sherri Ann, find Elaine for me." Elaine was the president of our breed club. Sherri Ann's lips formed what looked like a fleeting obscenity, but she silently departed in apparent compliance. Freida turned to Crystal. "Was the dog in question in poor condition? Is that what you said?"

"Dirty," Crystal agreed. "All of them are. And locked up in little, tiny cages. And with nothing to eat or drink, either."

Motivated, I thought, more by a desire to get Crystal out of the exhibition hall than by alarm about the dogs, Freida said, "Holly, see what you can do. Explain things to her, would you? And maybe you or Betty or someone . . . ? If the dogs really are . . ."

By now, Mikki Muldoon must've been halfway through judging American-Bred. Open was next—Kimi's class— and I desperately did not want to miss seeing Leah and Kimi in the ring. Like everyone else, however, I obeyed Freida. "I'm Holly," I told Crystal, taking her arm. "Show me where the camper is, and tell me what happened."

Out of curiosity, I suppose, Lisa Tainter trailed along with us. Crystal kept eyeing Lisa's furs and skins, but otherwise ignored her. As we passed the breed club booth, I caught sight of Betty Burley at the booth beyond it. "Lisa," I said, "would you get Betty? Ask her to come out to the parking lot and find me. Tell her what's going on."

Crystal, however, came to a standstill at the door and started fussing about the rain.

"All right," I conceded. "So we'll just stand here, and you can tell me about it. Tim Oliver offered to sell you a puppy. Is that right?"

"Yes, only it isn't a real puppy. What it is, is a dog, and who wants a big, grown-up dog?" she wailed.

"Anyone who doesn't enjoy washing floors," I said, more to myself than to Crystal.

"Can I ask you?" Crystal said. "Why is that woman dressed like an Eskimo?"

"It's a costume," I said inadequately. *We are one with our dogs*, I could have explained, *some of us more visibly than others.* "Look, selling dogs or puppies at a show is strictly against the rules. So, when you said what you did back there, it, uh, made everything very awkward for everyone."

"He told me we had to keep it sort of, uh, lowkey." Crystal caressed the sequins on her abdomen and pouted at the rain. "Like there was this rule, but, really, nobody cared."

"You're getting married today. This is a really big wedding. Aren't you going on a honeymoon?"

"Hawaii." She made it sound like a famous industrial wasteland.

"Well, what were you going to do with a puppy?"

"One of my friends was going to keep it for me till we got back," she answered defiantly. "My maid of honor."

"You know, a puppy is a lot of work—"

"But I wanted one! It's my wedding, and that's what I—"

"*I want, I want,*" mimicked Betty Burley, popping open an umbrella and raising it over Crystal's bedecked head. "Enough of what you want! Now stop whining and show us where this camper is."

The parking lot was thick with dog-show vehicles—campers, motor homes, vans, minivans, and four by fours—and especially crowded because the parking area at the opposite end of the hotel was cordoned off with crime-scene tape and unavailable to show people, wedding guests, and ordinary travelers and tourists. Despite Betty's injunction, Crystal groused her way across the blacktop. She knew when she'd been ripped off, she said, and she didn't take this kind of shit from anyone. Ask her father. Ask her mother. Ask Gregory. She wanted her two hundred dollars, and she wanted it *now*.

"That's it," she said, breaking off in the middle of what promised to be a bloodcurdling threat. "That one over there."

The beige camper at the far end of the lot looked exactly like dozens of others. Without bothering to knock or call out, Betty reached for the handle, opened the door, and stepped up into the camper. "The dogs are crated," she told us. The occasional malamute actually will defend property, especially a vehicle, and for all we knew, Tim Oliver's camper might've housed a loose dog of some seriously protective breed.

Even before I followed Crystal up into the dimness of the interior, the reek hit me, a nauseating combination of dog feces, urine, chemical toilet, and spoiled food.

Betty whipped open a big, ugly flower-patterned beige curtain. "Well, the dogs don't seem to be living any worse than Timmy is."

There were three malamutes in three big wire crates: a silver male as dirty as Z-Rocks had been and two big puppies, one male and one female. Both looked about four months old; by four months, a malamute is far beyond the little-ball-of-fluff stage. The adult dog's tail thumped. Happy to see anyone at all, the puppies scrambled through disgusting nests of damp, torn newspaper and unidentifiable junk, and nosed the doors of their crates. A fourth crate, a big Vari Kennel—Z-Rocks's, I thought—was empty. As Crystal had reported, the dogs had no food available, but, then, thirty seconds after I feed Rowdy and Kimi, neither do they. All four crates held small buckets of water. The dogs seemed well-nourished. If anything, they, like Z-Rocks, were heavier than I'd have liked. Maybe the secret ingredient in Pro-Vita No-Blo Sho-Kote really was some kind of fat, if not actual snake oil. Cardboard shipping boxes of the stuff stacked three deep in a corner bore telltale stains: The big male had expressed his opinion of Timmy Oliver's business venture.

As Betty said, the filth wasn't confined to the crates. Encrusted dishes spilled out of the tiny sink; greasy pans were stacked on the burners; and a cross-country trip's worth of fast-food wrappers, cartons, and drink containers lay on the floor. An open bottle of the miracle product lay on its side in a sticky-looking pool on the passenger seat. The dashboard and the open compartments under it were littered with wrinkled maps, crushed soft-drink cans, empty and half-empty cardboard coffee cups, a torn-open carton of cigarettes, a fat paperback book with the front cover missing, and what looked like a hundred dollars' worth of loose change. The only indication that Tim Oliver paid any attention to personal hygiene was evidence that he took off his dirty socks and underwear. There must have been at least a dozen dark-colored socks scattered around, and almost as many pairs of boxer shorts, some in prints, some in solid colors, none that could be called white. Even in the absence of puppies, I'd have been careful where I stepped.

Crystal was self-righteous. "See! I told you so! The one he wanted to sell me is the one there on the right. Now is that a puppy? No, that's a great big dog."

"She's probably four months or so," Betty said. "Really, they're—"

"Well, that's not what *I* mean by a *puppy*," insisted Crystal.

The stench was getting to me. I moved back to the door and pushed it wide open. How could a pregnant woman, even one past the phase of morning sickness, breathe in that camper without vomiting? As if to prove her immunity to nausea, Crystal paced to the front of the camper, pulled a pack of cigarettes from the carton, opened it, searched for matches, and, finding none, pulled a green plastic lighter from her own pants pocket and lit a cigarette. Spitting out grains of tobacco, she glared at Betty. "Well, you've seen for yourself! Now, how do I get back my two hundred dollars?"

Betty and I both knew that we could do nothing about the condition of the puppies. Tim Oliver could sell them as he pleased. In the meantime, they had water, they had enough to eat, they looked healthy, and their lives weren't in danger. It never even occurred to me to try to do anything about Crystal.

"You, young lady!" Betty began. "Put that thing out this second!" When Crystal failed to comply, Betty snatched the cigarette from her hand and tossed it past me and out the door. An odd look of relief crossed Crystal's face. "Babies having babies!" Betty exclaimed. "Well, now, you and I need to have a little talk, because, you know, it's terribly important to take responsibility for any life that you bring into this world."

"It's twins," Crystal told her.

"Two! Dear God! You can't be more than twenty."

"Twenty-one," Crystal mumbled.

"Aren't you supposed to be getting married? Isn't this your wedding that's . . . ?"

The pout reappeared on Crystal's face. "Yeah, but I'm not invited to this part. It's a wedding breakfast, and I'm not even invited. Do you believe it? My own wedding, and—"

"Oh, for heaven's sake," Betty sighed, "any puppy I raise is . . . Well, look. We have very little time, so let's make the most of it. First of all, forget about your two hundred dollars, because that foolish Timmy Oliver has spent it by now, and there's no sense wasting energy on something you can't change. Second, no dogs for you. Another responsibility is the last thing you need right now. And while we're on that subject . . ." Betty paused. "Catholic?"

Crystal looked stunned. So, I'm sure, did I.

"N-n-o," Crystal stammered.

"Well, that simplifies matters," declared Betty, with her familiar blend of optimism and practicality. "Two children are enough for you right now, and thank heaven, there are a lot of options these days." Betty cleared her throat.

Eager not to miss Leah and Kimi's appearance in the ring, I seized this opportunity to slip away. If I'd had time,

I'd have stayed, though. I really was curious. Although I'd heard Betty discuss reproductive responsibility with dozens of dog owners, I'd never before heard her deliver anything like a spay-neuter lecture concerning human reproduction. I couldn't help wondering how, and even whether, she'd adapt the standard version to its present purpose. Some points, of course, applied equally to dogs and people. Regardless of species, it is important not to create more creatures than there are loving homes, and it is vital to understand that the decision to bring life into this world means a lifetime commitment. Harvard Square, for instance, has at least as many homeless, abandoned human beings as it does stray dogs; and parents, like responsible dog breeders, often end up getting adult offspring returned when promising placements unexpectedly fail to work out. Myself, I'd have deleted the usual bit about the role of castration in preventing prostate cancer and testicular tumors, and I'd have downplayed such presumably irrelevant behavorial benefits as a reduced incidence of indoor leg-lifting. Oh, and I'd have found it impossible to make the routine promise that Greg would never know the difference.

CHAPTER 23 🔎

During my absence from the exhibition hall, the spectators had swollen in number. Now, in a fashion reminiscent of sociable protozoa, they teemed in a restless, blob-like colony around the ring. The heat of people, dogs, and fierce competition had raised the temperature by ten degrees. Enthroned on a parka-draped ringside lawn chair at the side of Victor Printz, Harriet Lunt kept her eyes on the judging. Her left arm rested in a makeshift sling. With her right hand, she shooed away would-be sympathizers. Out of the corner of her mouth, however, she murmured inaudible comments to Victor Printz. When I approached to ask how she was doing, she thanked me rather curtly for the help I'd given last night. Then, she hadn't seemed to recognize me. By now, I thought, she'd remembered the eyes and ears of the *AKC Gazette*, seen through my taradiddle, and learned that she had, in fact, been assisted by Alaskan Malamute Rescue.

"You saw no one at all, is that right?" Harriet demanded of me in that deep-bass voice, her eyes boring into mine.

No one, I assured her. Not a soul. As I moved away, Harriet muttered to Victor. I thought I heard her whisper Betty's name.

Soon thereafter, Harriet Lunt probably spoke my own. I know that she pointed me out. Detective Kariotis told me so. He led me to the same overwhelmingly bright function room we'd been in before. This time, though, our interview was brief. And I didn't make a fool of myself. I coldly explained why I'd been in the Lagoon in the middle of the night. "The stuff I bought was scattered all over," I reported. From the time I left my room until the moment I found Harriet Lunt, I said, I'd seen no one and heard nothing. When I'd come upon her, the door to the corridors had been closing. I hadn't even seen a shadow. I barely knew Harriet Lunt. I had no idea why anyone would assault her. What did I know of the, uh, Dowager Marchioness of Denver? For a second, I thought Kariotis must be asking about a character in some book. Then it dawned on me—Elsa Van Dine. Like everyone else, I knew she'd been murdered. A fatal mugging and robbery on a street in Providence, I'd heard. I'd never met her and never corresponded with her. If Detective Kariotis wanted to know about the older generation, he should ask an old-timer. I was new to the breed.

Throughout the interview, I desperately tried to conceal my impatience. With every succinct statement I made, I burned at the thought that as I spoke Leah and Kimi were in the ring. I elaborated on nothing and stuck to the facts of what I'd seen last night. Before long, Kariotis let me go.

Bolting back to the hall, I found that I hadn't, after all, missed Leah and Kimi. They had just entered the ring. Not far from them, a chunky woman fell to her knees in so genuflectory a manner that when she finished posing her bitch, stood up, and raised a finger, I expected her to make the sign of the cross. But the handler didn't have a prayer. Ignoring a jerk on her collar, the bitch sneezed violently, bounced up and down, skittered around, and capped the performance by attempting to mount her handler. Out of sympathy, I looked away. From one corner of the ring, though, the uncaring eye of the video camera recorded the whole episode, which in a month or so would be available for viewing and reviewing by anyone who ordered the tape from the professional company hired to make our national specialty the unforgettable experience it truly was.

I bought the tape and have repeatedly watched that display of naughtiness while fast-forwarding, stopping, and zipping on in search of the section that shows Leah and Kimi. But I have leaped ahead of myself. The tape has been heavily edited; long minutes have become seconds. And because the camera rested on a very low tripod, the viewpoint is odd and unfamiliar, as if the judging had been filmed by a very small child with a precocious interest in canine gait. Or perhaps an obsession with the lower halves of female human beings. In this foreshadowing of a radical-feminist future, the judge is female, and women handlers outnumber the men . . . five to one? Ten to one? So maybe what truly enthralls the child is ladies' legs. They vary so greatly in size and shape, bone and muscle mass, as to constitute a sort of all-breed show within this otherwise uniformly malamute ring.

Judge Mikki Muldoon's legs are fine-boned, and she toes out; judged by the official standard of the Alaskan malamute, she doesn't make it in her own ring. Kimi does. She moves with the power of a thundercloud and the grace of a big cat. At the time, I was silent. Each time I watch the tape, however, I coach Leah aloud: *Don't yank her in! Don't make her sidewind!* Leah's lesson-ridden childhood pays off: Eurythmics, Suzuki, and the Orff-Kodaly method have taught her tempo and discipline. And if Kimi's ear set is not the utter perfection of Rowdy's? Well, malamutes don't pull with their ears; and to some extent—fourth place, to be exact—Judge Mikki Muldoon agrees. First goes to a bitch bred, owned, and handled by Sherri Ann Printz. Two others are also ahead of Kimi. But fourth? Out of the highly competitive Open class? At a national specialty? With a young, if gifted, handler? I think that's damn good.

The hoots and wild applause were for Sherri Ann. My own cries of utter surprise were for Kimi and Leah. For obvious reasons, I did my best to hide the full extent of my astonishment from Leah and Faith. If Kimi knew, she didn't care. Dogs judge souls, not bodies. Kimi knows her own worth.

Leah thanked the judge, congratulated those who'd placed ahead of her, and accepted congratulations in return. Sherri Ann Printz smiled, chatted, and gesticulated with great animation. Sherri Ann could, of course, afford magnanimity. Her object, however, was obvious: to present herself to Leah as grandly rising above the false accusations and infantile food-fighting of madwomen. *Every vote counts*, I thought cynically: Leah belonged to our national breed club.

Even after leaving the ring, Kimi was still flashing her eyes, wagging her tail at everyone, and angling for liver. To spare Leah the need to keep an eye on Kimi, as well as to reclaim my own dog, I took Kimi's lead and was scratching her head and otherwise fooling around with her when Sherri Ann Printz turned from Leah to me and, just before leading her bitch back into the ring, exclaimed loudly, "These youngsters are the future, you know! And if this young lady is any example, it's my opinion that it's a very rosy one!"

I wasn't sure whether Sherri Ann meant Leah or Kimi, and not long thereafter, when Judge Mikki Muldoon again gave the nod to Sherri Ann—Winners Bitch—I couldn't help wondering whether the rosy future paramount in Sherri Ann's mind was hours rather than decades away: In picking a Pawprintz bitch, Mrs. Muldoon hadn't exactly dashed Sherri Ann's hopes for Bear's victory in Best of Breed, a triumph that would also serve as dandy revenge on the cake-smearing Freida Reilly. On the other hand (the frosting-free hand? sorry, no pun intended), if Mikki Muldoon was playing politics, this win and the championship points that went with it could be a sop, an advance consolation prize to Sherri Ann, who, as a VIP in the breed, would be a bad enemy for a judge interested in obtaining future assignments. How political Mikki Muldoon was, I didn't know. Her pleasure in judging was obvious: She radiated dignified elation. Her efficiency, too, was apparent: When she left the ring for a hard-earned one-hour lunch break, I checked my watch: ten past twelve. In a world in which schedules are usually optimistic approximations, she had completed her morning's work almost precisely on time, and she'd done it without creating any sense of rushed or careless judging. Striding confidently out of her ring, Judge Mikki Muldoon seemed an altogether different person from the woman who'd occupied the ladies' room stall next to mine yesterday morning, the nerve-wracked Mikki Muldoon who'd noisily lost her breakfast.

CHAPTER 24 🔍

As I stood at the take-out counter at the Liliu Grill handing over what felt like an awful lot of money for three sandwiches, Duke Sylvia showed up looking as confident as if Ironman had just gone Best of Breed. Duke nodded agreeably to me and asked for a pastrami on a bulky roll with extra mustard and a side of fries, not exactly what I think of as a remedy for a jittery stomach. For a few paranoid moments, I wondered whether Duke assumed that I was handling Rowdy myself. Was he trying to rattle the competition by ordering a lunch that wouldn't have made it past my uvula? Of course, I could have *ordered* pastrami myself. I just couldn't have forced it down.

"How'd you make out this morning?" I asked.

Duke momentarily looked as if he'd already forgotten the Kotzebue bitch. "She took her class," he said, as if it almost went without saying. "Sherri Ann took Winners," he added in the parlance of the fancy, which glosses over distinctions between dogs and their breeder-handlers, beings assumed to share a merged identity.

Almost as soon as Duke had finished paying, a white-coated waiter emerged through a swinging door with Duke's food and mine. To get to the exhibition hall and the grooming tent, we cut through the lobby together and circled around outdoors. Although the rain had stopped, the sky was still gray, and pools of water remained on the blacktop. How Faith intended to keep Rowdy's feet clean, I didn't know, but I hoped she'd take advantage of the lull in the rain to get him from the tent to the exhibition hall. I checked my watch: twelve-fifty.

"Ten to one," I told Duke. Rowdy's chances? Were they that good? I mentally reviewed the competition, top-winning dogs so famous that I knew their call names: Ironman, Bear, Casey, and lots of others, especially Casey, who was supposed to be utterly gorgeous.

Clustered near the entrance to the hall were at least a dozen people, a few standing alone, the others in twos and threes. A man I didn't know detached himself from one of the little clusters to approach Duke and mutter something I didn't catch.

"Thanks. I'll take care of it," Duke replied. Giving me his usual low-key smile, he said, "Sometimes it doesn't pay to do favors."

"Is this about Ironman?" I asked.

Duke shook his head: "That bitch of Timmy Oliver's. Z-Rocks. The thing is, Mikki's not going to look at her twice."

"Timmy's telling everyone that under Hunnewell—"

Uncharacteristically, Duke cut me off. As close to exasperated as I'd ever seen him, he said, "In Timmy's dreams. Besides, James'd never've lasted to now. He was sicker than anyone knew. He was supposed to be on oxygen. He told Karl so on the way from the airport. No way James'd've held out. Even if he had—like I said, in Timmy's dreams."

"Z-Rocks goes back to Comet," I said. "Besides, she's pretty."

With scorn, Duke said, "Comet was bone and muscle. He was all grit. Comet was not *pretty*."

Short on time, driven by nerves, I asked an abrupt question that Leah had asked me last night when she'd read the centerfold piece in the old *Malamute Quarterly*. "Duke, what did Comet die of?"

Duke spoke quickly and quietly. "Hit by a car." Duke's face and his whole body were stolid. "Most of the time, Comet was with me, but he was out of coat, and I was on the circuit, so James had him for a month." His voice was bitter. "James lived right by a major highway. And James *loved* to watch the dog run."

Someone told me later that Duke never discussed Comet's death and that I shouldn't have asked. I disagree. Duke, I think, told me about it because he knew I'd understand that Comet had been Duke's and that James Hunnewell had murdered Duke's great dog.

Before I could say anything, however, Duke excused himself and headed toward the grooming tent, where I intended to go myself to check on Rowdy and to give Kimi her unofficial prize as soon as I'd delivered lunch to Leah and Betty. Clutching the sandwiches, I dashed into the exhibition hall, where Leah was supposed to be helping Betty at the rescue booth, but was mainly devoting herself to fooling around with what I would immediately have recognized as a Poker Flat dog even if Robin Haggard hadn't been right nearby. This one turned out to be Joe—properly, Ch. Poker Flat's Rainman, C.D.X., T.D., W.W.P.D., W.T.D., C.G.C.—who, to judge from the way he was jabbing at Leah's pocket, was actually more Battering Ram than Poker.

"Leah," Betty said sternly, "get that dog out from behind this table before one of you smashes something! All we need is for one of those wolf prints to get knocked over, and there'll be broken glass all over the place. And if he swipes that lamp with his tail and does it some damage, I'll never hear the end of it!"

Almost before Betty had finished issuing the warning, the big, gentle dog rose up to give Leah a giant teddy-bear hug and, paws resting on her shoulders, fulfilled Betty's prediction by wagging his tail, tipping over what I was convinced was the murder weapon, and sending it crashing to the floor.

Leah was suitably ashamed of herself. "I'm sorry! I really am sorry. The bulb didn't break. Is the lamp . . . ?"

Retrieving the fallen relic, Betty rose like a diminutive Statue of Liberty struggling to hold forth a disproportionately large and radically redesigned torch. Our kind of help, she announced in a crabby voice, was exactly what she didn't need. "Out of here!" ordered Betty. "Every one of you!"

Catching the scent of food, Joe transferred his attention to me and had to be lured away midpoke. I thrust the steak sandwiches at Leah and said, "Here. One for you, one for Kimi, Go!" Then I bent over the lamp, which Betty had finally lowered to the table, and asked whether there'd been any damage.

"No," she grumbled. "More's the pity. The more I look at the thing, the more I hate the sight of it."

"Betty? I hate to tell you, but he's lost a big patch of fur. Down here by the base of his tail, he's shed to bare, uh, skin."

"Oh, that's nothing. That happened while he was on his little adventure. I meant to touch him up last night. We'll have to do it before the auction. They'll have glue back there somewhere at the registration desk." Replying to my raised eyebrows, she added, "Fur is fur. Rowdy's will do just fine."

"Speaking of—"

"Before you dash off, Holly, I want to remind you to keep

your eyes open for this Thacker woman. I am certainly looking forward to having a word or two—"

"We don't know what she looks like!" I protested.

Betty brushed off my objection. "Oh, you'll know her right away. The tone here isn't always what we might wish," she pronounced, glaring at the lamp. "Witness that ridiculous episode last night! But no one here is outright *slovenly*."

To get embroiled in a discussion of whether puppy-mill operators were necesarily slovenly seemed a perilous exercise. So I nodded compliantly and, reminding Betty that I'd brought her sandwich, took off for the grooming tent. Despite the schedule, the judging, I should note, was not about to start any second. Back from her lunch break, Mikki Muldoon was at the judge's table, where she was conferring with her stewards while securing the shoulder strap of her purse to the judge's chair, but a couple of show-committee members had just begun to embellish the arborlike gate to the ring with a long, thick garland woven from what must have been thousands of delicate pink and white flowers. The late Elsa Van Dine had sent Freida a special donation for flowers, I recalled Betty saying. The donation must have been very generous indeed.

There were, of course, no flowers in the grooming tent. It was a communal backstage dressing room forced to accommodate a big cast of stars and dressers. Portable tables and commodious malamute-size crates stacked on top of each other partitioned the space into a maze of open rooms, and everywhere were crate dollies, tack boxes, canvas bags of gear, heavy-duty extension cords, and those forced-air dryers that look like old-fashioned canister vacuum cleaners and sound like peaks in hell on the verge of volcanic eruption. The roar of the motors was so loud that I could all but see, taste, and smell the sound, but as handlers led their dogs out, the noise level diminished greatly, and what remained was the miasma of no-rinse shampoo, grooming spray, and clean, damp dog, the fervent odor of my own religion.

Faith Barlow was set up in a particularly jampacked spot near a canvas wall about halfway down the tent. The table on which Rowdy stood was so close to the one that supported Z-Rocks that in going over Rowdy with smooth, soothing strokes of her finishing brush, Faith came close to grooming Timmy Oliver as well. I'd known Faith for years. She looked the same as ever: same dimples, perfect skin, wavy hair in apparently permanent transition from blond to silver, same neat, conservative, multipocketed suits or dresses in colors chosen to camouflage dog hair.

But it wasn't a people show, was it? And I *am* a dog writer. Z-Rocks's coat, after what must have been wrist-spraining brushing, still retained a vaguely dead look. At the risk of making myself obnoxious by bragging about Rowdy, let me just remark in passing on the shiny, stand-off perfection of his coat, the gleam of vigor and health in his ideally dark eyes, the visibly and palpably well-conditioned tone of his musculature, and the indefinable yet unmistakable air of top-dog self-confidence radiated by this miraculous incarnation of the official standard of the Alaskan malamute. In truth, the dog was so beautiful that I could hardly believe he belonged to me. And he was just standing there on the grooming table wagging his tail. You haven't seen Rowdy until you've seen him move.

"Timmy Oliver!" Faith's voice was sharp. "Get that bottle off that table before I open it and pour the whole mess down your throat!"

Oblivious to Faith and Z-Rocks, Timmy Oliver was making his usual sales pitch for Pro-Vita No-Blo Sho-Kote to Finn Adams, who was ignoring Timmy to deliver his usual R.T.I. spiel to Duke Sylvia, who had Ironman up on the grooming table beyond Timmy's. I'd seen show photos of Ironman before, but in the flesh and bone and steel-gray coat, the dog was bigger and more imposing than I'd pictured him. To my eye, backed by the official breed standard, Ironman was too big; and his small, rather light eyes made him look strangely cold and frightening. The standard, of course, calls for dark eyes, the darker the better—Rowdy's eyes—and the correct facial expression is warm, sweet, and open, not icy or steely: nothing like Ironman's and everything like you-know-who's. Ironman was impressive, though. He had the kind of gorgeous coat that results from a combination of good genes, robust health, excellent diet, and regular grooming, and is never obtained just by dosing a dog with any of those magic-bullet powders, tablets, or liquids, including that stupid Pro-Vita No-Blo Sho-Kote, a large glass bottle of which now sat prominently on Z-Rocks's grooming table.

To promote his product, Timmy had set the bottle next to a bitch with the kind of ready-to-shed coat that the glop was supposed to prevent. As a time to try to sell Duke on R.T.I.'s services, Finn had chosen a moment when Duke was eager to get Ironman off the grooming table, past Finn, out of the tent, and into the ring. In jest, I assume, Duke told Finn that what Ironman liked was insemination without artifice, thank you; and furthermore, in Duke's experience, after people went to the trouble of freezing semen, they hardly ever used it anyway. Take Comet's. Why, on three separate occasions, he himself had taken Comet to—

Catching sight of Leah, Duke broke off. In her flowerprint dress, Leah could have passed for thirteen. Dog people speak with wholesome frankness about absolutely everything, but we occasionally remember to censor ourselves in front of other people's children. After kneeling by Kimi's crate to treat her to torn-up bits of steak sandwich, Leah had startled Duke by suddenly rising.

"Don't let me stop you," Leah told him.

But Duke took advantage of the interruption to get Iron-man off the table. As Duke led the dog away, Timmy Oliver resumed his effort to convince Finn Adams that that damned food supplement would make an ideal addition to R.T.I.'s product line. Gentleman that he'd been reared to be, Finn was doing his best to get out of the way of the handlers and dogs heading out of the crowded tent—he obviously wanted to join them—but Timmy had scooped up the bottle of Pro-Vita No-Blo Sho-Kote and was shoving it in Finn's face.

In the meantime, Faith had removed her grooming coat and was stocking the pockets of her gray wool blazer with bait, stashing a comb and a plastic spray bottle in her skirt pockets, and otherwise preparing to earn her fee by getting Rowdy into the ring on time. Attentive to the familiar cues, free of the grooming noose, Rowdy shook himself all over. The dog is a born performer. I stepped up to him, smacked my lips, and got a kiss. "Hey, big boy," I whispered in his ear. "Go out there and wipe the floor with them." Then I got out of Faith's way.

Faith showed none of Rowdy's extroverted energy. On the contrary, as she busied herself with last-minute details, her face wore an expression of cultivated composure. Tight-ening her grip on Rowdy's lead, she smiled at me, then at him. Snapping her fingers and gesturing to Rowdy to get his ninety pounds off the low table and onto the blacktop, she told him, "Okay! Let's go, Buster!"

Just as the Disobedience Champion of the Western World was about to do exactly as he was told, Finn Adams made his escape, and Timmy Oliver finally put down the glass bottle and got a grip on Z-Rocks. As he lifted her, her tail swept the glass bottle off the edge of the grooming table, where that stupid Timmy had left it, and sent it crashing down. I have never blamed Z-Rocks. Or Faith, ei-ther. She'd warned Timmy about that bottle, and until a

second earlier, it hadn't been sitting on the table where it
could tumble down and smash to pieces. And Rowdy?
When his feet left his grooming table, he had no idea that in
the second before he landed, the Pro-Vita No-Blo Sho-Kote
would get knocked to the blacktop.

I suppose that if the bottle had shattered into hundreds
of tiny fragments, Rowdy might have escaped unharmed.
Maybe, just maybe, fine shards of glass would not have pen-
etrated the thick leather of Rowdy's pads. As it was, the
power of Rowdy's descent drove his left front foot into a
thick chunk of jagged glass, and almost immediately, his
blood flowed into the foul-smelling brown pools of Timmy
Oliver's damned greasy snake oil.

To anyone who believes that show people treat dogs as
nothing but objects, let me point out that Faith Barlow, a
ferocious competitor, knelt in broken glass beside Rowdy,
and that in her determination to spare him further injury,
she shoved me aside, wrapped her arms under and around
him, and, murmuring gently, managed to lift him straight
up and back onto the grooming table.

Shaking their heads and calling out in sympathy, the exhibitors heading out of the tent took a safe route along the
opposite side, and people who weren't handling dogs scurried around cleaning up and offering help. Timmy Oliver,
who hadn't removed poor Z-Rocks from the glass-strewn
blacktop, made abortive efforts to speak, but the mere
sound of his voice inflamed Faith, who briefly raised her
head and snapped, "I am telling you *once*, Timmy Oliver.
You get yourself and your bitch out of here before you end
up hurting her, too. There's broken glass scattered all over.
Now, you pick her up and carry her, and don't put her down
until you're out of this tent, and the next time you lay eyes
on me, you turn in the opposite direction and run, because I
never intend to look at your ugly face again, and if I see it, I
intend to do something about it!"

I did not see Timmy leave. My eyes, my hands, too, were on Rowdy. A dog of another breed, maybe even another malamute, might have been whimpering and would have had a right to cry. A deep pad cut must be incredibly painful. This was not Rowdy's first. The last time Rowdy'd had one, I hadn't even realized that he was injured until we returned from a walk and he tracked blood all over the kitchen floor. He'd resisted my efforts to examine the wound. Now, unexpectedly hoisted back up on the grooming table, he wagged his tail and put his weight on all four feet. Oily brown splotches stained his forelegs. Blood seeped from his foot. Faith finally convinced him to raise it. With blood on her hands, she said, "It's way beyond me. We need—"

As if in reply, the little group of bystanders parted, and a tall, lean guy with green-blue eyes made his way calmly and purposefully toward Rowdy, who doubled the tempo of his tail wagging and sang a resounding peal of *woo-woo-woos*. Ignoring everyone but Rowdy, Steve Delaney moved immediately to him and, before examining the injury, wrapped gentle hands around Rowdy's head, brought his face so close to Rowdy's that the two rubbed foreheads, and spoke so softly that no one but Rowdy could hear him. Then Steve held out his hand, and Rowdy offered the injured paw.

Steve never hurries. I expected him to spend twenty minutes examining the wound before he uttered a word. I was wrong. After a glance, he lowered Rowdy's paw and, still addressing Rowdy, said, "Sorry, my friend. We'll patch you up, but for today, you're out of the running."

CHAPTER 25 🐾

M.D.s aren't the only M. Deities; they're not the only ones who think they're God. As Steve injected lidocaine and waited for the anesthetic to numb Rowdy's paw, he kept explaining why it was impossible instantly to undo the damage and rush Rowdy into the ring before it was too late. The jagged glass had sliced like the blade of a knife; the injury was far too deep for Nexaband, a sort of sterile Super Glue that's a miracle cure for superficial abrasions, but has to be used with care: Nexaband bonds skin to skin. Yes, imagine! My dogs and I are already as one. We don't really want to be Siamese triplets.

Watching Steve remove supplies from his emergency kit—it's actually a fishing bag from Sears—Rowdy's fan club had downcast eyes and sour mouths. Prominent among the sourpusses was Lieutenant Kevin Dennehy of the Cambridge police, my next-door neighbor, who'd arrived with Steve. Not being a malamute person, Steve, who has a shepherd and a pointer, had planned to come to the national only for Best of Breed. Bringing Kevin with him had been more my plan than Steve's, in fact, entirely mine, not that there's any enmity or ambiguity—Steve is my lover, Kevin's my friend—but if you kennel two alpha males in adjoining pens, you're bound to hear a few rumbles. Although you'd never guess it to look at Kevin, who has an Irish-cop face and the build of a mastiff, he feels intimidated in situations he can't control by the familiar expedient of putting everyone under arrest. In other words, he's more at home at a bank heist than at a social gathering where he doesn't speak the language and no one is likely to pull a gun. A dog show isn't exactly one of those Cambridge high-brow dinner parties where the host and hostess prepare dessert at the table by flambéing the peeled and diced remains of underpublished guests who didn't go to Harvard, but despite his affection for dogs, Kevin just isn't a real dog person, and if I hadn't intervened, he'd have stayed home. So in gratitude for the time he'd spent helping me run the dogs around Fresh Pond while listening to me blather about the national, I'd arranged to have him ride with Steve, who agreed to the plan only after, in a stroke of desperate mendacity, I promised him that Kevin would fix the hundreds of dollars' worth of Cambridge parking tickets that stood between Steve's and the renewal of its registration. But only, I cautioned, if Steve didn't mention anything whatsoever about the matter to Kevin, who, in his own way, was really very shy and would be deeply embarrassed by even a hint of thanks.

Anyway, I'd arranged to meet Steve and Kevin somewhere near the gate to the ring at a little after one o'clock, but before they'd entered the hall, Leah had flown out of the grooming tent, intercepted them, demanded Steve's keys, and dashed to his van for the kit that he always keeps there. And a good thing he does, too. The official show veterinarian for the national was on call, not at the site. Besides, I trust Steve. So, of course, does Rowdy.

When Steve had finished suturing and bandaging him, I eyed the morose faces around me. "Hey, would all of you please quit it? Rowdy thinks he's done something wrong, okay? In a few weeks or a month or whenever, he'll be fine. That's all that matters. So I would appreciate it if you would stop dumping your disappointment on my dog." Oddly enough, in speaking out for Rowdy, I experienced a feeling of liberation. It was as if the glass that sliced Rowdy's pad had cut through my knotted ties to him and severed the show dog from the dog.

Even the Buddha did not dwell in ceaseless epiphany. To my credit, everyone had to gang up to convince me to leave Rowdy in my hotel room, with Kimi crated next to him for company. He'd been stitched, bandaged, and started on antibiotics. Everyone would check on him. I'd been saving up for the national for the past year, hadn't I? There was no need for me to miss Best of Breed.

So only half an hour after my transcendent moment of spiritual reunion with Rowdy as just plain my dog, there I was in the aisle outside the ring with my mind's eye still on Rowdy and the other two on one of the top contenders, Williwaw's Kodiak Cub—Casey—and when I spotted Casey, I quit feeling guilty about leaving Rowdy back in my room. The solar system revolves around a single orb. Stuck outside the ring nursing his numb, gauze-wrapped paw, Rowdy would have hated playing distant planet to another dog's sun. Casey had tremendous carriage and a stand-off coat of dark, rich, gilded mahogany trimmed with pure Arctic white. To call that dog flashy isn't quite right. A flash is a swift burst. Casey was the sun at midday. In the aisle outside the ring, he worked a crowd that had stepped back in unconscious deference. Casey was a big dog, but not over-size, not like Ironman, and Casey's laughing, showoff eyes were dark and warm, not light and cold. I know a winner when I see one. I hoped that Mikki Muldoon did, too. Was

I unfaithful to Rowdy? Rowdy was out of the competition today. In his absence, I longed to see the best dog win.

The crowd in the hall now included spectators like Steve and Kevin who'd come only for Best of Breed. In addition to the people sitting and standing around the ring, throngs were shopping at the vendors' booths; placing final bids at Rescue's silent auction; taking chances on raffles for stuffed animals, kitchen implements, malamute coffee mugs, dog-portrait photography sessions; and accumulating brochures, sweatshirts, T-shirts, and tote bags promoting next year's national. Everyone who'd heard about Rowdy (and almost everyone had) asked how he was doing, offered sympathy, and condemned Timmy Oliver. "Leaving a glass bottle on a grooming table!" someone said. "Stupid, stupid! Just like him!" A few times I found myself in the peculiar position of defending Timmy: "He was careless, but he didn't do it on purpose," I heard myself say.

Kevin Dennehy interrupted my study of the catalog by is-suing a series of those hey-hey grunts that he uses to greet male police officers, and women he either considers to be good cops, or has a yen for, or both. As I've never remarked to Kevin, Rowdy, too, displays a single stereotyped greeting pattern for equal-status male dogs, respected females, and in-teresting bitches. Rowdy doesn't grunt and say *How ya do-ing?* of course. He lifts his leg on the nearest tree. Same difference.

With my view blocked by Kevin's bulk, I at first mistook the object of his hey-heying. I expected him to introduce me to a short, gray-haired woman who was shifting impa-tiently from foot to foot near the festooned gate to the ring and looking around with the vigilant expression I associate with presidential bodyguards. Nothing else about her sug-gested a career in law enforcement. She wore a black jersey dress that looked familiar and a print scarf that I definitely recognized from a recent visit to L.L. Bean, and over her shoulder was slung a black version of the handbag I'd ordered in tan from the same reliable source. The affinity I always feel for my sisters and brothers in Bean was quickly displaced by a sense of alarm. A cop at the gate had to mean danger. On a street in Providence at night, I'd have expected to be vigilant, especially if, like Elsa Van Dine, I'd been wearing a diamond ring. If, like James Hunnewell, I'd been elderly, ill, and unaccompanied by a big, strong dog, I'd have been wary about strolling across a dark parking lot. Last night, as I'd made my lone way through the deserted hotel, I'd been on my guard. I'd stepped briskly along, eager to return to the sleeping company of Leah and my big dogs. Moreover, I never wanted to look like an easy target, frail prey. Like Harriet Lunt. But *here?* In the exhibition hall? With hundreds of people? Hundreds of powerful dogs?

Within seconds, I felt foolish. I should have known better, I told myself. Unless the job stress of being a cop had prematurely aged the Bean woman by twenty or thirty years, she was far too old for active police work. But black jersey? At a hairy-beast specialty? That she was a dog person never crossed my mind.

As it turned out, the one to complete Kevin's ritual by grunting a return hey-hey was Detective Peter Kariotis, who appeared out of the crowd and ragged Kevin by asking whether he was one of the dog nuts. In reply, my friend Kevin gave a disloyal smirk.

After Kariotis moved away, I immediately took Kevin to task. I was citing Steve, Leah, and myself as typically sane and normal representatives of the dog fancy when some anti-dog agent of Fate sent our way who but Lisa Tainter, bedecked, as usual, in pelts, bones, teeth, and claws. Kevin was bug-eyed. And Lisa had no sooner departed than, practically right in front of him, Sherri Ann Printz directed the mist from her little blue spray bottle at Bear and then into her own wide-open mouth. Having dampened her dog and sated her thirst, she pulled out a metal comb and ran it though the dog's coat and then through her own hair.

Just then, Leah noticed a couple of seats being vacated in an ideal location near the judge's table and the gate. The long sides of the rectangular ring were lined with hotel-supplied chairs and spectators' aluminum lawn chairs three and four rows deep, but at this short end, the aisle between the single row of seats and the booths along the wall teemed with handlers and dogs awaiting further judging and with people visiting the rescue booth, which was directly behind the seats that had just opened up. Leah and Steve left to check on Rowdy. Naturally, as soon as Kevin had settled himself next to me, the handler in our direct line of vision, only a few feet away, stacked her male by unceremoniously thrusting her hand under the dog's tail (*Good God! Not THERE!*) and lifting and lowering him into position, thus leaving the dog and Kevin with identical expressions of consternation. The malamute, however, must've been used to the procedure. Kevin was not. In involuntary self-protection, his beefy hands flew to his lap, and when Mikki Muldoon came along and checked the same dog for the presence of both testicles, Kevin's face turned purple. He stood up and excused himself, thereby missing the opportunity to observe the same handler repeatedly transfer a single piece of liver back and forth between her own mouth and the dog's.

I took advantage of Kevin's hasty disappearance to find my place in the list of Best of Breed entries in the catalog— forty-five dogs, thirty-five bitches. The entire entry, of course, wasn't crammed in the ring all at once. With a big entry, you sometimes see the males judged first, then the females, but Mikki Muldoon was judging in catalog order, in other words, according to the arbitrarily assigned numbers printed in the catalog and on the handlers' arm bands that enable the spectators to tell who's who while supposedly keeping the dogs' identities secret from the judge.

Not to have recognized Ironman, Bear, Daphne, Casey, and the other top contenders, as well as their handlers, Mikki Muldoon would've had to stay away from shows and never open a dog magazine for a great many years, but she had a reputation for impartiality. Near the gate to her ring stood Duke Sylvia and Ironman. Standing up and turning around, I saw Al Holabach and Casey near the exit to the parking lot. Al's idea, I suppose, was to let Casey cool off in the fresh air. Far from availing himself of an offstage moment, the sable show-off was devoting himself to polishing his already gleaming act. In looking around for Casey, I'd intended to compare him with Ironman. Compare I did: Ironman had impelled me to look elsewhere; Casey, however, refused to let me look at another dog.

Thus Casey's charisma made me miss the start of the fracas. It broke out right near me when the Border collie of a hotel manager herded Freida Reilly up to Duke Sylvia and then backed off as Freida unsheepishly charged Duke with violating the absolute and universal show-site ban on bathing a dog in a hotel bathroom. By the time I looked, Freida was shaking a rolled-up show catalog at Duke so fiercely that the badge, the purple flowers, and the little gold team of sled dogs pinned to the bodice of her lavender dress jiggled wildly. "No bathing or grooming of dogs in hotel rooms!" she bellowed. "This is the first time you've encountered this rule? No, no, no! This is the ten thousandth time you have encountered this rule! Five other clubs are booked here this year, and *you* have taken it upon yourself to threaten their ability to use this site, and at *my* show!"

Karl Reilly forced his way to his mother's side, grabbed her elbow, and, in tones too soft for me to hear, somehow mediated the dispute. Within seconds, Duke Sylvia had pulled out his wallet and was offering the manager a fistful of cash. Everything about Duke's gesture, from the upraised hand to the angle of his head, was so familiar, so unmistakable, that I had to wonder whether the effect was deliberate: Except for the money in place of the usual liver, Duke looked exactly as if he were baiting a dog. Throughout the little episode, too, even when Freida was hollering, Duke made no observable effort to control Ironman, and no one—not Duke, not Freida, not Karl, not the hotel manager, certainly not Ironman himself—seemed to see the dog as any kind of threat. I believe that he was none.

I felt sorry for the hotel manager. Although human beings lack the Alaskan malamute's exquisite sensitivity to even the most subtle shifts in hierarchical position, the man must have known that in taking Duke's cash, he'd acknowledged Duke as master, himself as cur. Later, panicked in retrospect by his own apparent loss of sanity, he'd have waking dreams of Ironman, visions of the jaws and teeth of the huge dog with the cold eyes. Poor man! He couldn't have known that Duke Sylvia never, ever lost control—of a dog or of himself.

But that's just what Timmy Oliver had tried to provoke Duke to do. Timmy's object, as I see it now, was to cast a halo of guilt around Duke. At the time, I was mystified. As perhaps I haven't made plain, neither Freida's accusation nor Duke's immediate proffering of cash nor the admirable condition of Ironman's coat led me to suppose that Duke had precipitously decided to give Ironman a last-minute bath and foolishly left a hairy, stopped-up tub for a chambermaid who was bound to complain. The dripping-wet dog in the parking lot that morning had been Z-Rocks; the interior of Timmy's camper had been very dirty and equally dry; and Duke had regretted a favor. What escaped me at first was Timmy's cold-blooded calculation. Falsely charged with a demeaning offense, Duke could be counted on to take full responsibility for something he hadn't done. The pattern, I suspected, was lifelong. As a kid in school, Duke would've silently accepted punishment before he'd have stooped to pointing a finger at the real culprit. A whiny *I didn't do it—he did?* Not from Duke Sylvia. Not then. Not now.

Only when Timmy and Z-Rocks lined up directly in back of Duke and Ironman in the aisle behind my seat did I realize that Mikki Muldoon had also figured in Timmy's plan. Discovering that Z-Rocks came right after Ironman in the Best of Breed entries, Timmy had known (as I hadn't) that Mrs. Muldoon judged in catalog order and, consequently, that Z-Rocks and Ironman, Timmy and Duke, stood a good chance of ending up as they were now: with Z-Rocks and Timmy right behind Ironman and Duke.

Since the dogs were just behind my seat, I was perfectly positioned to overhear Duke's predictable demand to Timmy for reimbursement for the damage payment he'd just made to the hotel. I would've overheard it, too, except that a nearby seal-and-white male kept repeatedly bleating an oddly ovine version of *woo-woo-woo*. Besides, Duke spoke quietly. He talked so softly that he didn't even need a big stick. That little-boy Duke who'd've taken the punishment for another kid's crime? The same little-boy Duke who'd've stayed after for detention and then gone out and beaten the shit out of the poor sucker who hadn't known better, but learned fast.

Timmy's reply to Duke's request for reimbursement was loud and brash: "Your room, man, your problem." There was a pause; Duke must have spoken. Then Timmy said, "No can do! If I had a dime, I'd have my own room. Go ahead and try, but you can't get blood out of a stone." If Crystal was telling the truth, only yesterday she'd paid Timmy two hundred dollars. According to Betty, he'd probably already spent it. Or he was lying.

A hand descended on my left shoulder. Even before I saw whose it was, I flinched. Leaning across Z-Rocks, Timmy breathed into my ear. He reeked of aftershave and peppermint. "Too bad about that back there. These things'll happen. Nobody's fault."

As an alpha, I'm strictly self-made. I envied the naturals: Duke Sylvia, Rowdy, Kimi, Casey, Betty Burley. My mother, too. She'd have acted by instinct. But once I worked out what to do—not a damned thing—I knew I'd hit on the true alpha attitude. In my world, Timmy Oliver did not exist.

And that's *alpha*: Does God swat flies?

CHAPTER 26

Unable to outrun his predators, the horned lizard relies on crypticity and spines: He is hard to see and even harder to swallow. For canids, he reserves a unique defense: His lids swell, and out of minute openings in his eyes squirt fine streams of noxious and repellant blood. I am a sort of horny toad in reverse. Regardless of my surroundings, I stand out as a dog person, and far from sticking in the throats of dogs, I readily slip inside their skins. Confronted with a dog, I become all eyes. Into them shoots my life's blood. When it comes to dogs, I am utterly without protection.

So, when Timmy Oliver raced poor Z-Rocks up against Ironman, when he pulled that dirty old show-ring trick, I considered Z-Rocks ill-used, and I felt for Ironman.

Leah was vocal in her outrage: "Did you see that! Why doesn't the judge . . . ?"

"This is an insult to her," I said. "When she catches on, she won't put up with it."

"What does he think he's *doing?*" Leah demanded.

Timmy's immediate purpose, as I saw it, was to provoke Ironman. The sparring of terriers, of course, has no place in the malamute ring. If Timmy wanted an altercation between dogs, however, his effort was doomed. The peaceable and baffled-looking Z-Rocks was a wildly unsuitable choice for the role of aggressor, and even if she'd been a big, challenging male, the adroitly handled and self-contained Ironman would probably have continued to mind his own business.

I guessed what Timmy really wanted only when Mikki Muldoon intervened, as she'd been bound to do. To get Duke ordered out of the ring, Timmy had risked being booted out himself. An experienced judge, and no fool, Mrs. Muldoon called Duke, Timmy, and their dogs into the empty center of the ring, where she spoke briefly and softly while thrusting her finger first at one man, then at the other, and never at the dogs. The spectators, of course, eventually fell silent, but by the time everyone had quit talking and was straining to hear, Judge Mikki Muldoon had said whatever she'd had to say. The episode, by the way, does not appear on the commercial videotape of the national. I don't know whether the camera was stopped or whether the interchange was filmed and subsequently edited out. The outcome is, however, apparent on the tape: Instead of exercising her power to expel Duke, Timmy, Ironman, Z-Rocks, or all four from her little rectangular kingdom, Mikki Muldoon played absolute tyrant. For all I know, she may actually have threatened to behead someone: *Quick, stewards, the guillotine!* What I do know for certain is that Timmy Oliver immediately became a perfect little human good citizen in the realm of Mikki Muldoon, who subsequently ran her discards once around the ring before blocking them at the gate, where she said a polite thank you to everyone she was excusing, and thus let Timmy Oliver know that Z-Rocks had been cut.

As Leah and I watched Judge Mikki Muldoon, we began to make our own cuts from the list of murder suspects.

"Mikki Muldoon?" I said to Leah. "Hunnewell was a lot sicker than we knew. He told Karl Reilly so. Freida must've known, and she'd've told the judge who'd have to step in if anything happened. Even if Hunnewell had made it through yesterday morning, he'd probably have collapsed, and Mrs. Muldoon would be just where she is now. Why murder someone when all you have to do is wait? Besides, Mrs. Muldoon made a big point of keeping herself sequestered. Thursday night? When we had dinner? She could've had dinner in her room, okay? But what she did was to eat all alone out in public where everyone could see that she wasn't socializing. So it's hardly likely that a couple of hours later, at ten-thirty or whenever, when the Parade of Veterans and Titleholders was ending, she'd've been wandering around back here where—"

Leah interrupted me. "Wow! Isn't that . . . ?"

"Yeah, that's Casey," I said with approval.

Now that I saw my pick in the ring, I realized that what I'd mistaken for his performance had been a mere rehearsal. Clowning around for the passersby, Casey'd just been warming up his allure and stretching his magnetism, and in gazing at the eyes of his admirers, he'd been making a final check on the reflected glory of his own perfection. Now, muscles rippling and surging, he was the ultimate gorgeous show-off show dog . . . and I suddenly knew that Betty Burley had been right.

"Betty told me so," I said to Leah. "I just didn't listen."

"About . . . ?"

"Betty said it about . . . I can't remember. Maybe about Sherri Ann and Bear. No, about Daphne. Anyway, it doesn't matter, because what Betty said applies to everyone. We were talking about Best of Breed, and what Betty said was that because of Casey, nobody better count on anything. I

remember how she said it, because she never sounds that
way. 'Because Casey's here!' she said. And I didn't really get
it, because I'd just seen photos of him. Leah, the point is
that Casey is such serious competition that—"

"Under Hunnewell?" Leah asked.

"That's the point. You could go around mass-murdering
judges, and it still wouldn't guarantee anything, because as
long as Casey's here, Casey's going to do his damnedest to
win, and he's going to stand a good chance of succeeding,
because he is a hell of a dog and a hell of a showman. Furthermore, Sherri Ann Printz and Timmy Oliver and Duke
all knew that, because they've all seen Casey before, so they
knew exactly what they were up against, okay? So, Best of
Breed had nothing to do with the murder: With Casey in
the ring, you could murder half the judges on the AKC eligible list, and Casey could still win."

"So why does Timmy Oliver keep harping on . . . ?"

"Well, he's obviously right that Z-Rocks wasn't going to
go anywhere under Mrs. Muldoon—she got cut—but
whether Hunnewell . . . I don't know. Best of Opposite? An
Award of Merit? I suppose it's remotely possible, but she's
just not this caliber!" I pointed to the dogs in the ring.
Bitches, too, of course. "Just look! Look at what's in the
ring! She's—"

Almost against my will, my upraised hand and pointing
finger, however, drifted from my original target toward a remarkably accurate, yet smaller-than-lifesize and entirely flo-
ral representation that the florid-faced Harold Jenkinson,
Crystal's father, was positioning in the dead center of the
trophy table by the gate as solemnly and wordlessly as
though it were a spectacular bonus surprise Best of Breed
trophy offered as a tribute by the admiring wedding party.
And if the man's hands trembled? If his complexion turned
from red to white to scarlet? Why, what could be more natural in the father of the bride, the patriarch who had pre-

sumably just given away a gift more precious than an elaborate dog of flowers? And in another holy rite, too? The marriage of a daughter? A life event of sufficient moment in
itself to act as a sort of emotional surgery on the vocal cords,
thus transforming Harold Jenkinson into the grotesque and
pitiful human mockery of a poor debarked dog. His mouth
convulsively and silently opening and closing, Harold Jenkinson settled the elaborately florist-bred rose-red, white-
trimmed malamute on the trophy table. Driven, no doubt,
by the stress of a life transition and obviously frustrated in
his futile effort to speak his mind to Freida Reilly, he laid
hands upon the rope of flowers twined around the gate to
the ring and, with a swift yank, loosed the long garland,
sent the wooden trellis crashing to the floor. Then, like an
angry bride fleeing a ruined altar, he dragged away the train
of flowers, his own white veil.

Ignoring the departing Harold, Freida Reilly, arms
akimbo, scanned the crowd, spotted her objective, and
stormed toward Sherri Ann Printz. Jolting to a halt, Freida
turned so violently red that I feared for her physical and
mental health. "What have I ever done to you to deserve this
persecution?" she shrieked. "In the past year, I have spent
thousands of hours slaving over every last detail of this
show, and what do I get in return? A systematic campaign
organized by *you* to ruin *my* show! *You* got those entrees
switched last night! And *you* stage-managed this business
with the flowers! And *you*, Sherri Ann—"

"Holly," Leah whispered, "do you think that Sherri Ann
really . . . ?"

"Yes," I whispered back. "I think she really did. And I
think that Victor helped her, too."

"Mother," Karl interjected calmly. "Mother?" At his side
was a young woman I recognized as the doctor who had volunteered to examine Harriet Lunt last night. Together, Karl

and the doctor somehow convinced Freida to back off. They led her, red-faced and still sputtering, quietly away.

Sherri Ann, a caricature of generosity, exclaimed, "Poor Freida! Groundless suspicion of your old friends is a sure sign of mental illness, you know," she told us. "Watch and see. Cracking up under the strain." Shaking her head as if Freida were right in front of her injecting heroin: "Drugs! Poor Freida'll have to be all doped up."

Meanwhile, everyone nearby had pitched in to sweep up the scattered blossoms. As a couple of show-committee members raised the fallen bower, Leah commented, "Freida and that father of the bride are both pissed enough to—"

"Do not say *pissed!* This is a dog show, not a kennel. Besides, you go to Harvard."

"Everyone at school says everything. And," my cousin added in the clear, ringing tones of the expensively educated, "no one *there* goes around yelling about frozen semen and artificial vaginas."

"Leah!"

Finally lowering her voice, she said, "There's this sign you see all over the place in the Alps, warning you about not getting stuck up there, and anyway, what it says is, 'Distance distorts perspective,' and—"

"I thought distance lent enchantment to the view."

"They don't have to warn you about that part," Leah said. "Anyway, it's true, about distance and perspective, except that proximity does the same thing. And also, it works the other way: Perspective distorts distance." She paused. "And proximity." Taking a big breath, she continued, "So, subjectively speaking, the proximal-distal dimension is a function of perspective, and perspective—"

I'd had enough. "And the conclusion," I said, "is that since how close or how far away you are determines how something looks to you, and since your angle on it deter-

mines how near or far away it looks, there's never any way to
know where you really are."

"Oh, yes there is!" Leah crowed. "And that's the problem! Take the bride's father: The failure to avail himself of
the perspectives of others is responsible for his transparent
difficulty in obtaining a complex, multi-dimensional perspective on this wedding, which he is seeing from close up
and strictly from his own, inevitably distorted, point of
view."

"And how is he supposed to view it? It's his daughter's
wedding, and it must be costing—"

"Well, all that does is lock him more and more inextrica-
bly—"

"Leah, could I ask you something? Exactly what in God's
name does any of this have to do with anything else?"

With a triumphant smile she exclaimed, "There! You
see? You just showed it. Distance and perspective."

"I could strangle you," I hissed.

"Except," Leah impatiently continued, "that James Hunnewell was not strangled. He was bludgeoned. With a blunt
instrument." After waiting for me to follow, she explained.
"By someone stranded on the impasse of proximity and perspective who, instead of escaping via the route of multifac-
eted viewpoints—"

"Who *what?*"

"Meaning that killing Mr. Hunnewell represents the
murderer's maladaptive effort to rescue himself or herself
from an impasse or maybe an incipient avalanche that was
only apparent, but that *seemed* real because relative proximity distorts perspective, and perspective—"

"Meaning," I interrupted darkly, "that murder seemed
like a good idea at the time."

"Meaning," said Leah, "that the two people marooned on
self-created Alps were the bride's father and Freida Reilly,
who are obviously the two people who would've lost per-

spective. So either the bride's father was desperate not to have the wedding buried in an avalanche of malamutes, or else Freida was desperate not to have her show shoved off a cliff by—"

"Reasoning by analogy," I said. "Harvard should've warned you about that instead of teaching you to say 'pissed' all the time. Leah, the police could have declared this entire hotel a crime scene! They didn't. But they could have. No wedding, no national. Freida? Crystal's father? You've just picked the last two people on earth who'd ever have risked murder."

CHAPTER 27 🔍

"Myself," declared Pam Ritchie of Ch. Pawprintz Honor Guard, "I would say that he needs more neck and that he's oversized to the point of clumsiness, but far be it from me to stand between you and your own opinion, Tiny, and if you think he's nice, then nice he is." She paused. "In your opinion." She paused again. "Others, of course, may beg to differ. Mrs. Seeley, for instance, felt very strongly that . . ."

The better to tune in to today's episode of the Pam and Tiny spat, I'd turned my head away from the ring and was studying the object of dissent, Bear. The dog waited in the aisle behind my seat at the side of his breeder-owner-handler, Sherri Ann Printz. Mindful, no doubt, that Pam and Tiny wouldn't vote for her anyway, Sherri Ann boomed at her husband: "Victor! Victor, give me your opinion on something!" With her free hand, Sherri Ann directed Victor's attention and everyone else's to a gray dog who just happened to be of Pam Ritchie's breeding. "Now, Victor, if this wasn't a *malamute* national, wouldn't you swear to God that *that* was a *Siberian?*" Aiming her saccharine gaze straight at Pam, Sherri Ann drove the insult home: "And a fine-boned Siberian, at that!"

How Pam countered I cannot report. I was lost in thoughts of collaboration, collusion, and loyalty. Pam and Tiny: When James Hunnewell desecrated Short Seeley's sacred memory by spitting a stream of obscenities, Pam had zealously defended the matriarch of the breed: "If Short were alive today, you wouldn't dare say any of that!" Mrs. Seeley was dead, of course, but keeping her revered memory alive was a mission that Pam certainly pursued with religious fervor. Could Mrs. Lunt, too, have disparaged the matriarch of the breed in Pam's presence? And if zealotry had driven Pam to exact revenge on the defilers of her idol, Tiny would, as always, have been right at Pam's side. Sherri Ann and Victor Printz: Victor named her dogs. He mumbled to them. At ringside, he was Sherri Ann's ardent booster. When two Pawprintz dogs were due in the ring at the same time, he handled for her. He was her husband, her kennel help, her aide-de-camp. As I'd told Leah, I strongly suspected that Freida's accusations concerning Sherri Ann were correct and that Victor had served as his wife's co-conspirator. If Sherri Ann had committed murder, Victor, I knew, would have made himself as ruthlessly useful as ever.

Leah touched my arm. "Hey, that reminds me," my cousin said, pointing to the R.T.I. booth, where Steve Delaney was engaged in conversation with Finn Adams. "I forgot to tell you. Did you know that Steve and, uh, Finn already knew each other?"

"They don't. I mean, I've told Steve—"

"They met," Leah gleefully reported, "at a conference in Minneapolis. It was about—"

"A.I." Artificial insemination. "No, Leah, you're wrong. Because if they had, Steve would—"

"If they'd made the connection, which they didn't but—"

"But *you* . . . !"

"I did *not!* The un-romance of your romantic past is strictly your own—"

"Affair," I snapped. "And is not something I'm thrilled to have dragged into the present. Shit! It's not that Finn is . . . He's a decent person, and what happened was actually my mother's fault, not his, but I just—"

"He's a jerk," Leah said.

"Distance did lend enchantment," I conceded. "Well, if they haven't made the connection, they probably won't. Steve has a lousy memory for human names, and Finn doesn't know who Steve is, in relation to me, and even if he did . . ."

"Even if he did," Leah finished ruthlessly, "they're both more interested in dog sperm than they are in you."

I was pondering the ultimate consolation when, in the aisle behind us, new and acrimonious voices rose above Pam's and Sherri Ann's in what sounded like the escalation of their skirmish into a major battle in the sometimes un-civil civil war about malamute bloodlines that has raged for at least four decades. I want to report that in rising from my seat, I firmly intended to ally myself with neither militant faction, but to remain in the neutral role of a sort of United Malamutes observer.

As it turned out, however, Detective Kariotis had unin-tentionally changed the course of the battle by rallying the warriors on both sides in defense of one of their own, Betty Burley, against a common foe, namely, himself. The floor space near the gate, the trophy table, the breed club booth, and the rescue booth was so thick with handlers, dogs, and spectators that I had to keep tiptoeing around paws and begging everyone's pardon to get near the center of the es-calating fray. Sherri Ann Printz, backed by Victor Printz, Harriet Lunt, and an assemblage of other previously anti-Rescue and anti-Betty forces, was valiantly contesting De-tective Kariotis's attempt to seize the Comet lamp as a piece of evidence in the murder of James Hunnewell—indeed, as the murder weapon itself. Victor Printz, in a voice rusty with disuse, was demanding to see a search warrant. He was also threatening to file charges against Kariotis for harassing Betty Burley, who was calmly explaining what Alaskan Malamute Rescue was and how she would spend the money that the high bidder would pay for the lamp. With her neck stretched high and her small arms folded stalwartly across her chest, she insisted, "So, you see, since this beautiful and unique lamp is a very valuable collector's item, donated not to me personally, but to this organization and to the dogs that Mrs. Printz intends it to help, I am simply not entitled to—"

Sherri Ann broke in. Her voice trembled with sincerity. At first, I mistook it for the heartfelt candor of one who deeply and genuinely longs to win an election. "I'll have you know," she informed Kariotis, "that every person at this national is grateful to this woman for her efforts on behalf of this breed. Not one person here is going to stand by and watch you manhandle her and undermine her mission of helping these poor dogs. Practically every single one of us, myself included, has to live day in and day out with the terrible knowledge that in spite of our best efforts, our very own lines have ended up in the puppy mills! And I know! Because I myself was tricked into selling a beautiful Pawprintz puppy to one of those filthy, disgusting puppy-mill people! So if you think that we're going to just let *you* grab my beautiful lamp that I personally made and donated to help those poor dogs that go back to *my*—"

Kariotis valiantly interrupted Sherri Ann by saying something to Betty about probable cause. What he made of Sherri Ann's speech, I couldn't tell. The typical member of the general public doesn't even know what a puppy mill is, never mind what's wrong with puppy mills. Although the detective probably didn't understand that Sherri Ann had just made a brave and unusual public confession, he must have sensed the violence of her feelings. By comparison with Sherri Ann and the rumbling group around her, Betty must have seemed an easy target for an appeal to cool reason.

"I didn't hear him!" I complained to Harriet Lunt. "What did he say?"

"Piffle!" she replied. "He says they found dog hair in the wound or on the body or somewhere! And he thinks that because . . ." Switching abruptly from me to Kariotis, Harriet called out, "Young man! You there! You don't know much about dogs, do you? Well, don't you try and pull this probable cause nonsense here, because with all these dogs, you're going to find dog hair anywhere and everywhere! We eat it, we breathe it, it's all over us, it's all over everything we own, it's on our clothes, it's in our cars; if we don't find dog hair in our scrambled eggs and in our oatmeal, we know we've gotten someone else's breakfast; when we send letters, we mail dog hair with them, and when we go to the dentist, the hygienist finds it stuck between our teeth; and furthermore, whenever we cut ourselves, we wash and scrub and disinfect, and before we can slap on a bandage, there it is! If I'd actually been *killed* last night and you'd sliced into *me,* and guess what? Dog hair! In my guts, in my liver, in my arteries, everywhere! And not just little hairs, either, but whole big clumps! So if you found it in his blood and brains, young man, naturally you did! I happen to be an attorney, and what I'm telling you is, what you've got *isn't* probable cause. All you've got is *so what!*"

Mainly because Sherri Ann and Bear were wanted in the ring, the crowd dispersed with the dispute about the lamp still unresolved. What had happened was a phenomenon that Kariotis, I thought, should've seen coming: a large-scale version of a domestic disturbance in which the intervening cop becomes the target of the combatants.

"Leah," I asked, "where's Kevin?" Not that I expected or

wanted Kevin to aid his fellow officer. On the contrary, I was as eager as I'd been all along to shield Betty from inquiries about the lamp, as well as about Cubby's pedigree and the stud book page, items that must have been covered with her fingerprints. Since hearing Sherri Ann's speech, I was, if anything, more determined than ever to protect Betty. It sounded to me as if Sherri Ann had known all along about the Pawprintz dog that had ended up with Gladys Thacker. Surprised, shocked, and ashamed, Sherri Ann might have blamed Hunnewell, acted on her anger, and guaranteed his silence. But besides having apparently known all along, she'd just made a highly public admission. Sherri Ann could have reclaimed the Comet-reliquary lamp late on Thursday, at the end of the evening's events, when Betty had left it briefly unattended in her unlocked van. At the same time, she could have raided Betty's tote bag and grabbed the papers out of Cubby's file. But if she'd been choosing a weapon known to be in Betty's possession and pieces of paper bound to bear the clear prints of Betty's fingers, why the lamp she had made and handled herself? And why pages that bore her own name? Furthermore, if she'd gone out of her way to implicate Betty, why would she then have rallied her comrades in Betty's defense?

By comparison with a dog show, a session of the United States Congress is devoid of politics. In her pre-campaign campaigning for the breed club board, Sherri Ann might have been making a move that eluded me. Especially if she thought that Betty were supporting Freida, she might yet turn on Betty. Sherri Ann's loyalty to Betty was open to question. Mine was not. I needed to find out immediately everything Kevin knew about probable cause, warrants, and the seizure of evidence. Did the police have the right to demand Betty's fingerprints? "Leah," I repeated, "where is Kevin?"

"He got badgered into buying a lot of raffle tickets," she reported, "and he won something."

"And?"

"And it's supposed to be a secret."

"What's so secret about—"

"It's a present. For you. He wants to save it as a Christmas present for you. So he's stashing it in Steve's van. He'll be back. Hey, Holly, I wanted to ask you. Comet?"

"You read the centerfold. You looked at it last night."

"So a lot of people owned him."

"That happens with show dogs. You know that. A lot of top show dogs have a lot of owners all at once. Casey has four; Daphne has three. But, yeah, a lot of people owned Comet, and not at the same time."

"Remind me who."

"Well, J. J. Hadley. Hadley was his breeder. And then after Hadley died, his widow, Velma Hadley. Velma Hadley sold him to Elsa Van Dine. Then, uh, when Elsa Van Dine got engaged and was moving to England, she sold Comet to Timmy Oliver. Timmy got the money to buy Comet from James Hunnewell, and he and Timmy co-owned the dog. Except that Timmy was a co-owner in name only, I gather. It wasn't a normal co-ownership. Hunnewell didn't trust Timmy—"

"Surprise, surprise!" Leah was lighthearted. Even so, as I watched her face, I could see the thought cross her mind that my own prejudice against co-ownership could be overcome by just such a special arrangement.

"Yeah, who does trust Timmy? So Hunnewell had Harriet Lunt draw up some sort of elaborate contract that gave Hunnewell total control over everything. Hunnewell paid the whole purchase price and all the expenses, and Timmy paid nothing, so I guess it was fair. Duke told me that Timmy couldn't so much as say *boo* to Comet without Hunnewell's permission. And then, uh, I have the impression that it was just shortly before Comet died, Duke Sylvia managed to buy Timmy out. So then Duke co-owned him with Hunnewell. Duke had handled Comet all along, for everyone. Legalities aside, Comet was really always Duke's dog. I know it sounds like a lot of people, but it's not all that unusual, and—"

"So, Z-Rocks."

"She didn't make the cut," I said. "Weren't you looking?"

"What I want to know is, did Hunnewell really like Z-Rocks as much as Timmy Oliver says?"

"How would I know? Duke says . . . I'm not sure whether Duke said that he didn't or that he wouldn't have."

"And Duke would know."

"As well as anyone. He knew Hunnewell way back, and he'll tell you that you can't second-guess judges, but, yeah, of course. Duke is as good at knowing what judges like and don't like as anyone is. It's his business. So, uh, yes, I'd say Duke was probably right. Besides, Z-Rocks is linebred on Comet, and she's perfectly decent, but she's just not outstanding."

"So Timmy is lying."

"Let's say Timmy has a highly developed capacity for self-deception. Leah, if you don't mind, I want to go check on Rowdy. Do you have a room key? And if you see Kevin, tell him I want to talk to him, okay? Oh, and do me a favor, will you? If the opportunity arises, why don't you *not* introduce Kevin to Finn Adams."

"Oh, they've already met," Leah said blithely. "Kevin knows who he is. Kevin says you've told him all about Finn. Kevin recognized his name right away."

CHAPTER 28

My image of the Last Judgment owes more to the American Kennel Club than it does to Michelangelo. For one thing, although the Blessed and Damned huddle together, everyone is decently dressed, and the Judge, in particular, knows better than to turn up in a diaphanous loincloth that poses the insurmountable problem of finding a place to fasten the official badge where it won't look like a joke-shop fig leaf and inflict genital scarification if it comes unpinned.

And it's not just the Last Judgment. The Creation of Adam: Ever notice that sad little gap between God's hand and Adam's? Well, once you've torn your eyes away from the worrisome evidence that Adam suffers from the same demasculinization that afflicts those Florida alligators, you'll notice that although God and Adam are trying hard, God more than the languid Adam, I might add, divine and human don't quite touch. Feminist revisionist canine-cosmological Creation: The energetic Eve, her secondary sexual characteristics indicative of hormone levels in the high-normal range, eagerly reaches forth with not just one but two outstretched hands, as does the Great Breeder. In this version, the hands don't touch directly, either, but instead of an empty space? Pre-Creation Adam lazed around waving a finger in the air. Eve put down a deposit. He got a gap. She got a puppy. And at the Final Judgment? When the last trump sounds, Eve will not walk alone.

Nor, I hope, will I. But on the afternoon of the Eve of the Feast of Saint Hubert, after checking on the solidity of my links to the Infinite, I made a solitary sprint back to the exhibition hall and got there just as Mikki Muldoon was saying thanks, but no thanks, to a group of disappointed handlers whose dogs would doubtless make the Great Final Cut, but hadn't made this one.

Even celestial judgment is assumed to require paperwork, and in the earthly canine version thereof, the judge not only has to make entries in the official book, but, being human and fallible, has to keep taking and consulting notes, and, after temporarily excusing some dogs and then calling them back, is required to check handlers' armbands to make sure that those same dogs have, in fact, reentered the ring. Shuffling through the papers on her table, Judge Mikki Muldoon prepared for the culmination of her assignment. Lined up ready to go before her one last time were the dogs who'd made the final cut, among them some I recognized: Daphne, who'd both beaten and been beaten by Rowdy; a local dog called Burlimute's Malfeasance, sound and typey; a veteran whose name reliably aroused Pam Ritchie's fury, the unpronounceable Koonihc, "Chinook" spelled backward; Ironman, looking indefatigable; and pitted against Ironman, the blazing sable Casey, the dog of gold. Sherri Ann's Bear was not among the elect. Her Winners Bitch, however, could still get Best of Winners.

Near the gate, repeatedly pulling back the black jersey sleeve that covered her left wrist, was the L.L. Bean woman, as I thought of her, who had vanished for a while and now, like the dogs temporarily excused, had returned for the final judging of Best of Breed. Again, she checked her watch and then moved forward, almost as if she intended to speak to Mrs. Muldoon, who turned her head briefly in the woman's direction and, in apparent response to the woman's gaze, swiftly gathered her papers together, tapped them on the judge's table, consulted her own wristwatch, and gave a definitive, confident smile. A dog-show pro, I had no difficulty in reading the interchange. The Bean woman? In seeing her as a plainclothes cop, I hadn't been entirely wrong. Stationed by the ring, one eye on the judge, the other on the clock? She was, it seemed to me, a guard of sorts, and an official one, sent not by the police, but by the agency that rules the show ring. Monitoring the ring procedure, timing the speed of judging, the woman was—who else? at last!— a representative of the American Kennel Club, here to judge the judge. As she approached the gate, I noticed the inevitable layer of dog hair that now clung to the black jersey.

"Hey, you!" the L.L. Bean woman called to Mikki Muldoon. "You, there! Can I have a word with you?"

Wrong again. "Who *is* that?" I demanded of Lisa Tainter, who was squashed up next to me.

Lisa pulled back the fur hood of her authentic parka to reveal thin hair sweat-matted against her scalp. "She's, uh, Mr. Hunnewell's sister. It seems like she, uh, has some kind of thing about . . . It's weird. It's like she doesn't understand he's dead or something. Like she thinks his body is still him. She keeps talking about bringing him home and not wanting him to go home all alone. It's creepy, if you ask me."

What impelled me to speak the woman's name aloud was, I think, simple astonishment at the discrepancy between my image of Gladys Thacker as a sort of generic puppy-mill operator and the reality of a woman I'd mis-

taken, even momentarily, for an AKC rep. "Gladys
Thacker!"

In my surprise, I must have spoken more loudly than I'd
intended. Sherri Ann Printz, who stood nearby misting her
bitch's coat, jerked her head toward me just as the L.L. Bean
woman veered around and asked, "You talking to me?"

Up close, Gladys Thacker's hair revealed itself as a myriad of flattened curls, each crossed by the mark of a bobby
pin. Her foundation makeup was a few shades lighter than
her skin. Her eye shadow was green. She smelled musty, like
old powder.

Ignoring Sherri Ann, I cleared my throat and held out
my hand. "My name is Holly Winter. You're, uh, Mr. Hunnewell's sister?"

"If her name is Gladys Thacker, you bet your life she is!"
Her face cold with anger, Sherri Ann turned to the other
woman. "Is that who you are?" When Gladys Thacker gave
a baffled nod, Sherri Ann continued venomously, "Lady, do
you have any idea how much grief you have caused me? A
million times, I have cursed myself for shipping that lovely
puppy to you, all on your brother's say-so! What a fool I
was! I should never, ever have sold a dog to someone I'd only
talked to on the phone, never, ever! And you sounded so
sweet and all innocent, and all you wanted was a pet! And I
call you, I do my follow-up, and, yeah, yeah, he's just fine,
and then, *then*, a couple of years later, I discover . . . ! I get a
call from someone who says there's a malamute at a pet
shop, and she's managed to get a look at the papers, and
guess what? The sire is Pawprintz! He's *my* puppy that I
sent to you! You scum of the earth! How *dare* you show your
lying face—"

"You're one to talk!" Gladys retorted. "*You* breed dogs
yourself! You sell dogs! You sold one to me! I'm a breeder
same as yourself, and I don't see where you get off treating

me like dirt. I got as much right to be here as you! More! I'm here because of my brother! I'm not just here to make a stupid fuss about a bunch of dogs!"

I decided to intervene. "Sherri Ann, uh, wait, okay? This is really not the time to get into it. You're due in the ring."

One of the last people to feel any sympathy for a puppy-mill operator, I nonetheless pitied Gladys Thacker, whose eyes had filled with tears and whose powdered face showed not a trace of comprehension. I searched her features for any sign of resemblance to the late James Hunnewell and found only one: thin, lined lips. Gladys Thacker, however, was much younger than her brother had been. Perhaps his illness rather than genetics had made him look like a bloated horny toad.

Recalled to the present, Sherri Ann stashed her spray bottle and metal comb in one of the big pockets of her dress, a sort of housecoat of gray satin and turquoise chiffon. Like Gladys Thacker, she looked close to tears. "You just tell me one thing," she demanded of Thacker. "What do you think you're doing here? Here! This is the last place on earth anyone'd expect to find the likes of *you*, you—"

"Sherri Ann—" I started to say.

But Sherri Ann called loudly, "Victor! Victor, do you know who this person is? This is that puppy-mill woman who conned us out of that puppy! Harriet, this person is the one I was telling you about! She breeds malamutes for *pet shops!*"

"Sherri Ann, the ring!" Harriet warned, with more success than I'd had.

As Victor shepherded his wife down the aisle, Harriet Lunt, ignoring Gladys Thacker's existence, demanded of me: "Is that true?"

"More or less," I replied. "Mrs. Thacker is James Hunnewell's sister. Years ago, Sherri Ann shipped her a dog that's shown up in a whole lot of pet-shop pedigrees. But—"

"My brother," Gladys Thacker cut in, "is right now lying cold in some morgue, and I come all the way here to bring him home with me so's he can rest with his own, and do you people care? I think it's disgraceful, is what I think. My brother was murdered right here not two days ago, and here I am, come all this way so he don't have to go home all alone, with total strangers, and all you people can talk about is just dogs! It's the most disgusting thing I ever heard! It's sick! It's like you don't know the difference between a dog and a human! Sick!"

With a dignified snort that damned Gladys as an unworthy opponent, Harriet marched off.

"We do know the difference," I said quietly. "It's just—"

Someone tapped my shoulder. "Holly!" Leah said insistently.

I snapped at her. "What?"

"Holly, about Comet. Who exactly owned . . . ?"

"Leah, not now. I'm busy. If you want to know the exact details, the expert is Harriet Lunt. She's that gray-haired woman over there with her arm in a sling. She's the one who was attacked last night."

Without a word, Leah vanished.

"We're in the way," I told Gladys Thacker, who docilely followed me as I stepped back and thus ended up in front of the rescue booth. In the space behind the table, Betty continued to guard the lamp from Detective Kariotis. The policeman's face was damp with exhaustion.

"Betty," I said, "I want you to meet Gladys Thacker. Mrs. Thacker, Betty Burley. Mrs. Thacker has just had a run-in with Sherri Ann Printz. We have been having a discussion of the difference between dogs and human beings. Mrs. Thacker is James Hunnewell's sister. She's come here to, uh, accompany his body."

"To bring him home," Gladys amended. "When they let me," she added, glaring at Kariotis.

"Mrs. Thacker," he said, "we have explained to you that, given the circumstances—"

"Given that he was here with nothing but strangers," she replied acidly, "and given that his own sister's here to take him home—"

"I assure you that when the formalities have been completed, the body . . ." His voice trailed off.

Gladys was stolid. "Family is family."

"And?" I asked.

"The deceased," Kariotis reported somewhat grudgingly, "left clear instructions regarding his wishes in the event of his death. As I have informed you, ma'am, we are obliged to go by the document found in your brother's possession. It clearly stated that in the event of his death, his lawyer in Charleston was to be contacted. Acting on those wishes, we contacted the lawyer, who made the deceased's wishes plain. As I explained to you, they make no reference whatsoever to you and no provision for shipping the body to Missouri or anywhere else. You have no authority whatsoever to act in the matter."

"Your brother's your brother," Gladys stubbornly insisted, "your sister's your sister, blood's thicker than water, you can't change that, and I come all this way to get him, and I'm not leaving him here!"

Betty and I exchanged shrugs.

"Cremation?" Betty asked.

Kariotis nodded. "And the ashes sprinkled over one of these, uh, malamute shindigs."

"Some people find the idea of cremation very repugnant." Betty sounded sympathetic. "It really all depends on your point of view." She cleared her throat. "Speaking of which, Mrs. Thacker, why don't you step back here, behind the booth, and have a seat? Because you and I need to have a long talk about everything, including James, and the dog that you bought from Mrs. Printz, and her, uh, feelings on the subject." With one hand resting protectively on the remains of Northpole's Comet, Betty gestured invitingly to two folding metal chairs. When Gladys Thacker complied, Betty lifted the lamp, placed it on the floor, and seated herself in front of it. "Now," she said resting one elbow on a stack of handouts about the evils of puppy mills, "the first thing to get out in the open here is that what we are experiencing, you and I, is a radical clash of cultures, if you will, and I, for one, see this situation as a golden opportunity to hear your point of view. But let's start with your brother. You came here because you wanted to get his body, isn't that right? To bury at home? With, uh, other members of the family?"

Gladys Thacker nodded. "With his own people."

"Except that once you got here, you discovered that you have no authority in the matter, because . . . He didn't leave you anything, did he? You must have felt very hurt, that your own brother went and . . ."

"It's crazy," Gladys said. "Jim's brain wasn't right, you know. He'd go on and on about dogs. But it wasn't him—it was his brain! It wasn't getting oxygen. He hadn't been right for a long time. You could tell. I'd call him, and he'd go on and on about dogs—not that I've got anything against dogs; I've got dogs myself—and at Christmas, we'd keep sending him cards, and, one year, what he did was pack up all the ones we sent and mail 'em back to us! And the one time Jim come to visit, he had a fit, because he didn't like the looks of the dogs I had, and I told him, yeah, they're not your show dogs, but they're real good producers. And I shovel out once a week, and they get enough to eat, and all that. It's not like I run one of them puppy mills, you know. I'm licensed and everything. But he wouldn't listen."

"Yes, I can see that there was a, uh, a problem in communication," Betty said tactfully. "And part of the problem is that your brother really felt that, uh, people like everyone here were like family. That his friends in dogs had *become* his family."

"That's why I come here today!" Gladys Thacker cried. "I figured, well, Jim treated them like family, and so maybe they'll understand that his brain wasn't right, and they'll help me get him home! And then I get here, and I get sent back and forth, and then I wait and wait for that one over there"—Gladys pointed to Mikki Muldoon—"so's I can talk to her and ask her to help me get these people to let me bring him home!" She ended on a wail.

"Well, I for one," said Betty, "have no objection to your taking his body back to Missouri, and I will be glad to say so to anyone you like, for all the good it'll do. After all, James is beyond caring, and if it's so important to you, I don't see what the big objection is."

"The objection," Kariotis contributed, "is that the deceased explicitly—"

"Died," Betty finished tartly. "And isn't it illegal to go around distributing ashes here and there? It's not exactly sanitary, is it? Maybe there's a loophole for you there, Mrs. Thacker. We'll ask around. But while we're on the subject of disease"—Betty seized a puppy-mill handout—"I want to discuss with you one of the concerns that many of us have about, uh, commercial kennels. You see, in *our* experience, all too many of the dogs that . . ."

I had heard enough. Confronting Gladys Thacker, a genuine, if timid, representative of the archenemy, Betty was a woman without violence. She was, as always, determined to make her own views clear, but I trusted her to fulfill the promise to hear everything that Gladys Thacker had to say in reply. I was as convinced as ever—and as sure as I thought Betty was, too—that the Comet lamp had been the blunt instrument used to murder James Hunnewell. I was equally convinced that Betty hadn't been the one to use it.

CHAPTER 29

Judge Mikki Muldoon was going over a group twice the size of any she'd previously had in her ring, twenty dogs, perhaps more. The video shows me looming in back of Pam Ritchie, who'd stolen my seat, as I peer solemnly into the ring. Visible behind my shoulder is the aged-child face of Tim Oliver. Even more than usual, his half-baked countenance suggests a squishy interior of warm, damp feeling. In the camera's eye, Pam Ritchie bears a weird resemblance to a barefaced Alaskan malamute inexplicably sporting chestnut curls. Although I have forgotten Pam's words and cannot hear them on the video, I am sure that as she bobs her head and jabbers to Tiny, she emphasizes, as always, the incomparable excellence of the old Kotzebue dogs. In the ring, Duke takes Ironman out and back. Duke is a master of timing and gait. With another handler, the dog could be ponderous. With Duke, he is athletic. Ironman remains serious competition. My own group is smaller than Mikki Muldoon's. Pam Ritchie joins my discards. To the best of my knowledge, she has no connection with Harriet Lunt and hadn't even known Elsa Van Dine. Besides, far from killing off opposition, Pam cultivates it. James Hunnewell's blatant insult to Mrs. Seeley's memory, instead of driving a desperate Pam to murderous reprisal, merely secured her all the more as Mrs. Seeley's ardent defender. No, Pam hadn't murdered James Hunnewell.

My other discards: Mikki Muldoon, who'd have judged anyway; Freida and Crystal's father, Harold, who'd never have chanced the cancellation of their respective, if parallel, events; Sherri Ann Printz, who wouldn't have bashed in Hunnewell's skull to conceal a secret she'd just broadcast herself. I'd cut Betty Burley, too. One of the mean-spirited people Jeanine and Arlette had overheard on the night of the showcase was, I believed, the deep-voiced Harriet Lunt, who favored that horrid phrase: "trash dogs." If, as Jeanine feared, Betty had also heard the cruel words, and if the other speaker had been James Hunnewell, both he and Harriet Lunt would even now be pinned in a corner somewhere while Betty told the pair of them everything that was on her mind. Besides, I had a hunch that the people whose words had wounded Jeanine hadn't been Harriet Lunt and James Hunnewell, but Mrs. Lunt and Victor Printz. With some re-luctance, I also discarded the obviously guileless Gladys Thacker. She'd sat with that Comet-hair lamp right there on the floor at her feet and had shown no reaction to it at all.

Who made my final cut potential murderers? Duke Sylvia. Timmy Oliver. On Thursday, when I'd first encoun-tered the wedding party in the hotel lobby, both Timmy and Duke had just arrived. The night before, either might well have been in Providence murdering Elsa Van Dine. Any of the others could, of course, have made the three-hour round-trip between Danville and Providence on Wednesday night. But Timmy or Duke might naturally have been pass-ing through. Both men had known Elsa Van Dine. Duke had handled Comet for Elsa. She had sold Comet to Timmy. Either man could have stayed in touch with her and could have known exactly where she was staying in Providence. She had taken Timmy under her wing; she had a soft spot for him. Duke knew that the marquis had died and Elsa was now a dowager. When Elsa Van Dine had sold Comet, she'd offered the dog to Timmy Oliver. Why not to Duke? Had there been something about Duke she didn't like? James Hunnewell had liked him, I thought, or at least liked his handling. And Hunnewell had trusted Duke to co-own Comet. On the other hand, Harriet Lunt had drawn up a special co-ownership contract for Hunnewell because he hadn't trusted Timmy. Was it the only one she'd drawn up? Had Hunnewell *really* trusted Duke Sylvia?

Having lost my ringside seat to Pam Ritchie, I pressed up against the back of her chair, with Steve to my left, and beyond him, Finn Adams. The latter had abandoned his booth to pursue the kind of promising client he must have been trained to plague, a veterinarian interested in reproductive high tech who, as Finn was not saying outright, could fill his own coffers by funneling dog sperm into the freezers of R.T.I. Mashed against a chair back between Steve and Finn, Leah, in what I took to be a merciful effort to interrupt Finn's copious flow, kept bursting in with queries about the legal ownership of frozen sperm. Personal property, Finn kept telling her, an asset like any other, an asset separate from what Finn kept calling the "donor dog."

In the ring, Al Holabach took Casey out and back.

"That's my pick," I told Steve. "Beautifully presented, too. Damn! Kevin is missing everything!"

The last time I'd seen Kevin, he'd been lugging a malamute-size cedar-filled dog bed that he'd confessed was one of quite a few items he'd won by buying an evidently extraordinary number of raffle tickets. Now, finding him near one of the raffle tables, I said, "You know, you don't really have to buy all that many tickets. It's nice of you, but . . ."

Awkwardly fingering a set of kitchen utensils bearing hand-painted images of—what else?—Alaskan malamutes, Kevin said, "Hey, heart of gold." With a shucks-ma'am smile, he beat his chest with a wooden spatula.

I insisted that it would be a shame for him to miss the final moments of Best of Breed, but as he followed me, I made the mistake of using the word "climax." Kevin's face promptly turned an orangutan orange-red that clashed with his hair. For a second, I entertained the thought that in his profound ignorance of dog shows, Kevin might imagine that I was exhorting him to witness some sort of ritual mating of the Best of Breed and Best of Opposite Sex in an orgasmic grand finale that I could hardly wait to applaud myself. Although I dismissed the possibility—Kevin really did know better—it occurred to me that from Rowdy's point of view, such conventional trophies as punch bowls, trays, commemorative plates, tea sets, and engraved platters were of no interest whatsoever, whereas a bitch in season would be a prize *really* worth taking home.

The action in the ring did not, of course, consist of ritual mating. Rather, the dogs—an elite group of polished show dogs, not a slinker among them—were arrayed, one in front, one in back, in a zigzagged double row across the narrow end of the ring, near Leah, Steve, and Finn. Facing the dogs, studying Ironman, narrowing her eyes to peer at Casey, taking long, slow strides, tilting her head as if to get a fresh look at Daphne, Mikki Muldoon wore the grave expression universally seen on the faces of judges who, as the entire gallery realizes, have finished picking their winners, but aren't quite ready to bring the drama to its conclusion by ending the delicious tension of uncertainty. What makes the ploy work is that there's nothing sham about the absolute power of a judge: At the last second, Mikki Muldoon really could change her mind.

As we worked our way toward Steve and Leah, Kevin caught sight of Finn Adams. Respectful of the hush that had fallen, he poked one of the wooden kitchen implements toward Finn and Steve and whispered salaciously in my ear, "The two of them caught on yet?"

"There's nothing to catch on to," I whispered indignantly, "and, no, they haven't, and please do not—"

With as much dignity as can be summoned by a gorilla-built cop in mufti carrying a set of malamute-embellished spatulas, spoons, and pancake-turners, Kevin gave his head a perish-the-thought shake that drove from my consciousness the lesson that most women learn by the age of eighteen, if not earlier, and that I'd certainly gleaned from my experience with Finn Adams: Never, ever under any circumstances trust a man who, by word or deed, says, "Trust me!"

As it turned out, however, in Kevin Dennehy's ears, the most alarming words in the male vocabulary were not "Trust me!" The particular expression that drove Kevin wild is, in fact, still uncertain. It could have been any one of a number of those being innocently pitched sotto voce by Finn Adams to Steve Delaney when Kevin, considerately positioning himself where he wouldn't block someone's view, found a place between two other tall men and thus accidentally overheard my ex-lover utter to my present lover such phrases as "always ready" and "last forever," and refer in passing to proven studs and ripe bitches . . . meaning dogs, of course, and not me.

Alas, as Kevin—in his role of defender of fair maidens—drove the handle of a wooden spoon into Finn's solar plexus, Leah compounded my humiliation. Nimbly stepping between Pam and Tiny, bending far into the ring, Leah called out to Duke Sylvia, demanding to know who had owned

Comet when his sperm had been collected for freezing. For-
tunately, since my father is possibly the most embarrassing
person I have ever met, I grew up being disgraced at dog
shows. Leah's inappropriate behavior, which could have
been taken as a deliberate attempt to distract Ironman,
didn't faze the big steely dog at all. Maybe Ironman's sire
was as mortifying as mine. Duke, however, jerked his own
head around. Despite his obvious and justified anger, he
wisely shut Leah up by loudly answering her question:
"James Hunnewell," he said. "And Timmy Oliver."

"And who owned the *sperm?*" Leah demanded in that
ringing voice of hers.

"James Hunnewell," Duke told her. "No one else."

An unusual arrangement. As unusual as the co-ownership agreement itself.

On the videotape, you can't hear Duke. He just turns his
head for a few seconds. You can see Timmy Oliver's pasty
face. Timmy's closer to the gate than I am. He takes a step
toward it. In the background, Steve flourishes the wooden
spoon that he's managed to wrest from Kevin's enraged
grip. Then the camera zooms in on Casey, who, with consummate self-possession, goes to the far end of the ring and
comes back one last time. You can see on tape that the beautiful sable dog expects to win. As the camera zooms back
and pans the dogs, you can see that Ironman does, too. So
does Daphne, who is used to beating the boys and considers
her sex no disadvantage at all. Mikki Muldoon makes a
show of considering Daphne. Perhaps this is one judge who
notices, as I do and often have, that Daphne's ear set is
slightly incorrect. No one, however, has informed Daphne
of her minor faults. Here in the ring at the national, Daphne
is at her showiest, and she's very showy, indeed. Duke draws
joy from the solemn Ironman. Way in the background, if
you look closely, you can follow Leah as she snags first Kevin
Dennehy, then Detective Kariotis, and succeeds, she tells

me, only in embarrassing both of them by talking about bitches and sperm. The flower-print dress probably didn't help. As the videotape does not reveal, Leah gave up on the police to seek out Betty Burley, who would grasp an abbreviated explanation and, having understood, would act.

I apologize for my inability to give a firsthand account of Betty's subsequent movements. My excuse is that at the very moment Betty must have pointed her finger in public accusation, Judge Mikki Muldoon took a flamboyant giant step backward toward the center of the ring and swept her arm up to send the entire group of malamutes around the ring. As those beautiful dogs melded together in a circle of gray and silver, black, white, and gold, Betty Burley's voice rang out above the cheers. "Timmy Oliver, you slimy little hypocrite!" Betty cried. "You smarmy, greedy, *evil* little lump of blubber, *you* did it!"

In front of me, Pam said loudly, "High time, too! Selling puppies on show grounds! The nerve! I don't know what made him think he could get away with it! Good for Betty! At least someone here's got the guts to let that jerk have it!"

As Timmy edged toward the gate, passed under the denuded trellis, and actually entered the ring, Freida Reilly joined Betty in pursuit of him. Freida's accusation, I am told, was rather different from Betty's. Despite what I assumed was a tranquilizer from the doctor's emergency bag, Freida's rage was similarly intense. "Timmy Oliver, you stinking little rat!" she bawled. "So it was *you*! Of all the damned unmitigated gall! Trying to ruin *my* national specialty! And leaving *me* stuck with the job of moving the body of *my* judge off the grounds of *my* show!"

Timmy Oliver's actions in the ring are shown on tape. You can see that he bends over the judge's chair and sends his hand darting after Mikki Muldoon's handbag. And when Timmy stands upright, you can see the gleam of what Kevin Dennehy informs me was a Colt Mustang Pocket

Lite, a .380 caliber autoloader that Mikki Muldoon had no
business carrying in the Commonwealth of Massachusetts
and no business leaving around anywhere at all. The presence of a handgun in the ring, though, certainly made
Kevin feel right at home, and Detective Kariotis must've
shared Kevin's sense of *finally* belonging in the show world,
because the two cops pressed forward confidently to the gate
and were just entering the ring when Mikki Muldoon, determined not to cede her kingdom to an upstart, shot out
her arm, pointed her finger straight at Casey, and picked her
Best of Breed.

As Timmy Oliver marched toward Casey, the nasty little
Colt in his hand abruptly silenced the screams and "bravos."
Reaching Casey and taking the dog's lead, Timmy told
Casey's owner-handler, "Sorry about this, Al, but I got no
choice." You can hear Timmy on the videotape. I've listened
again and again. And you can see him press that gun right
up against Casey's gorgeous head and dig it into that gold-
mahogany coat until the trusting dog must have felt the
cold of metal on his warm skin. You can't hear what Al says
to Casey, but you can tell that he says something, and you
can see the color drain from Al's face as Timmy leads Casey
away.

With no word or signal, the people outside the ring
moved back to clear a broad path to the open door. Casey
parted crowds all the time; he was used to it. And Mikki
Muldoon was equally accustomed to exerting authority. Furious at having her judging interrupted and her Best of
Breed stolen from her ring, she was on Timmy's tail when
through the wide door to the parking lot burst the four big
heads of Poker Flat's Risky Business, Poker Flat's Hell's
Belle, Ch. Poker Flat's Snow Flurrie, C.D., and Ch. Poker
Flat's Paper Chase, C.D. The four big bodies of this team
entry of Battering Rams followed. Confronted with Casey,
they came to a halt and spread themselves across Timmy's

escape route. The five big, beautiful dogs—the team and Casey—knew nothing of Colt Mustangs. Poke-Poke-Pokers though they were, the Battering Rams, show dogs all, knew that the one place they were never to stick their noses was straight into the face of another dog.

As Timmy Oliver and Casey paused before the canine blockade, Judge Mikki Muldoon stepped swiftly to our breed club's preview display of auction items, seized that historic sign that had hung over one of Eva B. Seeley's own kennels, raised it swiftly in the air, and smashed it down on top of Timmy's head.

"Not loaded!" she announced authoritatively. And after getting a grip on Casey's lead, she took her Best of Breed back into what was unquestionably her ring.

CHAPTER 30 🔍

How Timmy Oliver's mug shots turned out, I don't know. They couldn't have been flattering. By the time they were taken, I guess he'd had the splinters removed from his scalp, but his hair was probably messy. Although he'd no doubt had a Teflon-coated comb or a finishing brush in one of his pockets when he was arrested, the police must have confiscated all his possessions.

I suspect, though, that Timmy didn't look too much worse than the rest of us. Even the official show photographer who took the picture of Casey's win failed to make the occasion appear normal. On the far right, Mary Jane Holabach, Casey's co-owner and human Mom, is as pretty and well groomed as ever, and she's managing to smile, but the malamutes in the framed print she displays seem to be standing on their heads: She is holding the picture upside down. Freida Reilly's show chair badge, purple flowers, and gold dog team are askew; her closed eyes suggest that instead of presenting the malamute quilt she's holding to Casey and the Holabachs, she'll wrap it around herself, drop to the floor, and take a long, drugged nap. Although Mikki Muldoon hides her feet behind several pots of flowers and a collection of trophies, you can see that her slip is showing. Furthermore, her once-carrot hair is a little disheveled. Her bearing, however, is flawless, and as usual, she is fastening the ornate purple-and-gold Best of Breed rosette to her own midriff. Al's color has not returned. He looms over Casey, as if fearful that the dog might again be taken hostage. Casey's ears are, as always, alert. His broad winner's smile reveals a red tongue. Every single hair is exactly where it should be. Indeed, everything in Casey's world is just as it should be: He is used to creating a stir. This time, he thinks, he has simply outdone himself.

Or so it seems in the photo. I wasn't there when it was taken. I left even before Judge Muldoon picked Daphne for Best of Opposite—Best of Opposite Sex to Best of Breed. (Since Best of Breed was a male—Casey—Best of Opposite was a female—Daphne.) The female of Sherri Ann's who'd gone Winners Bitch defeated the Winners Dog for Best of Winners. (Still not fluent? *Winners Bitch:* the winner of the championship points in the competition among the bitches who weren't yet champions. *Winners Dog:* same thing, but for males. *Best of Winners:* She's defeated the other girls who were vying for points. He's defeated the other boys. Both have won championship points. Now we have the battle of the sexes: Winners Bitch versus Winners Dog. The victor? Best of Winners. Okay, so what about Casey and Daphne? Best of Breed and Best of Opposite? Why didn't *they* win the points? Because they weren't competing for points, that's why; they were *already* champions and thus entered only in the Best of Breed competition. Ah, but could the Winners Dog or Winners Bitch also have gone Best of Breed? Yes, thereby automatically becoming Best of Winners. Confusing? Consider tennis. Fifteen, thirty, forty, game? And "love"? What on earth does "love" have to do with tennis? Love is no racket! On the contrary, love is a warm you-know-what.) Anyway, I wish I'd been there. I hated to miss the judging of the Stud Dog, Brood Bitch, Brace, and Team classes, too, but Betty needed help with Timmy Oliver's dogs. Seconds after Timmy was arrested for the murder of James Hunnewell, Betty, of course, started to worry about his dogs. Timmy, she declared, belonged in a jail cell. But what had the innocent Z-Rocks and the silver male and, especially, the two puppies done to deserve incarceration? Her concern was well founded. Detective Kariotis did, in fact, try to claim the dogs as evidence. But Betty held out, and before long, she and Kariotis worked out a trade. Betty would have had to surrender the lamp, anyway; in bartering the murder weapon for the dogs, she got a good deal.

As we started across the parking lot toward Timmy's camper, I said, "You know, Betty, I feel so stupid. Duke told me so much that I can't help thinking that he knew all along. I mean, he's the one who told me about Timmy Oliver and James Hunnewell's co-ownership agreement: that Timmy co-owned Comet in name only and that Hunnewell controlled absolutely everything. Harriet Lunt drew up the agreement. Duke knew that. He's the one who told me. He also said that when Comet was alive, when Timmy and Hunnewell co-owned him, Timmy had a bitch he wanted to breed, and he wanted to use Comet, but Hunnewell absolutely refused. Timmy didn't even have stud rights on his own dog. And out in the grooming tent, Duke *said* that Comet's semen had been frozen. And never used. I just didn't finish putting it all together: that if Hunnewell controlled everything else about Comet, including using him at stud when he was alive, he'd hardly have let Timmy own half those straws of sperm."

"Usually," Betty said, "if you co-own a dog and you have his semen frozen, then half the straws are in one person's name, and the other half are in the other person's. Isn't that how it works?"

"*Unless* you make some other arrangement. Hunnewell didn't trust Timmy. Who does? If Hunnewell hired Harriet Lunt to cut Timmy out when he bought Comet, he probably got her to make sure that the contract about the frozen semen was the way he wanted it, too."

Betty sighed. "So that's why Timmy's been making a fuss about Z-Rocks. He knew as well as I did that that bitch didn't have a chance against this kind of competition. He was just setting the stage for what would happen after she produced a litter out of Comet. I can just hear him: 'See? Didn't I tell you James loved her? Didn't I tell you she was just his type?' "

"So everyone would believe that Hunnewell had let him use Comet," I said. "Comet's sperm. I wonder if Timmy ever even asked Hunnewell. Or if he just assumed that Hunnewell would refuse."

"And went ahead and killed him. And forged his signature. And left that damned lamp under *my* van!"

As we later found out, Timmy did forge Hunnewell's signature. In his camper, the police found transfer-of-ownership forms for Comet's sperm, papers signed with James Hunnewell's name, but not in James Hunnewell's own hand.

When we reached Timmy's camper, Detective Kariotis wasn't there. Crime-scene tape was strung all over, and two police officers guarding the camper didn't want to let us in, so we hung around waiting. The camper, of course, was crammed with real evidence. For example, the open carton of cigarettes I'd noticed that morning, the carton that Timmy must have lifted from Hunnewell's hotel room. Timmy didn't smoke, but Hunnewell sure did, and a heavy smoker like that doesn't arrive at an unfamiliar destination without the means to satisfy his addiction. As I now piece things together, Timmy must have gone to Hunnewell's room at about ten o'clock on Thursday night. At nine-fifteen or nine-thirty, when I was helping Hunnewell with the ice machine, he offered me a cigarette, and he didn't ask anything about the location of a cigarette machine. Furthermore, Freida Reilly says that after Hunnewell's spat with Pam, at quarter of ten or so, when Freida took him back to his room, he didn't ask her, either. So Timmy must have shown up there at around ten o'clock and left, probably soon thereafter, with Hunnewell's entire cigarette stash. Exactly how he filched it, I don't know, but I understand why he didn't want to commit the murder inside the hotel. There, a guest passing by in the hall could have heard a shout, or he might easily have been observed leaving the rooms with traces of the deed visible in the expression of his face, if not actually on his hands and his clothes.

By ten-thirty Timmy was back at the exhibition hall. Sherri Ann remembers seeing him. The Parade of Veterans and Titleholders was still going on. Sherri Ann Printz is sure that Timmy was there when she showed some people the lamp and explained what it was and how she'd made it. Sherri Ann *is* running for the board of our national breed club, by the way. For office: president.

Anyway, at about the same time that Sherri Ann was politicking with the lamp, Betty Burley remembered that she'd left the lamp and the other valuable auction items, as well as her tote bag, at the booth, and she went out and drove her van to the unloading area just outside the hall. On Betty's first trip from the booth to the van, she had her tote bag over her shoulder, and she carried the lamp in her arms. It must have been while she was returning for the framed wolf prints and the other stuff that Timmy slipped into her van, grabbed the lamp, and raided her tote bag. The theft of the lamp, I am sure, was a last-minute inspiration. His camper overflowed with the detritus of travel—maps, fast-food wrappers, old coffee cups—but the amount of loose change was extraordinary, and there were all those socks, too. The Comet lamp, I think, was a substitute for the coin-packed sock he'd intended to use as his blunt instrument. In contrast to a cosh, the lamp was a meaningful weapon: a sacred relic of Northpole's Comet. And Timmy must have known that if he could get the lamp back in Betty Burley's possession, she'd do her best to see that it got auctioned off to raise money for her rescue dogs. Then, after the auction, the murder weapon would vanish forever into the living room or den of the highest bidder.

Exactly where Timmy waited to intercept Hunnewell is unclear. Running out of cigarettes, Hunnewell would certainly venture from his room. Timmy must have hung around watching for him, perhaps in a linen closet or in the stairwell. In any case, he must have approached Hunnewell and told him that he had cigarettes in his camper. Hunnewell was so out of touch with the times that he hadn't even known how to open a pop-top can. I guess that whoever did his shopping for him bought nothing but bottles. Anyway, I don't think he'd have been surprised to hear that Timmy smoked. If Hunnewell ever entered the camper, he didn't leave any prints that the police found. Probably Timmy told him to wait outside. Then he returned not with cigarettes, but with imminent death.

Although I don't know exactly where Timmy murdered Hunnewell, I know that very early on Friday morning, Freida found the corpse under a camper. Timmy's must have been in the line of campers when Leah and I played at choosing one for ourselves. Freida continues to insist that the body was either on show grounds or close enough to show grounds to threaten the cancellation of the national, and she is as furious as ever at Timmy Oliver for depositing it there and leaving her stuck with the obligation to move it to the little shed where Finn Adams subsequently came across it. According to someone who told someone who told me, Freida swears that Mikki Muldoon had no idea how sick Hunnewell really was. Consequently, according to rumor, Freida just took it for granted that Mikki Muldoon had murdered him to get the judging assignment. Freida apparently also confides to people that she'd eventually have shared her suspicion with the police. Further, she assures everyone that she'd have waited until Mikki had completed the judging. Freida is running for the board, too. For president.

But back to that Saturday afternoon. By the time Detective Kariotis showed up, the crime-scene experts were more than ready to get rid of the dogs, who, as it turned out, were destroying evidence. Toss anything into a dog crate occupied by a puppy, and what can you expect? Actually, Timmy Oliver expected the destruction to be greater than it really was. As we found out afterward, in addition to shredded newspaper and miscellaneous filth, the puppies' crates contained bits of the paper towel that Timmy had used to clean off the base of the bloodied lamp, as well as numerous scraps from the files that Timmy had stolen from Betty's tote bag. I suspect that Cubby's pedigree and the page from the stud book were touches that Timmy added well after he'd murdered Hunnewell. Betty's tote bag is always so crammed with paper that she still isn't sure what he stole, but the information on several other dogs is also missing, and I think that he looked through all of it, selected those particular pages, and planted them on Hunnewell's body. He really was furious at Betty for refusing to tell the hotel that his camper belonged to her.

Betty's initial hypothesis that Sherri Ann and Victor Printz had murdered Hunnewell was not, I think, part of Timmy's scheme. Betty now confesses that mistrustful of Sherri Ann's sudden generosity to Alaskan Malamute Rescue, she decided that Sherri Ann had donated the lamp for her own use as a murder weapon. Betty, of course, knew that

Sherri Ann was furious that one of her Pawprintz puppies had ended up in Gladys Thacker's puppy mill. Sherri Ann now claims that she, Sherri Ann, has only herself to blame for shipping a pup to someone she didn't know. Betty still says that Sherri Ann has always held James Hunnewell responsible for referring his sister to her to begin with; and that if Sherri Ann was murderously angry, she had every right to be. Victor, Betty maintains, was the one who left the material about Cubby, which Betty viewed as equivalent to a soldier's playing card. Until Betty advanced the idea, I hadn't even known that soldiers left playing cards on bodies.

Anyway, when the police finally let us have Timmy's dogs, the crime-scene experts inadvertently turned over to us the single most damning piece of evidence against Timmy Oliver. And I was the one who found it! *Found*, however, is not quite the right word . . . I picked it up in a plastic bag. Not an evidence bag, either. Not an *official* one, anyway. So here's how I brilliantly, resourcefully, and single-handedly obtained absolute, undeniable proof of Timmy Oliver's guilt: I walked a puppy. I cleaned up after him. Truly, that's all there was to it. Well, a little more. Instead of letting Betty and me go into the camper to get Timmy's dogs, the police protected what they supposed to be the crucial evidence by bringing the dogs out one at a time. By then, Steve and Kevin had arrived. Steve's van held the two crates he uses for his own dogs. The plan was that he'd take Timmy's two adult dogs, Z-Rocks and the silver male, back to Cambridge, where he'd board them at his clinic. That part went fine: A couple of crime-scene guys led out the dogs and turned them over to Steve and Kevin. Then a woman brought out both his sturdy puppies. Betty took the lead of the female Timmy had tried to sell to Crystal. I took the male's. And we started toward Betty's van. A dog show was no place for puppies this age, Betty had insisted. Neither was a veterinary clinic. Consequently, she was going to drive the two puppies home and leave them with her sister, who was taking care of Betty's own dogs. As we crossed the asphalt, both sizable puppies kept biting their leashes and bouncing around. My puppy, however—the male—started to sniff and circle, and as he settled into a squat, I reached into my pocket and extracted one of the plastic bags that I, Ms. Responsible Dog Owner, am never without. And when the pup had finished, I, Ms. Responsible Dog Owner, reached down to clean up after him. What I found, in the middle of the expected, was a tiny plastic packet carefully sealed with tape. For obvious reasons, I did not unwrap the little package with my bare hands, but immediately turned my evidence bag over to the police. This indelicate vignette has a moral: *Always, always clean up after your dog!* For in doing so, you, too, may one day find a diamond ring. You, however, may get to keep *yours*. I had no right to the one I found. My diamond ring had belonged to Elsa Van Dine.

At the banquet that night, everyone kept asking me about the diamond ring. At first, I avoided the topic. My mother would not have considered the episode a suitable subject for the dinner table. After drinking more than I probably should have, however, I revealed the whole story. My mother, after all, had belonged in a federal penitentiary. Who was she to make me feel guilty about a trivial impropriety? Although Betty, I am certain, was as astounded at the discovery as I was, she maintained that she wasn't in the least surprised. "Timmy always did go whining to Elsa about everything," she reported. "I have no doubt that he tried to buy that semen and that when James refused, he went sniveling to Elsa."

After dessert, I carried my coffee cup and bravely took the vacant seat next to Harriet Lunt. Keeping my voice low, I related the full history of Jeanine and Cubby, including the ugly words spoken in the darkness of the parking lot. And Jeanine's tears. Harriet did not produce the confession

I'd hoped to provoke. Her only reaction was to Cubby's ancestry. "*Comet!*" she cried. "Good God! Duke Sylvia or no Duke Sylvia, that was obviously a *trash dog.*"

At the post-banquet auction, Rescue's special items brought in a satisfying amount of money, mainly because Freida and Sherri Ann got into a vicious bidding war over the print of the wolf disemboweling the elk. Both responded to the symbolism, I suppose. Each, I'm sure, saw herself in the victorious wolf, her rival in the vanquished elk. Although I made a few bids, the only item I'd coveted, the sign from the Chinook Kennels, had been reduced to fragments of old board that were now in police custody. Pam Ritchie will never forgive Mikki Muldoon for smashing that relic. A tiff broke out. Mikki Muldoon swore that she'd grabbed the first weapon that came to hand. According to Pam, Mikki deliberately destroyed a significant piece of the breed's history while delivering a posthumous insult to Eva B. Seeley. Then Freida charged Pam with trying to spoil the occasion by picking a public quarrel with the judge. Betty and Sherri Ann, in contrast, moved to a distant, deserted table at the back of the banquet room and commiserated about what both considered the theft of the Comet lamp. As to the mix-ups of the entrees, the cake, and the flowers, Sherri Ann managed to convince Betty of her innocence. I, however, continue to believe that Sherri Ann was guilty. She will not, of course, get my vote.

After the auction, Duke Sylvia and I left the banquet hall together to get a drink. We sat on tall stools at the outrigger bar. I told him that Leah was convinced that he, Duke, would have been Timmy's next victim. Duke just laughed. Although he must have realized that Timmy was trying to cast a halo of guilt around him, he didn't say so. It's possible, I suppose, that Timmy really would have tried to murder Duke. If so, Timmy'd have failed. He'd never have gotten the best of Duke. I did not confront Duke with my

firm belief that he'd known all along who murdered James
Hunnewell. I know what it is to have a great dog die. What
it must be like to have one murdered, I can't imagine. Duke
said, and still maintains, that Hunnewell refused to sell
Comet's sperm because he didn't like the direction the breed
was going in and wanted to guarantee that if the breed improved, there'd be a worthy stud available. As I didn't tell
Duke, I don't think that Hunnewell's objection to a particular bitch had anything to do with his refusal. It is my con-
viction that Hunnewell wanted that remaining viable trace
of Comet, those precious straws of frozen semen, to remain
intact in the freezers of R.T.I.

As to Timmy's motive, Duke took the practical view that
Timmy had just wanted a litter out of Comet, puppies sired
by the long-dead legend. About winning and losing, Duke
was a realist. He said that there were fashions and fads in the
ring just as there were everywhere else and that, these days,
there was no telling how Comet himself would do out there.
I think that in killing for control of those last drops of
Comet, Timmy ached to own the living remains of a great
dog who'd never really belonged to anyone but Duke Sylvia.
Where Timmy was raw, Duke was polished. Timmy was a
badly aged child. Duke was a man. I believe that in longing
to control Comet's sperm, Timmy wanted not only the dog's
power, but Duke's, as if anyone who owned even a few drops
of Comet would thereby become Duke.

Now, months later, Comet's future is as frozen as ever. In
one respect, James Hunnewell proved himself a wise judge
of men and dogs. He willed the bulk of his estate to the Dog
Museum, which happens to be in his home state, Missouri.
He left Comet's sperm to Duke. If the immortal Comet ever
sires a litter, I will look for his sons and daughters in the
ring. As I've mentioned, it's always a pleasure to watch
Duke handle. And, after all, James Hunnewell would have
been the first to agree that Comet was a dog to die for.

My own are dogs to live for. On the day after the official end of the national, Kimi went Winners Bitch at our independent area specialty, thus picking up her first championship points. Rowdy, of course, was temporarily out of competition. In my judge's book, however, they eternally tie for Best of Breed. Oh, and speaking of braces of beauties, I must not forget to mention Greg and Crystal's twins, Gregory, Jr., and Lindsay, whose names and little wrinkled faces appeared on the front page of the Boston papers almost exactly two months after the national, on January the first, when the twins took the breed, so to speak, by arriving in the early hours of New Year's Day. Crystal and Greg are in the picture, too. Both are smiling.

Oh. After Duke and I left the bar, did we . . . ? Certainly not! But I sure was tempted. And while I'm on that subject, I am thrilled to report that the recent restoration of the Sistine Chapel has revealed that Michelangelo did not, after all, shortchange Adam in the matter of . . . *one-fourth*? Really, we should have guessed. As it was, where did Cain and Abel come from? Never mind the rest of us. And the gap? Authorities maintain that what fills the previous emptiness between God and Adam is a primitive version of the Italian greyhound. Myself, I think that Michelangelo's pup is hairier than that. The muzzle, as I see it, is blocky. The bone is heavy. In brief, when it grows up and starts to talk, it's obviously going to say *woo-woo-woo*. That's just my interpretation, of course. Genius that Michelangelo was, though, he may actually have created something of a cosmic and universal looking glass that reflects the soul of the beholder. The Sistine Chapel is not for sale. I own the next best thing. As high bidder at the silent auction, I bought that hand-painted malamute mirror. I paid a lot, but I got a bargain. In the gap between human and divine, I see myself as my own dogs. I sense Creation. Like God and Adam, I am newly restored.

A NOTE TO THE READER

The Alaskan malamute rescue group and the national breed club depicted in this book are imaginary. For information about the real Alaskan malamute rescue organization, write to:

Alaskan Malamute Protection League
P.O. Box 170
Cedar Crest, NM 87008

Information about the breed may be obtained from:

Cap Schneider
Public Relations
Alaskan Malamute Club of America
21 Unneberg Avenue
Succasunna, NJ 07876

Information about other breed rescue groups and national breed clubs is available from:

The American Kennel Club
51 Madison Avenue
New York, NY 10010